T0346257

J. J. Connington and The Murder Room

>>> This title is part of The Murder Room, our series dedicated to making available out-of-print or hard-to-find titles by classic crime writers.

Crime fiction has always held up a mirror to society. The Victorians were fascinated by sensational murder and the emerging science of detection; now we are obsessed with the forensic detail of violent death. And no other genre has so captivated and enthralled readers.

Vast troves of classic crime writing have for a long time been unavailable to all but the most dedicated frequenters of second-hand bookshops. The advent of digital publishing means that we are now able to bring you the backlists of a huge range of titles by classic and contemporary crime writers, some of which have been out of print for decades.

From the genteel amateur private eyes of the Golden Age and the femmes fatales of pulp fiction, to the morally ambiguous hard-boiled detectives of mid twentieth-century America and their descendants who walk our twenty-first century streets, The Murder Room has it all. >>>

The Murder Room
Where Criminal Minds Meet

themurderroom.com

J. J. Connington (1880–1947)

Alfred Walter Stewart, who wrote under the pen name J. J. Connington, was born in Glasgow, the youngest of three sons of Reverend Dr Stewart. He graduated from Glasgow University and pursued an academic career as a chemistry professor, working for the Admiralty during the First World War. Known for his ingenious and carefully worked-out puzzles and in-depth character development, he was admired by a host of his better-known contemporaries, including Dorothy L. Sayers and John Dickson Carr, who both paid tribute to his influence on their work. He married Jessie Lily Courts in 1916 and they had one daughter.

Sir Clinton Driffield Mysteries

Murder in the Maze
Tragedy at Ravensthorpe
The Case with Nine Solutions
Mystery at Lynden Sands
Nemesis at Raynham Parva
The Boathouse Riddle
The Sweepstake Murders
The Castleford Conundrum
The Ha-Ha Case
In Whose Dim Shadow
A Minor Operation
For Murder Will Speak
Truth Comes Limping
The Twenty-One Clues
No Past is Dead

Jack-in-the-Box
Common Sense is All You Need

Supt Ross Mysteries
The Eye in the Museum
The Two Tickets Puzzle

Novels
Death at Swaythling Court
The Dangerfield Talisman
Tom Tiddler's Island
Murder Will Speak
The Counsellor
The Four Defences

Nemesis at Raynham Parva

J. J. Connington

An Orion book

Copyright © The Professor A. W. Stewart Deceased Trust 1929, 2012

This edition published by
The Orion Publishing Group Ltd
Orion House
5 Upper St Martin's Lane
London WC2H 9EA

An Hachette UK company
A CIP catalogue record for this book is available from the British Library

ISBN 978 1 4719 0601 5

www.orionbooks.co.uk

CONTENTS

NOTE

I take this opportunity of acknowledging my indebtedness to Mr. Victor Gollancz, who suggested the basal idea of the following story. For certain details in the narrative I have drawn upon the information given in the League of Nations paper C.52.M.52.1927.IV. and Mr. Albert Londres' book *The Road to Buenos Ayres*.

J. J. C.

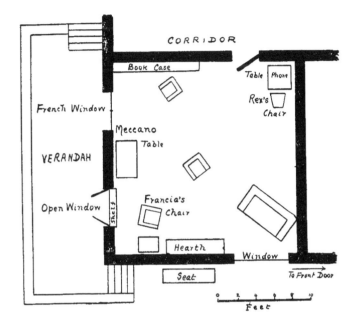

PLAN OF SMOKE-ROOM AT FERN LODGE

CHAPTER I

THE AFFAIR BY THE ROADSIDE

The big car ran smoothly through the darkness, opening up vista after vista of the road with the long beams of its headlights ; and Sir Clinton Driffield, alone at the wheel, reflected contentedly that he might have fallen upon a worse night for his journey. He liked to drive late in the evening when the heavy traffic of the day was over ; and now for the last half-hour he had not seen the lamps of another car. A pleasant feeling of isolation from humanity, tempered by the company of the machine, fitted in well with his mood and served to make him forget the annoyance of disarranged plans.

He was just back from a holiday, and had intended to drive down in time for dinner at the house which his sister had leased at Raynham Parva. But the breakdown of an engine had disorganised the Continental service ; and when at last he reached London, it was too late to keep to his original programme. He had telephoned his news, so that there might be no anxiety at his non-arrival ; and then, after dining at his club, he had started out in time to reach his destination about midnight.

Sir Clinton diverted his gaze momentarily from the pale ribbon of the road under his headlights and glanced across at the milometer on the dashboard. He had never been over the route before ; but he had a mental picture of the map to guide him ; and the figures on the dial showed that he was near a point where he would have to leave the main highway for a by-road.

1

His eyes turned to the illuminated clock beside the speedometer, and he noticed that it was rather later than he had believed.

Half a mile farther on, he swung off into the expected side-road ; and with the change came a feeling of even more complete solitude. Except for the hum of the motor, the night was silent. The air was pleasantly cool ; and as he swept through a little pinewood, Sir Clinton caught a whiff of aromatic scents drifting from the trees. Then once more he was under the open sky, running between low hedges, over the tops of which he could catch faint glimpses of fields under the stars.

A small dark object hurried laboriously across the road in the beam of his headlight, and Sir Clinton relaxed his pressure on the accelerator lest he should run over the creature ere it could get out of his way. When it had scuttled into safety at the wayside, he let the car out once more.

" A hedgehog ! " he said aloud to himself. " This is the peaceful country and no mistake. I wonder if it would have punctured a tyre if I had run over it."

The hedges gave way to a high stone wall enclosing some large estate ; and a couple of miles farther on, Sir Clinton had to take another turn. Inspection of the milometer told him that he was nearing the outskirts of Raynham Parva, and two or three scattered lights ahead suggested the village itself. He slowed down, for the road had become crooked. Then, as he rounded a turn, his headlights broke on a scene which contrasted strangely with the peace out of which he had come.

A car with only sidelamps lighted stood by the road-side ; and in the free space of the road, Sir Clinton's headlights glared upon the figures of two men who had come to grips with each other. Close by, but in the background, stood a woman, with something which looked like a suitcase at her feet.

Sir Clinton had all the decent man's dislike for getting

mixed up in a brawl, especially one in which it was impossible to distinguish the right side. The presence of the girl influenced him to some extent ; since she might be left at the mercy of the victor in the struggle, if no help were at hand. Apart from all other considerations, this factor weighed with him as he checked his car and cautiously drew nearer to the three figures.

But his mere arrival momentarily disturbed the balance. As the blaze of the headlights fell upon the group, one of the combatants, dazzled by the unexpected glare, fell back a pace ; and the smaller man seized the opportunity to launch a not unsuccessful kick. The heavier figure stepped back under the shock and desisted from his attack while he rapidly explored the extent of the damage.

The advantage gained was merely momentary. Finding himself undisabled, the bigger man paused as though gathering himself together; then, with a dash, he fell upon his antagonist, shook him by the coat-collar, and swung him round.

" So kickin's in the game, is it ? " he demanded furiously. " All right. Turn about's fair play. It's my turn."

And at once he put his suggestion into practice, administering a brutal punishment to his adversary.

The girl made a movement as though to interfere ; but the burly man, with an angry gesture, warned her back to her place. Sir Clinton pulled up his car and stepped out ; but before he could reach the group, the affair was over. The bigger man, after a last kick, flung his opponent from him so violently that he stumbled and fell to the ground, where he lay groaning.

" That'll perhaps learn you not to come sniffin' round after other men's girls ! " the victor commented sneeringly, as he stood over his adversary.

Then, seeing Sir Clinton's figure approaching, he turned away and beckoned to the girl.

3

" You come along with me," he ordered. "I'll see you safe home."

But the girl ignored his order, still keeping her place by the roadside. For a moment the man seemed to think of using force to compel her obedience ; then, with a glance at Sir Clinton's approaching figure, he turned and walked past the tail of the standing car. Before he could be called back, he had slipped into a by-road out of sight. From round the corner came the sound of a self-starter ; gears were engaged ; and soon the noise of the motor had died away in the distance.

Coming up to the standing car, Sir Clinton stooped over the figure on the road and offered his hand to assist the man to rise. Evidently the kicking had been a vicious one ; but it seemed to have done no permanent damage ; for when the man got to his feet again he was able to hobble painfully to the door of his car. Apparently he was in a furious rage, for he did not even pause to thank Sir Clinton for his help. Instead, he climbed painfully into the driving seat of the two-seater and worked the self-starter.

As he lifted his head after reaching forward to the knob, his face came into the full glare of Sir Clinton's headlights and revealed his features, contorted with passion. Sir Clinton noted that he had a sort of coarse handsomeness ; and that the cast of his looks was un-English. He might have been a southern Frenchman or Spaniard, had it not been for the suggestion of some other race which Sir Clinton failed to identify. In spite of well-cut and inconspicuous clothes, there seemed to be a hint of showiness in his appearance which accentuated his divergence from the normal English type.

Paying no attention to Sir Clinton, he leaned out of the car and addressed the girl, who was still standing where she had been throughout the scene.

" Strap your suitcase on the grid and get in," he said curtly.

4

But the girl's attitude showed more than a little hesitation. She glanced from the man in the car to Sir Clinton, as though weighing the position in her mind before she spoke.

" I don't think I'll come," she answered doubtfully. This seemed to infuriate the man in the car.

" Get in when I tell you," he said angrily. " Don't stand there gaping ! That fellow may change his mind and come back again, any minute. Come on, now, quick ! "

The tone of his voice seemed to stiffen the girl's resistance.

" I'm not going with you," she answered in a firmer tone.

The man examined her face in the glare of the head-lights, and seemed for a moment or two as though he were calculating his chance of swaying her from her decision. But the presence of a stranger evidently hampered him. He cast a glance of annoyance at Sir Clinton ; and decided to give up his attempt.

" All right," he snarled. " Stay where you are. It's your loss."

And without wasting more words, he started his car. The girl watched him stonily as he drove away round the corner and out of sight. A glimpse of her face, brightly lit by the headlights, gave Sir Clinton the impression of a conflict between relief and disappointment on her features.

The affair was no business of his, obviously, however out of the common run it might appear, but he could hardly leave a girl by the wayside at that time of night without offering some assistance, since her suitcase might be a heavy one. It was a case for tact ; and he determined, even at the cost of absurdity, to ignore what he had seen.

" You seem to be left stranded," he said, as he approached her. " I'm driving into Raynham Parva ; and

5

if it's any use to you, I'll be glad to give you a lift in my car."

He pointed to the empty back seats, by way of suggesting that she need not sit beside him unless she wished to do so. For a moment or two, the girl seemed to hesitate ; then, with a glance at the pine spinney which fringed the road behind her, she shook her head decidedly.

" I'll manage all right, thank you."

As she turned her head to answer him, Sir Clinton saw that she was a pretty girl. Her voice, with its slight quiver of agitation, was a pleasant one ; and only the faintest accent betrayed that she did not belong to his own class. A single incurious glance had shown him that she had good taste and carried her clothes well, though they were not expensive ones.

" If it's any help, I'll take your suitcase for you and drop it in Raynham Parva. There's no need for you to drag it along, even if you don't feel inclined to risk yourself with a stranger at this time of night."

" No, thanks. I'll manage quite well."

Sir Clinton had no intention of forcing his company on her. After all, she knew her own business best ; and it was not his affair to look after her if she preferred to be left to her own resources.

" That's Raynham Parva just ahead, isn't it ? " he asked, by way of taking the awkwardness out of the situation.

The girl nodded.

" Keep straight on," she volunteered. " You'll come to it in two or three minutes. It's only half a mile or so along the road."

Sir Clinton thanked her and was about to turn away, when a thought struck him.

" Perhaps you could save me some trouble. I'm going to Mrs. Thornaby's—at Fern Lodge. I don't know the village—never been here before ; and by the time I get there, everyone will have gone to bed long ago and I'll

6

find no one to tell me my road. Perhaps you could direct me ? "

A new expression came into the girl's face, something with more than a tinge of dismay in it.

" Oh, then you're Sir Clinton Driffield ? " she exclaimed.

She stopped abruptly, biting her lip as though she had let the question slip out in spite of herself and now regretted that she had done so.

" You seem to know me," Sir Clinton admitted, restraining his surprise.

He examined the girl closely ; but could not recall that he had ever seen her before. He felt a slight touch of vexation at this, for he prided himself on his memory for faces.

She seemed uneasy under his scrutiny ; and made no reply to his implied question. To relieve her, he took his eyes from her face and made a gesture towards his car.

" Well, since you know who I am, now, perhaps you'll change your mind and let me take you in to the village. There's no point in your dragging that suitcase along the road."

But again the girl shook her head, this time so definitely that Sir Clinton saw her mind was clearly made up.

" I can tell you how to get to Mrs. Thornaby's," she said. " You go right on till you come to the village. . . . Wait a moment, I must think. . . . Yes, go down the main street till you come to the Black Bull Hotel—you can't miss it. Turn up the road on the right, just beyond it. There's a grocer's shop at the corner, so you can't mistake it. Then you go on along that road till . . . let me see. . . . Oh, yes, till you cross a bridge with stone walls on each side of the road. Then you take the first road on your right again. Mrs. Thornaby's house is in that road. It's on your left hand side. You'll know it at once

7

because it's got two beasts carved on the tops of the gate-pillars ; and the name of the house is on shield-things on the pillars, too. You can't possibly mistake it."

" Thanks," said Sir Clinton. " I'd better get on my road. You're sure you'll be all right if I leave you here ? "

Again the girl refused the invitation which he implied.

" I'll manage all right," she assured him.

Sir Clinton had no further excuse for lingering ; but he was still puzzled, and he hated to be perplexed by an unsolved problem.

" I wish you'd tell me how you recognised me," he said. " You don't know me by sight, obviously, or you'd have spotted who I was when I came up at first."

For a second or two the girl remained silent, evidently uncertain what to say.

" I knew you were coming to-night," she said at last, " and I guessed who you were when you spoke to me."

She stopped, as though a fresh aspect of the situation had occurred to her, and it was only after a pause that she went on :

" Please don't ask questions, Sir Clinton. And, please, if you see me again, don't say anything to anyone about this affair to-night. You must have seen that it wasn't nice. I want to forget all about it. And I don't want anyone to hear a word about it. Don't let anyone know that you've seen me before. You won't, please ? "

Her distress was apparent ; and Sir Clinton could see no valid objection to giving his promise.

" Sounds a bit mysterious, doesn't it ? " he said lightly. " You seem to think we're likely to come across each other again. Well, if it'll ease your mind, I certainly won't say anything about it to anyone ; and you needn't recognise me when we do meet. That's all right. Now about these directions you gave me. Let's see if I have them right. Straight on till I come to the Black Bull ; then up to the right past the grocer's shop ; then on till I come to a bridge ; and the first road on the right brings me to Fern Lodge. That's correct, isn't it ? Thanks for putting me on my way."

He did not repeat his offer of a lift, but made his way back to his car. The girl showed no sign of leaving her post, but stood on the grass edging of the road with her suitcase at her feet as he drove slowly past her. A few yards down the road, he turned and glanced back in her direction ; but by that time her figure seemed to have been swallowed up in the darkness.

A few hundred yards farther on, he ran into Raynham Parva, and had little difficulty in finding the Black Bull Hotel. The village was asleep ; and he congratulated himself on having secured directions about his route beforehand, for there was no one in the streets whom he could have questioned. Taking the turn at the grocer's shop, he found that a couple of minutes driving took him beyond the outskirts of the village into the open country once more.

His thoughts, however, were less on the road before him than on the scene which he had just witnessed. On the face of it, the meaning of the affair was plain enough : the quarrel of two men over a girl, ending in a rough-and-tumble struggle. The girl's suitcase pointed clearly to some projected elopement which had apparently been interrupted by the arrival of the second man.

Sir Clinton's eye was trained to catch minor details ; and he had noticed that the girl's ring-finger was bare. But that in itself meant very little. A married woman leaving her husband might very well take off her wedding-ring, even if the removal of it was a mere emotional gesture.

The foreign-looking fellow in the car seemed an obvious interloper. If he had been posing as a lover of the girl, the pretence had been stripped bare by his actions at the last moment ; for all the emotion which he had shown was easily to be accounted for on other grounds, and his manner to the girl had been anything

9

but lover-like. He had behaved like a bad loser confronted by an unexpected disaster.

The second man's doings presented an even greater puzzle. If he was the girl's husband, why had he left her by the roadside ? Village manners would suggest quite another line of action for him. If he were either a lover or a brother, why had he not waited until the other man drove away and then settled matters to his own satisfaction, if possible ? There must have been some fairly strong motive in his mind if it impelled him to leave the girl stranded on the road with a suitcase at that hour of the night, especially when he had a car in waiting round the corner.

The girl's behaviour furnished yet another problem. Her voice, Sir Clinton recalled, had not suggested any local accent, though she obviously did not belong to his own class. She spoke nicely—with an intonation quite different from that of the second man. But in country places it is not uncommon to find a girl with a cleaner accent than that of the men in her circle.

One thing was fairly apparent. She had arranged to meet the foreigner at an hour when the coast was clear ; and she had brought a suitcase. The whole affair was obviously clandestine ; and on this basis it was clear enough that she could not be picked up by the car at the very door of her own house. On the other hand, if the car was available, there would be no point in letting her carry her suitcase for any considerable distance from her home. The conclusion seemed to be that she must live somewhere close to the point where Sir Clinton had left her by the roadside ; and this, in addition to other possible reasons, would account for her refusal of a lift in his car.

Finally, there was the question of her recognition of himself, which at first sight seemed the most puzzling point of all. Very brief consideration gave Sir Clinton a possible explanation of that side of the problem ; and, as he thought it over, he found that it fitted neatly into the rest of the affair.

While he was thinking, the car had run for the best part of a mile, and yet there had been no sign of the bridge which was one of his landmarks ; and he had almost come to the conclusion that the girl had misdirected him when he saw the stone parapets lining the road. And when he had crossed the stream, there was no sign of any road leading off to the right. He held to his instructions, however, though he knew that by this time he had left Raynham Parva far behind ; and at last he came to a hairpin corner formed by the expected tributary road.

Sir Clinton had a good head for locality ; and after he had gone a mile or so along this fresh route, it became obvious to him that he was now returning on a line which would bring him back to the vicinity of the village. When he realised this, a faint smile crossed his face ; for it was just what he might have expected, if his guess at the situation had been correct.

" Very smart, on the spur of the moment," he confessed to himself. " She's evidently got her wits about her even when she's shaken up a bit."

His suspicion that he had been entirely misdirected died away ; and his faith in his interpretation of the affair by the roadside was strengthened when the gates of Fern Lodge appeared in the beam of his lights, unmistakable with the carved lions surmounting the pillars.

The way was clear, and he turned his car into the entrance. Before him, a short drive opened up ; and at the end of this Fern Lodge itself appeared, a substantial house decked with creepers, which gave it an old-established air. Light streamed from the hall door across the gravel sweep ; and the windows of one room glowed in the night. Except for this, the building was dark against the sky.

A glance at the clock on the dashboard showed Sir

Clinton that the détour he had made since leaving Raynham Parva had been longer than he had supposed. Evidently the Fern Lodge household had gone to bed, with the exception of someone who was sitting up to await him on his arrival. He sounded his horn gently as he drew near the door ; then, pulling up his car, he got out and entered the house without ceremony.

CHAPTER II

THE MAN FROM THE ARGENTINE

As Sir Clinton entered the hall, he heard a light step ; a door opened, and Mrs. Thornaby came forward to welcome him. Though she was slightly older than her brother, few people would have realised this at first acquaintance. Her looks did not betray it ; and she had a personality which seemed to take her out of the normal limitations of age and to let her mix with young people as easily as with those of her own generation. A marked capacity for making allowances for the prejudices of others was one of her most salient characteristics ; and it made people turn to her for sympathy in their difficulties with a certainty that they would go away again with fresh courage.

" I heard your horn," she said, after they had exchanged greetings. " Just as well you telephoned. I'd have been worried about you if you hadn't turned up at dinner-time."

She turned to the door.

" You'd better put the car into the garage now. It'll save going out again later on. Drive down that path there, and you'll find the place."

She watched him start the engine, and then turned back into the house. Sir Clinton put his car into the garage, locked the front door of the house as he returned, and took off his overcoat.

" Come in here, Clinton," he heard his sister directing

from the room out of which she had appeared on his first arrival.

As he crossed the threshold, he threw a quick glance of inquiry round the room ; but if he was surprised to find his sister alone, he did not let it appear in his expression.

" You must be cold after that long drive. There's whiskey and soda over yonder. If you'd rather have coffee, I can make it in a minute or two ; I've got the machine here. When you telephoned that you'd be late, I didn't keep the maids up ; and I expect they're off to bed long ago."

Sir Clinton nodded, declined the coffee, and helped himself to some whiskey and soda. With a gesture, Mrs. Thornaby invited him to take a comfortable chair near her own. Part of her charm lay in the fact that she always seemed more interested in other people than in herself ; and it was characteristic that now, although she had news which concerned her deeply, she put it aside for the moment and questioned her brother about his own doings.

" Had a good holiday, Clinton ? "

" Not bad."

Sir Clinton also had the habit of suppressing his own affairs and showing a greater interest in other people's.

His sister laughed gently.

" Really, Clinton, this police work of yours seems to be converting you into a sort of human oyster, so far as your own doings are concerned. One would think you were losing the gift of expression. I suppose it's all this official secrecy business ; but surely, after a couple of months on the Continent, you might come back with something more detailed than ' Not bad ' as a report. It sounds a trifle bald, somehow."

Sir Clinton laughed in his turn at this thrust.

" What do you expect ? Detailed descriptions of Dutch windmills ? You've seen 'em yourself. The Eiffel Tower's still standing, and I don't see much change in the view from the Lucendro Pass. I just wandered about and met a lot of interesting human specimens, here and there."

" And left no address behind you."

" How could I ? I didn't know, one day, where I'd go on the next. I wanted a real holiday, not a Cook's tour with a time-schedule. When I got tired of a place, I just moved on to a fresh one that took my fancy."

He drew a case from his pocket, chose and lighted a cigarette. In some indefinable way he made the gesture put a closure on the discussion of his own affairs.

" Now what about yourself ? " he demanded, as he laid down the spent match. " Johnnie's in bed long ago, I suppose ; but where's Elsie. I thought she'd have stayed up to see me."

His quick eye detected a faint tinge of trouble in Mrs. Thornaby's face at the mention of her daughter's name ; but when she spoke, it was evident that she was trying to treat the matter lightly.

" If you insist on cutting yourself off from your family for weeks, Clinton, you can't complain of surprises when you turn up again. I've got one for you. Elsie's married."

Sir Clinton seemed less astonished than she had expected.

" Married, is she ? Well, Rex Brandon's a sound young cub as cubs go ; and he certainly deserved to win. I've seldom seen any youngster so keen on a girl."

Mrs. Thornaby shook her head.

" It isn't Rex Brandon. It's someone you've never heard of, Clinton."

The tone of distrust in his sister's voice was faint but unmistakable. Sir Clinton's careless manner fell from him at the sound of it ; and the face which he turned to Mrs. Thornaby was that of the official Sir Clinton.

" That's rum," he said slowly. " Tell me about it, Anne. You've managed to spring a surprise on me all right."

Those who knew Sir Clinton only as an efficient and somewhat cynical Chief Constable would have been surprised if they had seen him with his nephew and niece. They would have discovered an entirely fresh side of his character ; for since the death of his brother-in-law, ten years before, he had taken the two children under his wing and made an effort to fill the gap left in their lives by their father's death.

Mrs. Thornaby made a gesture which seemed to suggest that she herself knew very little about the matter.

" I was never very keen on Elsie's going to London, you know," she explained. "I'd much rather have kept her beside me, though perhaps I'm a bit old-fashioned in that. But one can't deny that she's good with her violin. She's quite worth the best training I could afford for her. And when she wanted to go to the R.A.M., I hadn't the heart to refuse, once I found she was really eager about it. You know how one feels, Clinton. If she had her chance, then there was no grievance ; but if I had objected to her going, she'd always have felt she'd missed something that might have made a big difference to her playing. She wouldn't have groused about it ; but I'd have felt all the time that I'd stood in her way. Let her have the experience, I thought, and then she won't feel she's missed an opportunity, even if nothing comes of it in the end. Besides, I felt that in a case of that sort, one's better to weight the scales against oneself— just to make sure. I wanted to keep her ; and I had a sort of notion that I was being selfish and disguising it by telling myself I was prudent. You see what I mean ? "

Sir Clinton nodded, but said nothing. He and his sister understood each other ; and this problem was one which Mrs. Thornaby had settled for herself. Comment was needless.

" Well, I'm afraid it didn't turn out quite as I'd

hoped," Mrs. Thornaby went on. " Elsie didn't neglect her work—trust her for that. She's too keen on her fiddling. But she seems to have got among a rather weird lot of people in London. Some of the musical set introduced her to people outside, and they introduced her to others, and so on."

Again Sir Clinton nodded without speaking.

" What I didn't like about it was that she seemed to pick up a lot of futile ideas from these people ; and if one didn't agree at once that these notions were the last touch in up-to-dateness, then one was classed as mid-Victorian. I don't mind being called Edwardian, but really mid-Victorian is a bit unkind, at my age."

Sir Clinton's face relaxed in a smile.

" They seem to have stirred you out of your senile torpor, anyhow. What sort of notions were they ? "

" Oh, all about freedom, and living your own life without bothering about other people's feelings, and so forth. Getting away from all the petty restrictions that hampered the older generation."

Sir Clinton's smile deepened.

" That comes well from people who can't buy a cigarette or a box of chocolates in a shop after 8 p.m. without running the risk of being run in. We weren't quite so hampered as all that in King Edward's days."

" Most of their notions seem mixed up with the sex question," Mrs. Thornaby continued, disregarding the interjection. " Some of them seem to me simply silly. For one thing, they don't believe in a girl getting engaged to a man ; it seems that's a case of a petty restriction. A man and a girl go about together for a while ; and then, one day, they decide to get married—if they take even that trouble—and they drop into a registry office and fix it up without telling anyone. And that's that. It may be a new way of doing things, but I don't think much of it."

Sir Clinton made no effort to conceal his amusement.

" It's none so new, you know, Anne. When I was a boy, it was the ordinary method of getting married which servant-maids used. ' Walking out ' they called it. I don't see much novelty in that. Mid-Victorian's no name for it. They must be a very unsophisticated bunch if it's fresh to them."

" It's no laughing matter to me, Clinton. That's just what Elsie did."

The " official " expression returned to Sir Clinton's face.

" Let's hear about this, Anne."

Mrs. Thornaby seemed to find relief in putting the matter into words. She was not the type which discusses its private affairs with friends ; and the return of her brother had given her an outlet which hitherto she had lacked.

" Well, it seems that a man Francia was one of the circle she drifted amongst."

" Francia ? What is he ? Spanish ? "

" South American, I believe. He comes from the Argentine, Elsie told me. It seems that he fell in love with Elsie—violently in love."

She paused for a moment, as though the subject grated on her indefinably.

" You'll see him to-morrow," she continued, as Sir Clinton made no comment. " Perhaps it's jealousy on my part—quite likely. You know how much Elsie is to me, Clinton, and naturally I don't like the idea of her going away to South America. It's selfish, perhaps, but there you are. I can't help it."

She halted again, as though expecting some remark from her brother. Sir Clinton threw away the stub of his cigarette and chose another from his case, as though to fill the pause. He was evidently following his sister's story closely, but had no intention of interrupting the narrative.

" Elsie attracted this man's attention," Mrs. Thornaby continued with some hesitation, as though she were picking her words in dealing with a disagreeable subject. " They seem to have gone about together a good deal. He managed to make her care for him—she's quite keen on him, I can see. And the result was that they put these modern notions into practice : arranged everything and went off one day to a registrar's and got married without a word to anyone beforehand. She's of age of course, and it's all in order ; but they didn't even tell me about it till it was all over. That cuts one a bit, you know, Clinton."

Sir Clinton nodded gravely. He had had a different picture of his niece's wedding in his mind. Elsie's excitement over an announced engagement ; her surprises over her wedding-presents ; all the fun of choosing a trousseau ; a pretty wedding, with her friends as bridesmaids and herself as the star ; and, instead of all that, a visit to a dingy registrar's office, a business with as much romance in it as taking out a dog-licence.

" H'm ! She's missed a lot of harmless pleasure," he commented, as though to cover his sister's emotion. " The new method doesn't seem to offer the same opportunities as the old one, to my mind. However, if she's fond of him, that's always something."

He seemed to ponder for a moment.

" A bit rum to come home and find the kiddie married. It seems not so long ago since she was climbing on to my knee clamouring for fairy tales. And now she's the wife of a fellow I'd never even heard of. I can appreciate your feelings, Anne."

Mrs. Thornaby had recovered herself.

" Elsie wired me after it was all over," she went on. " They went off for a week-end together. Then Elsie brought him down here, and they're staying till they go out to Buenos Ayres. I've done my best, Clinton. I was quite prepared to take second place, now. But he's foreign—not our sort. His manners are all right, you know, only too much so, if you see what I mean. Somehow, I feel as if I'd never get to know the man."

For his sister's sake, Sir Clinton tried to put the best face on things.

" Spanish ? " he said thoughtfully. " After all, Spaniards aren't necessarily dagoes, you know, Anne. Some of them are sound stuff. One mustn't get too prejudiced merely because a man doesn't come from our own part of the country. Though I admit I'd have been better pleased if Elsie had kept to her own people and left foreigners alone. Rex Brandon was the man I was betting on. He may be a bit sharp-tempered at times, but he's a likeable cub. Pity ! "

" Well, perhaps I'm prejudiced," Mrs. Thornaby admitted, with a tired smile. " I expect this wrench of Elsie going off to the other side of the world may have a good deal to do with my feelings. One can't help that. It's only natural."

Sir Clinton seemed to be following a fresh train of thought.

" He can't have married Elsie for money," he said at last. " She hasn't a penny of her own, and she knows that quite well."

" Oh, that had nothing to do with it," Mrs. Thornaby admitted frankly. " He seems to have plenty of money, so far as one can see. Elsie's dropped one or two things which point that way. I gathered that he's got quite big interests in the Argentine."

" What's his line ? " Sir Clinton inquired.

Mrs. Thornaby's gesture showed that she had little definite to tell.

" I don't really know. I'm not inclined to cross-question Elsie too much, you see, Clinton. I'm doing my best to conceal my feelings from her. I don't want to stir up trouble in these last few weeks that are all I'll have of her for long enough. I don't want to seem too curious, because, if I talk too much about him, I'm afraid she'll see clearly enough what I feel."

Sir Clinton nodded understandingly.

" But you've got some notion, haven't you ? " he asked.

" Nothing much," Mrs. Thornaby answered doubt-fully. " I think he does something with horses."

" That's not unlikely in the Argentine. Anything else ? "

" He seems to have something to do with theatres—or else some friend of his is interested in them and he has influence in that line. That reminds me, Clinton. They've got a couple of girls here—Elsie asked them down. It's something to do with this theatre business. You'll see them to-morrow."

Sir Clinton nodded rather absent-mindedly at this information. He was evidently still trying to bring himself to new bearings in the matter of his niece.

" She was always such a pretty, trustful kiddie," he said reminiscently. " Never been hurt, and thought everybody was as straight as herself. The worst of the marriage system is that, if the husband comes a smash, he drags his wife down with him. It's hardly fair, when one comes to think of it."

He glanced at his sister's face, saw that he had let something slip out which had done no good, and changed the subject abruptly.

" What about the other half of the family ? At the age of eleven, Johnnie's hardly likely to have got involved in troubles of that sort, anyhow."

" Johnnie's all right," Mrs. Thornaby confirmed. " He was looking forward so much to seeing you to-night ; and when he found you wouldn't be here till late, and I wouldn't let him sit up for you, he nearly rebelled. I expect he'll be hammering at your door to-morrow long before you're awake. He's got a lot of things he wants to show you. He's got a regular menagerie round by the garage, and he's frightfully keen over some hutches he's made. Don't omit to be enthusiastic."

" Is he still worrying round with Meccano and that sort of thing ? "

" He's still quite keen on it. Some of the things he makes are really quite good—most complicated working models. He seems to have a turn for that sort of thing."

" It's always a sound thing if a cub can use his hands. I've brought him a lot of supplementary stuff—it's in the car and he'll get it to-morrow. That'll infuse some fresh interest into the business for him."

Mrs. Thornaby nodded.

" You spoil the boy," she said, with a faint smile. " But I don't think he likes you merely for what he can get out of you. The latest is that he's ' going into the police, like Uncle Clinton,' when he grows up. By the way, Clinton, are you really dropping the Chief Constableship ? "

Sir Clinton glanced up whimsically.

" No. Shouldn't dream of it now," he said, with a purposely solemn face.

" You aren't sending in your resignation, then ? "

" No. Once is quite enough. I resigned the other day. You see, Anne, when old James left me his money, I knew there was a string tied to it. He didn't put it in black and white because he knew he could trust me. But he wants the old place decently kept up ; tenants looked after and so forth. James had very conscientious views about the duties of the country landlord towards his dependents. So I'll have to step into his shoes and run the thing properly ; and that's a whole-time job if one takes it seriously. I haven't time for that and the Chief Constableship, obviously, unless I let one or other of them down—or both. So I cleared out. No more police for me. I've earned a change of occupation, at any rate."

Mrs. Thornaby's face showed her satisfaction at the news.

" Well, we shall see more of you in future, Clinton. You won't be tied down so much as you used to be."

" It'll be a change, certainly. And this affair of Elsie has altered things a good bit. You'd better come and help me to look after things at the old place. I'm short of a Lady Bountiful at present ; and there's nothing to keep you here when Elsie's gone."

He rose slowly to his feet, glancing at his watch as he did so.

" It's getting well on into the morning. I'd no notion time had gone so fast. Suppose we turn in ? I've got a suitcase in the hall, if you'll show me where my room is. The geography of this place is new to me."

CHAPTER III

SERGEANT LEDBURY

Mrs. Thornaby's overnight prophecy was fulfilled to
the letter. Long before the normal breakfast hour,
Sir Clinton was awakened by a peremptory rapping
at his door and the incursion of a small boy into the
room.

" Good morning, uncle. I say, here's your shaving-
water ; and I've told them downstairs to have breakfast ready for you in half an hour."

He put down the steaming can and flew to the windows to throw back the curtains, through which the
sunlight was already making its way. Sir Clinton, wide
awake on the instant, inspected his watch.

" Easy with those curtains, young man," he directed.
" You'll wake the whole neighbourhood if you slam
the runners about like that. This is an ungodly hour to
rouse a travel-worn relative."

Johnnie turned back from the window and perched
himself on the edge of the bed.

" They wouldn't let me sit up to see you, last night,"
he complained, " and I've got heaps of things I want
to talk to you about."

" That last one's a commoner complaint than you
seem to think, Johnnie. Quite a lot of people suffer from
a mania for talking about their own affairs," Sir Clinton
pointed out. " Like this place in the country, after
having been a town-bird all your life ? "

Johnnie nodded vigorously.

" It's A1. I never thought I'd live in a place like this,

24

just stuffed full of interesting things. Do you know, uncle,
I saw a badger yesterday, wandering along under a
hedge. I didn't know what it was when I saw it, but
somebody told me afterwards. I'd no notion badgers
were as big as that, had you ? "

"Not knowing how big it was, I can't say."

"Well, it was ever so much bigger than I expected.
And there's a rabbit-warren in the wood behind the
house. You can see them come out into the fields just
about dusk. And I've seen two weasels in the wood. I
don't like weasels. And there's a dovecote on the top of
a pole in the yard ; and there's any amount of fowls
and pigs and ducks and turkeys. And two collie dogs.
And, do you know, uncle, I've got a pony all to
myself."

His uncle made a pretence of being galvanised by this
last item of news.

"All the modern conveniences, evidently. Hop off
the bed, young fellow, and let me get up. We must look
into all this."

Sir Clinton slipped out of bed and put on his dressing-
gown.

"Now you can show me where the bathroom is.
This house is new to me, and I forgot to inquire
my way about last night. If I happen to fall asleep
while I'm dressing, please wait for half an hour
and then waken me again—gently, this time. Meanwhile, kindly lead the way, and don't talk at the top
of your voice when you pass the door of anyone's
bedroom. Show some fellow-feeling and let 'em sleep,
even if I mayn't."

Johnnie grinned at his uncle's suggestions. He had
carried his point and managed matters so that he would
have Sir Clinton to himself during breakfast ; and he
hoped to carry him off immediately afterwards to inspect
the grounds, before any of the rest of the family put
in an appearance. He led the way to the bathroom,

chattering eagerly as he went ; and it was with obvious reluctance that he turned away when Sir Clinton cut him short by closing the door in his face.

" I forgot one thing, uncle," he communicated via the keyhole. " There's a lake runs up into the grounds. It's got fish in it and a lot of water-fowl live there. And I've learned to row a boat on it. I'll row you, by and by."

" I don't mind if you do. I can swim. Now clear out ! "

Twenty minutes later, Sir Clinton descended the stairs to find Johnnie restlessly wandering about the hall, in evident impatience at what had seemed to him an interminable delay.

" Come on, uncle. Along this way. Staffin's just taking in the grub. I told her you took coffee. Do you know, there's a couple of owls about the place—huge ones. I've never seen a live owl before, except at the Zoo. But you'll need to wait for dusk to-night. In here, this is the breakfast-room."

He stood aside to let his uncle enter ; but at the door they almost collided with the table-maid, who was hurrying out of the room. Her eyes met those of Sir Clinton for a moment, and he recognised the girl he had left by the wayside with her suitcase on the previous night. She looked anxiously at him as they met ; but Sir Clinton, mindful of his promise, let no sign of recognition escape him.

As he helped himself to breakfast, he reflected that his inferences had been correct. The point where he had encountered the girl was obviously quite close to Fern Lodge ; and she had deliberately misdirected him over a roundabout route in order to give herself time to re-gain the house before he arrived himself. Obviously it might have been difficult for the girl to re-enter the house and slip off to her room undetected, if she had come back at the moment when the place was astir at his arrival. She could hardly guess that only Mrs. Thornaby would be sitting up to welcome him. And, naturally, when she met him on the road, she guessed his identity as soon as she heard that he was bound for Fern Lodge, since he was the only visitor expected.

" There's a pine spinney running down to the road near here, isn't there ? " he asked Johnnie, merely to clinch the point to his own satisfaction.

" Oh, yes. There's a short cut through it, down to the road. It's in our grounds. I found a toad there, the other day."

Johnnie was so eager to exhibit the resources of the neighbourhood that Sir Clinton found breakfast anything but a quiet meal. Good-naturedly, he made as little delay as possible ; and they rose from the table before any other members of the family appeared.

" Now where's this pony of yours, Johnnie ? "

The pony occupied some time ; and, after it had been fully admired, Sir Clinton was conducted round the chief sights of the farmyard and out-buildings. At last, when Johnnie had exhausted the sights in the immediate environs of Fern Lodge, his uncle turned resolutely towards the house.

" Elsie will be downstairs by this time, Johnnie. I haven't seen her yet, you know. By the way, which is the shortest way to the garage ? There's something we've got to pick up there."

Johnnie, feeling that his uncle was passing into the hands of unappreciative grown-ups, led the way reluctantly to the garage door. Sir Clinton's luggage had been removed from the grid of his car and taken up to the house ; but a large wooden box had been left in the back of the tonneau. Sir Clinton went to take it out, whilst Johnnie glanced round the roomy garage in manifest surprise.

27

" Why, where's Vincent's car ? " he demanded.

" Who's Vincent ? " Sir Clinton inquired, as he lifted out the box.

" Elsie's husband, of course," Johnnie replied. " She calls him Vincent. His real name's Vicente, though. I know that because he told me himself. Vicente's the Spanish for Vincent."

" Well, what about his car ? " Sir Clinton asked.

" It isn't here," Johnnie explained. " It's a two-seater and he keeps it in our garage. This is our own car," he added, pointing to a four-seater saloon which was standing beside Sir Clinton's touring car.

" Never mind about it just now. Here's something for you," his uncle answered, indicating the wooden box. " It's a new set of Meccano parts, and a few other things I picked up for you a while ago and didn't send on at the time. There's a couple of electric motors to make the wheels go round ; and a battery or two for the motors."

Brushing aside Johnnie's thanks, his uncle picked up the box.

" A bit too heavy for you to carry. I'll take it up to the house and you can unpack it for yourself."

When they reached Fern Lodge, Sir Clinton was surprised to find Staffin, the table-maid, in the hall. The girl was making a pretence of setting something to rights ; but it was obvious at the first glance that she was doing this merely as an excuse for her presence. Sir Clinton was about to pass her, when over the head of Johnnie she made it clear that she was anxious to speak to him in private.

" Hardly like Anne to have a table-maid who vamps casual visitors at second sight," Sir Clinton reflected amusedly.

A glance at the girl's face convinced him, however, that she was in real trouble.

" Cut along and get your box opened, Johnnie. Put

it down somewhere where the packing won't make too much of a mess," he directed.

Then, as Johnnie disappeared towards the back of the house, Sir Clinton turned to Staffin.

" Well ? "

The girl threw an apprehensive glance towards the stairs and the breakfast-room door, as though afraid that she might be overheard.

" Oh, sir," she said breathlessly, " I've just heard that Mr. Quevedo's dead and they've arrested Teddy . . ."

" Mr. Quevedo being the man in the motor-car, and Teddy your other friend ? " Sir Clinton interjected.

" Yes, sir. Teddy's hot-tempered ; but he'd never go that length, or anywhere near it. It's all a mistake . . ."

She had some difficulty in restraining herself as she broke off. Sir Clinton offered her no assistance. It seemed better, since she had a story to tell, to let her tell it in her own way without leading questions. In a moment or two she regained control over herself and was able to continue.

" It was like this, sir. Teddy's the son of a small farmer close by ; and when I came down here with Mrs. Thornaby, he took a fancy to me. We'd talked in a sort of way about getting married ; and I suppose he thought it was all settled up. Then Mr. Quevedo came to the village ; and *he* seemed to take a fancy to me too. He made Teddy jealous ; and Teddy and I had a row over the head of it ; and I sent him about his business."

Sir Clinton refrained from showing by his expression that he had inferred most of this from what he had seen with his own eyes.

" Then," the girl went on, " Mr. Quevedo got a bit more friendly ; and he was always telling me that a girl like me was wasted in service. I could do better for my-self than that, if I'd go to London. He was going to find a good post for me. He seemed so kind about it, and he

29

never seemed to expect anything for himself. All he wanted, he said, was to see a girl making the best of herself and getting a good screw."

She threw another apprehensive glance at the door of the breakfast-room, from which came the sound of voices.

" They'll be finishing breakfast any minute," she went on. " When things got this length, Mr. Quevedo found he had to go back to London himself ; and he offered to give me a lift in his car. He was very careful, and said that he wouldn't like to drive up to the house and take me away. People would get all sorts of bad ideas in their heads if he did that. And, of course, so they would."

Sir Clinton nodded without speaking, but the glance which he threw in his turn towards the breakfast-room had the effect of keeping the girl to the point.

" Mr. Quevedo arranged to pick me up on the road last night. I was to slip down through the spinney and meet him where you saw us. He said he could find a place for me to stay in London, if I had no friends there. Very particular people, he said they were. They'd prob-ably take me to church on Sundays, he said ; and he asked if I thought I could stand that, just so as not to give them a bad impression."

" And you believed all that ? " Sir Clinton demanded, almost incredulously.

" I don't now, of course," the girl admitted frankly, " but then it sounded quite all right, sir. He seemed so anxious to give me a chance ; and he never made any suggestions or took any liberties with me. I thought he was just being kind. And he had a way of talking that made it all seem just as simple as anything. Looking back I see—oh, what a fool I've been ! "

She showed signs of breaking down, but again she managed to recover her surface composure.

" Then I met Teddy, sir, and he was so anxious to

make it up and begin again. But he'd hurt my feelings badly with some things he'd said in his quick temper before ; and I just wanted to even up with him. So I told him I'd better things to think about than him. And somehow, with our getting a bit angry with each other, I let slip something that showed him how the land lay—about Mr. Quevedo meeting me that very night."

She glanced rather piteously at Sir Clinton, as though expecting some comment on her tale ; but none came.

" You saw what happened, sir. Teddy's got a terrible temper. But he'd never—he'd never have killed Mr. Quevedo. It's all some dreadful mistake. Teddy's not that sort of man, sir. He's as kind as kind, really. I can't think what made me behave like a fool and not know when I'd got what I really cared for. It was just Teddy making me lose my temper, and his losing his, that did it."

" And why do you tell me all this ? " Sir Clinton asked in a colourless voice.

" Why, sir, we know all about you, being Mrs. Thornaby's brother. They all say you're so clever at finding things out, Sir Clinton. Can't you do something to help poor Teddy ? It nearly drives me out of my mind when I think of him in gaol, and knowing no more about Mr. Quevedo's death than I do, I'm sure. That's why I came to you, sir. Please help us, and get Teddy off. Please, please, do ! You're in the police yourself, and they'd listen to you."

" I'm not in the police now," Sir Clinton corrected. " And that makes no difference in this kind of case. I'll give you one bit of sound advice, Staffin. When you're dragged into this, as you may be, then stick to the plain truth. Don't try to make up a story in the hope of helping Teddy—what's his other name, by the way ? "

31

" Barford, sir. You will help him, Sir Clinton, won't you ? "

Sir Clinton's face betrayed his sympathy with the girl in her trouble, but his reply was guarded.

" It's everybody's business to see that an innocent man isn't condemned. But I can't suppress what I know myself about your doings last night, remember."

" But that's the worst thing there is against Teddy ! " the girl exclaimed. " If that comes out, everybody'll be sure he went after Mr. Quevedo and killed him."

" They'll have to prove it, though ; and that's harder than merely saying it. Take my advice, and make a clean breast of the whole affair, if they ask you about it. If you don't, it'll be dragged out of you sooner or later ; and it'll make a very much worse impression that way."

The girl was obviously about to make another appeal to him when the sound of a chair colliding with something in the breakfast-room arrested the words in her throat.

" They're coming," she muttered, and she hurried away towards the servants' quarters before the breakfast-room door opened.

Sir Clinton glanced after her as she went. A faint, but not altogether pleasant smile crossed his face as he thought of the trouble she had raised by not knowing her own mind in time. Of course some men had the gift of a plausible tongue ; and no doubt Quevedo had played his game well enough to take this girl in completely. Barford's temper had probably precipitated the whole business and thrown the girl straight into the foreigner's hands at the crucial moment ; though luckily for her he had upset the arrangement and let Quevedo show himself in his real colours in the end. On the face of it, the whole business seemed to be a sordid enough little affair ; and it was the duty of the local police to clear it up. But would the local police get to the bottom of it ? Sir Clinton discovered a certain sympathy in his mind for Barford, in the circumstances.

His train of thought was interrupted by the opening of the breakfast-room door. He heard his niece's voice speaking to some people who were evidently still at table. Then, as she came out of the room, she caught sight of him and hurried forward.

" Oh, there you are, uncle ! You must have come down very early. When we turned up, Johnnie had carried you off somewhere or other, and no one knew where you'd gone."

She held up her face and Sir Clinton kissed her. As he did so, he became aware of a second figure in the background.

" This is Vincent, uncle. Mother's told you all about us, I expect, hasn't she ? "

Francia came forward as she spoke and bowed to Sir Clinton with a certain foreign politeness which seemed to suit his appearance. Sir Clinton let his eyes travel unobtrusively over his new relative. He did not wish to let himself be prejudiced by anything his sister had said ; and, at the first glance, he found little to cavil at in Francia's appearance. The man would never have passed for an Englishman ; but Sir Clinton was enough of a cosmopolitan to judge other races by their own standards rather than by British criteria ; and he mentally ticked off the externals of the man before him. Foreign-looking, Francia undoubtedly was ; handsome, by some standards undeniably, though to Sir Clinton's taste the Argentiner's looks were a trifle florid. As for his clothes, " good tailor " might have been inferred at a glance from their appearance. Altogether, the result of his survey removed one of Sir Clinton's apprehensions. This new nephew-in-law was at least outwardly presentable ; though Mrs. Thornaby had been quite fair in describing him as " foreign."

33

"He's not Anne's sort; that's plain," Sir Clinton reflected rather ruefully. "The main thing is, though, does he suit Elsie?"

He seemed to find an answer in a glance which his niece shot at her husband. Despite himself, he felt a twinge of jealousy as he saw it. All of them would have to take a back seat now, evidently. The old relationships might go on, but this new one had altered all former bearings; and Sir Clinton could not help realising how acutely his sister would feel the change.

Elsie slipped her arm into her uncle's and led him towards the hall door.

"Now I've rescued you from Johnnie's clutches, I'm not going to let you go," she announced. "I've heaps of things I want to hear."

She turned to her husband.

"Vincent! Please bring some camp-chairs out to the lawn. We'll sit there for a while—over yonder under the lee of the rhododendrons. You'd better fetch four chairs when you're about it. Mother may come out when she's got through breakfast."

Her husband, with a gesture of excuse towards Sir Clinton, went off obediently in search of the chairs, while Elsie led her uncle out into the open air.

"Well?" she demanded eagerly, as soon as Francia was out of earshot.

Sir Clinton had guessed the reason which had led her to despatch Francia on his errand; but he wished that he had more time in which to reply to the implied question.

"You seem to favour the compendious in your conversation nowadays," he said teasingly. "I suppose your 'Well?' means 'What do I think of your husband?' He seems all right and he says 'Good morning' better than most people. Beyond that, our acquaintance hasn't provided much material, has it?"

He glanced down at his niece's eager face.

" Quite happy ? " he demanded seriously.

" Just ever so, and a bit more," Elsie answered, with equal seriousness. " You've no notion what a dear Vincent is. You'll like him, uncle, once you get to know him. He's so thoughtful—seems to spend his time thinking of things that'll please me."

" H'm ! Spoils you, in plain English," said Sir Clinton, with a glimmer of a smile.

" Well, what if he does ? You did your best yourself in your day, uncle, so you can't afford to put on airs."

Sir Clinton's smile vanished abruptly. The sting of the phrase ' in your day ' was all the sharper owing to Elsie's complete unconsciousness that she was marking the vanishing of the old order of things. His day was over now, as it was bound to be, sooner or later. That was inevitable, of course. No one wanted a girl to spend all her life in circling round an uncle. But at the back of Sir Clinton's mind there had always been a fairly definite idea of the sort of man who would supplant him : not necessarily young Brandon, of course, but at least someone of the young Brandon type, a youngster one could take to and trust with Elsie, because he was one's own sort. This man from the Argentine was different— " foreign," as Mrs. Thornaby had put it the night before. He might be all right ; one hoped he was ; but he wasn't young Brandon or anything like him.

" You mustn't be jealous, you know," Elsie said mpulsively, as though she had been able to read her uncle's mind. " You needn't think anything of that sort. I'm not that kind."

" Jealous ! " Sir Clinton laughed to conceal the shrewdness of the stroke. " What would I be jealous about ? I couldn't have married you myself, could I ? " All I want is to see you happy, Elsie. You know that well enough."

" Then I am happy, so that's all right."

Her smile vouched for her even better than her tone.

" Here's Vincent with the chairs. Put them down over here, Vincent, please. Oh, by the way, you'd better get a couple more. I'd forgotten that these two girls may be coming out later on."

" Time enough when they turn up," Sir Clinton suggested.

He had no desire to pursue the conversation with his niece at the moment. It was getting on to dangerous ground, and he knew that by an incautious phrase or even a failing in enthusiasm he might open a breach which would be hard to re-close. Besides, he was curious to learn something at first-hand about Francia. He helped to set up the camp-chairs, and watched Elsie's husband arrange a cushion at her back when she sat down.

" That's nice," she said, leaning back luxuriously. " Nobody arranges a cushion so comfortably as you do, Vincent. You must have taken lessons or something."

" A correspondence course," Francia admitted, with a smile which showed white, even teeth. " Seven lessons, $10, with a diploma thrown in."

He gave the cushion a final touch and went over to his own chair. Sir Clinton also smiled, but without amusement. Francia was obviously an old hand at settling a girl's shoulders comfortably on a cushion ; and the joke about a correspondence course seemed rather pointless.

" Have you been long in Europe ? " he asked, as he sat down in his turn.

" A few months," Francia answered concisely.

He pulled a cigar-case from his pocket.

" You allow me ? " he asked, glancing at Elsie for permission to smoke.

She nodded, and he selected a cigar with some care.

" I do not like your climate," he continued, turning to Sir Clinton with another smile, which showed his teeth under his moustache. " We are not accustomed to this particular kind of dampness over yonder. Brrr ! "

He shrugged his shoulders as though a shiver had gone up his spine.

" I shall be glad to be back in Buenos Ayres, I can tell you, Sir Clinton."

" You aren't thinking of leaving immediately, I suppose ? "

" In a month or six weeks," Francia answered. " I shall be much pleased to taste *café con lèche* again. England is, of course, a wonderful country ; but it cannot make *café con lèche* as we can."

" That's *café au lait*, uncle," Elsie explained.

Sir Clinton needed no assistance in the matter, but he nodded his thanks for the information.

" Six weeks ? " he said, returning to the earlier subject. " I'd no idea you were leaving so soon as that."

" It does seem short," Elsie interrupted. " But won't it be a lovely trip when it does come ? We're joining the boat at Havre, you know, uncle ; and then we go down the coast of Spain. I've never seen Spain before. And then on to Teneriffe and Dakar—fancy seeing Africa ! I never thought I'd get as far as that."

" Neither did I," Sir Clinton admitted, with an assumption of cheerfulness so good that it deceived his niece. " And then ? "

" Oh, Rio. You know, the place where the armadillos come from. You used to make me sing ' Roll down, roll down to Rio ' when you gave me the *Just-So Stories*, you remember, long ago ; and I used to wish I could roll to Rio. I was only about six then, wasn't I ? "

" About that, I suppose."

" And then Santos, Montevideo, and Buenos Ayres." Elsie wound up, disregarding him. " I've looked it all up in the atlas, you know, uncle. What a trip ! "

Sir Clinton agreed with a gesture.

" If I had the time, I'd go out with you and have a look round myself. Nice to see you settled down in your own house."

" I wish you could," Elsie exclaimed. " Oh, uncle, now you're out of the police, couldn't you manage it ? "

Sir Clinton saw from the tone of her voice that, although he might have dropped into the second place in her life, he still had his full share of her affection. Quite obviously, she was eager to see him come out. The tail of his eye swept round to Francia's face in time to catch a totally different feeling displayed there. It was a mere fleeting expression, but Sir Clinton saw it clearly enough before it was suppressed.

" Can't be done, I'm afraid, Elsie," he said regretfully. " I'll have my work cut out for me this year in getting to know my way about the estate business. I'm new to it, you know."

Elsie's face betrayed her disappointment.

" Then you'll come out later on," she decided.

A mischievous expression crossed her face.

" What a pity you can't come. You'd have been such company for Estelle."

" What's Estelle got to do with it ? " Sir Clinton demanded.

Estelle Scotswood was one of Elsie's oldest friends, and in the days when the two children had been almost inseparable, Sir Clinton had been elected to the post of Estelle's " Honorary Uncle." The honorary uncleship had its perquisites later when Estelle grew up into a tall, graceful girl who was never bored when taken out to dinner or to a theatre.

" It was Vincent who suggested it," Elsie explained. " He said he was afraid I might be lonely, going away out yonder, at first."

Francia nodded gravely to Sir Clinton as though in confirmation.

" A new country, new faces, a new language," he said, " it might be rather trying at first if one had no friend at hand. So I thought."

" And so we're taking Estelle out with us, and she'll

stay with me for a couple of months. Wasn't it nice of Vincent to think of it ? Of course, we're paying Estelle's passage, as she's our guest. She's tremendously keen to come ; and it'll be so nice to have her there, instead of starting off with no friends at all. Won't it ? "

A weight fell from Sir Clinton's mind when he heard the plan. Elsie couldn't have picked a better companion than Estelle ; and it was a relief to know that she wouldn't be landed out in Buenos Ayres with not a soul she knew, except her husband, on the whole western continent. Estelle would bridge the gap until Elsie picked up some acquaintances. He had to admit to himself that Francia had shown the thoughtfulness for which Elsie had praised him. An idea of that sort needed some sympathetic imagination to produce it. And there was a certain amount of sacrifice involved as well. Most men would shrink from having a friend of their wife's planted on them for a couple of months immediately after marriage and before there had been time for the inevitable adjustments which marriage brings in its train.

Before he could answer his niece, however, there came an interruption. The figure of the table-maid came across the lawn towards their group ; and as she drew near Sir Clinton saw that her face was white.

" Sergeant Ledbury's in the smoking-room, sir," she said, addressing Francia. " He's called about a motor-car, he says. And," she added, turning to Sir Clinton with a look of appeal in her eyes, " he says he's heard that you're here ; and he'd be very glad if you could spare time to have a word with him."

Francia was evidently taken by surprise.

" What can he want to see me about ? " he asked.

" A motor-car was what he said, sir."

Sir Clinton dismissed the maid.

" We'd better see what it's all about," he suggested quietly.

He was careful to betray no hint that he had any clue

in the matter. Francia looked doubtful, and a puzzled expression passed over his face as he offered Elsie his excuses for leaving her. Sir Clinton said nothing ; but the unspoken message in his glance served to reassure his niece as they left her and turned towards the house.

CHAPTER IV

ACCIDENT OR HOMICIDE?

Sergeant Ledbury proved to be a burly, red-moustached man whose general air of dullness was curiously belied by the sharpness of his rather small and close-set eyes. Sir Clinton, after a shrewd glance of inspection, inclined to the view that the dullness was wilful rather than natural ; and he waited with some interest to see if his inference would prove accurate.

" You're Sir Clinton Driffield, sir ? " Ledbury inquired respectfully as they came into the room. " And this will be Mr. Francia, I suppose ? Just so."

Sir Clinton nodded ; and the sergeant subjected both of them to a polite but detailed scrutiny, as though he had not quite decided what to say next and was merely occupying his eyes while he turned over his phrases in his mind.

" I've called about your motor-car, sir," he explained, turning to Francia. " Isn't it a grey two-seater Alvis with the number JX. 7079 ? "

The sergeant's query stirred Sir Clinton's recollections. He recalled that Johnnie had drawn attention to the absence of Francia's car from the garage that morning ; and this linked itself in his mind with the two-seater which had played a part in the affair by the roadside on the previous night. Though apparently indifferent, he was watching Francia keenly ; and he detected a fleeting expression of surprise and uneasiness on the face of the Argentiner when the sergeant put his question.

41

"Yes," Francia admitted, "that is a description of my car."

The sergeant waited for a moment, evidently in the hope that Francia might be drawn into something further if he were given time ; but, finding that nothing was volunteered, he assumed an expression of condolence.

"I'm sorry to say, sir, that it's met with an accident. The radiator's smashed and one of the wheels is badly buckled. You weren't driving it yourself, of course ? "

Sir Clinton mentally gave the sergeant a good mark. Ledbury knew, of course, that Quevedo had been driving the car and had been killed ; but in all probability he had ascertained from the servants that Francia was still in ignorance of the tragedy ; and he was keeping this card up his sleeve until the proper moment arrived for playing it. Evidently the sergeant believed in giving himself every chance of eliciting information before he was forced to be frank himself.

The effect of the news upon Francia was what might have been expected from any man who learns that he has had a valuable car smashed up.

"That *is* a bad business," he ejaculated. "I hope no one was hurt ? "

Ledbury's face showed that his hand was being forced.

"Well, sir," he said, "might I ask who was driving your car last night ? I take it that it hasn't been stolen."

"No," Francia admitted, after a pause so slight that it might easily have passed unnoticed, "it wasn't stolen. I lent it to an acquaintance of mine. He had to get to London in a hurry, and he borrowed it."

"Ah, just so," said Ledbury, producing a notebook. "I'll take the particulars, sir, if you don't mind. One likes to have things ship-shape, and I never trust my memory. Now, would you let me have the name of the driver ? "

"Quevedo is his name—Pedro Quevedo."

Ledbury, slightly accentuating the dullness of his expression, requested Francia to spell the name, and then took it down in his notebook after laboriously moistening the tip of his pencil.

" Pedro Quevedo," he said at last ruminatively. " A friend of yours, sir, I suppose ? "

" An acquaintance," Francia amended.

" Ah, just so," Ledbury corrected himself. " An acquaintance."

He moistened his pencil once more and made a note. Sir Clinton watched him amusedly. He was afraid that the sergeant was overdoing things a little ; but possibly a foreigner might not see through the acting. As Ledbury looked up from his notebook, Sir Clinton glanced at him with a twinkle in his eye ; but the sergeant stared owlishly at him with no answering flicker in his face.

" An acquaintance ? " he repeated heavily. " You didn't know him long, then ? "

Francia shook his head definitely.

" I met him on the ship coming from Buenos Ayres."

Sir Clinton was following the interview with a certain mild amusement. Quite obviously, Francia had made up his mind to volunteer no information ; and the sergeant was finding his task more difficult than he had expected.

" I thought perhaps you might have had some information about him," Ledbury confessed, with an air of disappointment. " You see, sir, in this country one doesn't lend one's car to chance acquaintances. It's not usual."

Again there was an almost undetectable pause before Francia replied.

" I think I had better be quite clear," he suggested. " Mr. Quevedo was not a friend of mine, you understand ? But we had some business dealings—private business transactions—and naturally I went, perhaps, a little out of my way to oblige him in the matter of the

43

car. A business acquaintance, that is how I should describe him."

" Quite so," Ledbury answered, as though the point had been cleared up to his satisfaction. " I quite see how it is, sir. You'll have his home address—I mean, his business premises in America—of course ? "

This time the pause was a shade longer than before.

" No," Francia said, at last, " I don't remember it. I had his address in London at one time. But when he came down here to stay at the Black Bull Hotel, I threw his London address into the wastepaper-basket— having no further need of it—and I cannot recall it now."

At this answer, the sergeant's face brightened slightly. The information seemed to have taken a weight off his mind.

" I see, sir," he said briskly. " This Mr. Quevedo, then, was nobody of much interest to you personally ? That's all the better ; for I'm sorry to say he was killed in this motor-smash. Very sad, isn't it ? " he added perfunctorily.

Sir Clinton, knowing that this revelation was bound to come sooner or later, had kept his eyes on Francia's face ; but the Argentiner betrayed no particular sorrow at the news of Quevedo's fate.

" Very sad," he agreed, in an almost formal tone. " How did it happen ? "

" A skid, sir. It took him smash into a stone wall. He's been badly cut about by the glass of the windscreen. Later on, perhaps, we'll need to ask you to identify him, just for form's sake, sir. But that won't be immediately."

Francia nodded as though agreeing to this.

" I'm quite at your service," he volunteered.

Then, as though a thought had struck him, he inquired :

" Was anyone else hurt in the accident ? "

Ledbury shook his head.

" Nobody, sir."

He seemed to have elicited all that he wanted from Francia at the moment.

" I think that's all just now, sir. I'll let you know later on about the identification."

He turned to Sir Clinton, but seemed doubtful about dealing with him so long as Francia was present. Sir Clinton saw his difficulty and helped him out.

" I think you wanted to speak to me about something, sergeant ? Right ! Then I tell you what we can do. I've got my car in the garage, and I'll run you down to the village. Save you a bit of a walk, and you can do your talking in the car. That suit you ? "

Ledbury accepted the invitation eagerly ; and, taking leave of Francia, they walked round to the garage. As Sir Clinton drove down the short approach to the house, he turned to the sergeant.

" I don't know this neighbourhood—only arrived last night after dark. You'll need to pilot me."

Ledbury nodded.

" Turn to the left at the gate, sir, and then, if you don't mind, you might take the first on the left. The fact is, I'd like you to see the state of affairs with your own eyes ; and then perhaps you'd be good enough to give me your advice. You've had experience, sir, and I'd be very glad if you'd give me the benefit of it."

Sir Clinton turned an innocent face to his passenger.

" Advice ? What do you want advice for, sergeant ? I gather a man's been knocked out in a car accident. Well, the coroner will have to look into it. You know the routine, surely ? "

Ledbury fidgeted slightly in his seat before replying.

" It's not quite so simple as all that, sir."

45

Sir Clinton made no effort to restrain his smile.

"Ah, I see, sergeant," he suggested, "It's this murder case you have in your mind—Teddy Barford, I suppose ? "

The sergeant was evidently taken aback.

" Well, you do seem to know more than one expects ! It's what I'd heard about you, sir, if you don't mind my saying it. How . . ."

Sir Clinton had no desire to encourage a roving inquiry into the sources of his information. He changed the subject abruptly and decisively.

" You didn't say anything about a murder to Mr. Francia, I noticed ? "

Ledbury seemed to take the hint.

" Well, sir," he explained, " when you're out to get all the information you can, it seems to me there's two ways of doing it. One's to pretend you know all about it before you start, and let on you can check every fact as it comes out. That wants a good bluffer to work it properly. Then there's the other way : to pretend you know nothing at all and take all you get as if it was a treat to get it. That's the sympathetic way, and the stupider you look while you're working it, the more you're likely to fish up. I'm more fitted to look stupid than to bluff well, sir ; so I take the easiest line."

" Ah," commented Sir Clinton, " then that would account for the laborious pencil-licking and so forth, I take it ? "

Ledbury recognised that he had met a kindred spirit.

" Just so, sir. It all helps, you see. When people see me licking away at my pencil, they put me down as a blank idiot, naturally ; because anyone with a grain of common sense would sharpen the point before it got to that state. I've thought out one or two things of that sort : like scratching your ear as if you were puzzled, or breathing noisily, or losing your place in your notebook.

It's easier to pretend that you're stupider than you are than that you're cleverer than you are."

" A bit involved, that last sentence. But I get a dim notion of your drift, I think. Now suppose, sergeant, that for a moment or two you contrive to be just as clever as you are, no more and no less ; and kindly tell me what it's all about."

The sergeant struggled for a moment with a nascent grin and succeeded in repressing it at last. Sir Clinton's reputation had led him to expect this kind of thing ; and he was pleased to find himself ready for it.

" Turn to the left here, sir," he directed, as they came to a cross-road.

Sir Clinton obediently swung the car round ; and as he came into the fresh road, he recognised that it was the one which had brought him into Raynham Parva on his arrival. The pine spinney on the left was where he had left Staffin with her suitcase. She had evidently sent him on a long wild goose chase by her mis-directions.

" Well, sergeant ? " he prompted.

" This is what happened, sir. About a quarter to one this morning, Constable Peel was cycling home along this road a bit farther up—coming in this direction. He'd been out to some spree or other—he's young and unmarried—and he'd stayed pretty late. Of course he was off duty."

" It sounds like it. Go on."

" He was pedalling along, not expecting anything on the road at that hour of the morning ; and he'd come within a few hundred yards of the lodge gate of Screvesby Manor. There's a stone wall on each side of the road there, sir, with a deepish ditch."

Sir Clinton nodded as though accepting informa-tion ; but he had no difficulty in recalling the long high wall past which he had driven on the previous night.

" He turned a corner, sir," the sergeant continued,

" and in front of him was the glare of a motor's head-lights. He expected it to be down on him in a second or two ; but it turned out that the car was standing ; so he cycled along towards it. By the time he came level with it, he was pretty dazzled by the lights, but as he passed the car, he saw it was empty and the door was open. Then, a few yards farther down the road, he made out —after he'd got his eyes free from the glare of the lamps —something big on one side of the road, and somebody standing beside it."

" Was that near the lodge gate ? " Sir Clinton demanded.

" A couple of hundred yards on the other side of it from here," Ledbury explained, " You'll see it all for yourself in a few minutes, sir."

Sir Clinton nodded, and the sergeant went on with his tale.

" When Peel got his eyes a bit undazzled, he made out that the thing in the ditch was a car, pretty badly smashed up. So he got off his bike and wheeled it over to where the man was standing. Peel recognised him, of course, at the first look. It was Teddy Barford. So Peel, not rightly understanding what was afoot, spoke up and asked Teddy what it was all about and if anyone was hurt in the smash. Meanwhile, he was peering about as best he could with his dazzled eyes, trying to see for himself. I always keep one eye shut myself, when I'm passing motor-lights ; but Peel never thinks to do a simple thing like that."

Sir Clinton had a suspicion that Constable Peel was not altogether a favourite with his superior.

" Teddy Barford looked a bit taken aback, it seems, when he saw Peel," the sergeant proceeded. " He's rather a rough-spoken man when he's angry, and I gather he asked Peel what the hell he was doing there —or words to that effect," Ledbury added hurriedly. " It sounds as if he'd been a bit surprised by Peel turning up like that—hadn't noticed him coming up, I expect. Anyhow, Peel pushed past him and looked at the smash-up ; and there was the body of a man lying in the ditch, and a lot of stuff that Peel took to be blood. So Peel laid down his bike and had a good look at things. It seems the poor chap was a deader—complete—but quite warm. Knocked out only a few minutes before, by the look of things.''

Ledbury paused for a moment, as though his last words had completed one section of his narrative.

" Peel climbed out of the ditch, after he'd seen all he could see with the help of his bicycle lamp ; and then it seems to have struck him that Teddy Barford wasn't doing overmuch to help in the affair. He'd had a good look at the deceased's face ; but it was so cut about with the glass of the windscreen that he made very little of it. So he turned to Teddy and asked if he knew who it was. Teddy glowered at him and said : ' Yes, it's that swine Quevedo. That settles the score I had against him.' And a few more things that showed there'd been bad blood between 'em. Peel pricked up his ears at that.''

" Death settles most scores," Sir Clinton commented, with wilful sententiousness.

Ledbury glanced round as though he detected something more in the phrase than appeared on the surface.

" Just so, sir,'' he agreed. " It might mean that. But Peel, being one of these young fellows that's keen on promotion and getting their names into the papers, didn't quite take that out of it all. There'd been a bit of talk about the place lately about Teddy Barford having his nose put out of joint by Quevedo over some girl or other ; and Peel, putting one thing to another, made up his mind that likely enough Teddy Barford had lost his temper and gone for Quevedo. Peel's got one of these leaping intellects, sir, that don't seem to need to wait for evidence before they get set like a bit of concrete."

Sir Clinton smiled covertly at this further revelation of Ledbury's distaste for his subordinate.

" Some people go one way to the truth, others go another, you know, sergeant. It takes all kinds to make a world."

Ledbury stared suspiciously at his companion. This flood of platitude was hardly in keeping with his pre-conceived opinion of Sir Clinton.

" Ah, just so," he admitted grudgingly, after a slight pause. " Well, the end of it was, he asked Teddy if he'd any objection to being searched—just as a kind of guarantee of good faith, or something of that sort. And Teddy Barford was so mad at the notion, that he fairly damned Peel's eyes for him—just as I expect I'd have done myself in his place. That made Peel more set on his notions than ever, of course. He's one of these obstinate fellows—you know, sir. And the upshot of it was that he arrested Teddy Barford there and then for murder. No warrant, of course, and no evidence worth a hen's whistle."

His face showed clearly enough what he thought of the affair. Sir Clinton made no comment ; and the sergeant, after waiting for one, decided to go on with his story.

" He made Teddy take his bike into the car as well as himself, and then they drove into Raynham Parva and got me roused up. By that time, Teddy Barford had got cooled down a bit. He'd had time to think things over. So when I tackled him, he just said that he'd make no statement till he'd seen a solicitor. Wisest thing he could have done, of course ; and I didn't dissuade him. If I'd thought it was murder, I'd have had a turn at him my-self, to see if I could get him to talk. But the whole thing was obviously an ordinary motor-smash, from all I could get out of Peel. So I explained to Teddy Barford that he'd better let us lock him up for the rest of the night and it would be all right in the morning, no doubt. He'd sobered up a good bit, and he agreed to this. He knows he'll get a square deal from me."

" Humorous situation you all seem to have got into," Sir Clinton admitted. " And meanwhile the unfortunate dead man was left by the roadside to horrify the next passer-by ? "

" No longer than I could help, sir. I got hold of another constable and sent him out with a waterproof sheet to make things decent, and I gave him orders to stand by until he was relieved. Much better to leave things as they were until daylight, when we could see clearly."

" And then ? "

" Well, of course, by breakfast-time, the whole place was buzzing with the news. I took Peel with me and went down to the smash-up. Once I'd had a look-round in daylight, the thing was clear enough. It was just an ordinary motor-smash. The tracks are plain enough on the road. Quevedo's car had swerved, hit the ditch, half-overturned with the jerk. He'd gone clean through the windscreen and got frightfully cut about the face and neck by the glass. The car had brought up short against the stone wall—the radiator's crushed and the bonnet's all burst. Then, as the tracks show, Teddy Barford had come along behind in his car. His track overlies Quevedo's car-marks and travels on a bit beyond the place where Quevedo went into the ditch. There's no doubt he arrived after the smash. He pulled up at the sight of the wreck, got out, and walked back. And then Peel must have come down on top of him before he'd time to do much."

" Well, that sounds simple enough," Sir Clinton pointed out. " What am I doing here, if I may ask ? "

Ledbury grinned at the thrust.

" It's this way, sir," he explained. " The car's well

enough known round here. We've all seen Mr. Francia and his wife driving it. So we had to inquire about it, anyhow, in case it had been stolen by Quevedo, or anything of that sort. And we had to let the owner know it had got into a smash. Well, you'd hardly believe it, sir, but even after I'd shown Peel the track of Teddy Barford's wheels overlying those of Quevedo's car, he still stuck to it that it was a murder case. He's got his knife into Teddy hard. They never liked each other ; and now, what with a chance of a bit of notoriety and a chance of paying off scores, Peel's that obstinate that he won't give in he's wrong. Now I want to let Teddy Barford out as quick as may be, for the whole thing's a mare's nest. But Peel's obstinate ; and he's been as near insolent as he dare be about my ' favouring the escape of a criminal '—that's his way of putting it."

To Ledbury's astonishment, Sir Clinton interjected a question which suggested that his mind was wandering from the main track.

" What sort of driver is Mr. Teddy Barford ? A good one ? "

" Oh, quite good," the sergeant admitted in a puzzled tone. " He drives hard, but I never knew him come near an accident for all that. He's no patience, Teddy, though. I've often had a lift in his car ; and when he starts off, it fairly jerks the inside out of you."

" Let's the clutch in with a bang, you mean ? "

" Just so, sir. Makes the car jump about two feet as it gets off the mark. Cruel on the machinery, sir."

" Sorry I interrupted," Sir Clinton apologised. " Go on with the story. I'm still unable to see why I'm here."

" Well, it's this way, sir. Peel wouldn't give way and nothing I could say to him would shift him from his notions. So at last I said to him : ' There's no use our arguing this thing up and down any more. You say it's a murder done by Teddy Barford. I say it's just a plain motor-smash. Suppose we call in an umpire to settle it one way or the other ? ' You see, I'd got word you were coming down to stay at Fern Lodge, sir. So I said to him : ' You've heard of Sir Clinton Driffield that's just retired from the Police ? You're so keen on the papers that you must have seen that and know all about him. What about asking him to settle who's right ? You won't go against his opinion, will you ? Nor I, either.' Well, Peel hummed and hawed, but at last he had to give in. ' You'll never get him to come,' he said. ' If he's the sort of person I've heard he is,' I said, ' he won't refuse. And I'll go up now and fetch him if he'll come. You wait here and see no one stands round gaping. And keep your mouth shut,' I said to him as I went off. And I left him thinking."

" You didn't leave me much chance of refusing, did you ? " Sir Clinton pointed out, with a smile. " Well, if it's really going to be of any help to you, it's very little trouble to me. But I must have a look round, you know. I can't hazard an opinion on second-hand evidence in a matter of importance."

" Of course, sir. That's understood. And it's very good of you to fall in with the idea, sir. Peel won't have a word to say if you agree with me."

" And if I happen to agree with Peel, by any chance ? "

" I've heard a good deal about you, sir. I'd trust your opinion even if it went against my own."

" There's a third possibility on the board," Sir Clinton remarked. " Ah, here we are ! "

The wrecked car had come in sight as he spoke ; and he slowed down, bringing his car to a standstill long before it reached the point where the lodge gate broke the line of the wall on the left of the road. Ledbury's surprise at this was evident. He had expected Sir Clinton to drive straight up to the scene of the disaster, where the constable was awaiting them, on guard over the wreckage.

" Aren't you going on, sir ? " the sergeant inquired, holding the car-door open in a tentative manner, as though he expected to be told to keep his seat.

" No use bringing an extra set of car tracks to mix things up, is there, sergeant ? " Sir Clinton answered. " It's safer to stop a decent distance away, just in case of need. We'll walk the rest. By the way, have any cars passed this way since the smash ? "

" None, sir, up to the time I left Peel here."

" H'm ! " Sir Clinton commented ruminatively. " There's been at least one car through, if you look at the tracks there on the road. Lucky the surface seems to have been just right for taking impressions of the tyres. Now we'll interview your friend."

Constable Peel proved to be a young man with a certain cockiness of demeanour which suggested that he was not likely to under-estimate his own merits. Sir Clinton questioned him about passing cars, and found that his inference had been correct : one car had passed up the road not far ahead of their own.

" I signalled them to stop, sir," Peel explained, " and then I went down and made them drive carefully past. Got them in as close to the ditch as possible, so's they wouldn't mix up the other wheel-tracks with theirs. That's their track—the fresh one yonder."

Sir Clinton's nod conveyed his appreciation of this caution ; and Peel threw a glance at the sergeant as much as to say : ' There ! *You* wouldn't have thought of that ! ' Ledbury ignored this, and contented himself with explaining that Sir Clinton had come to look into things on the spot.

" This is how it was, Sir Clinton . . ." Peel began. But Sir Clinton cut him short in a tone which combined politeness and decision.

" I'll have a look round myself, first, constable.

54

Then I'll know better what questions I want to ask you."

Constable Peel's jauntiness declined slightly.

" Very good, sir," he agreed.

He fell in alongside his superior, and both of them followed Sir Clinton over to the wreck of the car.

CHAPTER V

SOME FACTS IN THE CASE

For several minutes, Sir Clinton stood on the grassy border of the road, apparently trying to reconstruct the sequence of events which had led up to the tragedy. Quite evidently, the car had been travelling at a fair speed when it went over the edge of the ditch and collided with the wall beyond. The radiator was smashed and twisted with the impact, and the near forewheel was badly buckled. Glass from the broken windscreen was scattered over the seats and the floor, as well as on the ground near by ; and the floor-boards of the car, as well as the grass, showed ominous dark stains on which the blood was still moist. Quevedo had apparently been thrown through the windscreen when the shock occurred ; and he had landed on the grass, clear of both the car and the wall.

Constable Peel manifestly found Sir Clinton's silence rather long ; and at last he decided to speak himself.

" The way I look at it is this, sir. The deceased had a skid or something, and his car went into the wall. He wasn't killed outright. Then Barford—who'd a grudge against him—came up ; and, seeing the man was all cut up with the glass, he saw his chance and finished him, thinking that a knock on the head would pass as having happened in the accident itself. And so it would, if he'd had time to get away. That would explain his saying to me . . ."

Sir Clinton looked up, evidently none too pleased at being interrupted.

" A skid, you say ? Very well. Let me see the trace of that skid in the track of the car. Facts are what I want, constable."

With rather less confidence in his air, Peel retraced the wheel-marks of the shattered car along the road.

" There ! " he said, after walking a few yards, " that's what I would say was the beginning of the skid, sir."

Sir Clinton stooped over the marks and scrutinised them with care.

" It's a matter of terminology, I suppose," he said sarcastically. " Skid seems to convey something to your mind which it fails to suggest to me. What do you say, sergeant ? "

Ledbury, concealing his joy at the constable's down-cast appearance, bent over the track before offering an opinion.

" What I mean by a skid," he explained, " is when the wheel slides sideways instead of rolling forwards. I don't see anything like that in the tracks."

He paused for a moment, and then added in a doubt-ful voice :

" That's a rum start ! "

" Very rum," Sir Clinton agreed in a colourless tone. " But it's a fact. You'd better make a note of it."

Ledbury nodded and drew out his notebook. Sir Clinton was faintly amused to see that the pencil which the sergeant produced was one which required no lick-ing to make it write. Peel also fished out a notebook and made a jotting.

" You think there wasn't a skid, sir ? " he demanded.

" Do you yourself think there was, after examining the track closely ? "

Peel's assurance was replaced by a slight nervousness as he heard Sir Clinton's tone.

" Well, sir, perhaps I made a mistake."

Sir Clinton's expression was hardly reassuring ; and his next words took the last trace of swagger out of Peel.

"A minute ago, you'd have been prepared to take your oath that this car skidded. If the coroner questioned you about it, that's what you'd have testified, apparently. By that time, these tracks would have disappeared and there would be no way of checking your evidence. This isn't one of your chicken-stealing cases, constable. You've charged a man with murder. And you don't seem to think it worth while to look at things carefully. You'd simply got the idea that if a car smashed into a wall, there must have been a skid ; so you took that for granted and never bothered to look. Isn't that about it ? "

Peel's face showed that this shot was near the truth, and he refrained from attempting to answer.

"That comes of preconceived notions," Sir Clinton pointed out. "What we really want are the facts, first of all. I don't suppose either of you can tell me, but I'd like to know if this man Quevedo drove his car on the throttle or on the accelerator."

Neither official could answer this query ; but it prompted Ledbury to walk back to the car and examine the steering-wheel.

"You mean, sir, that the throttle's full open ? "

"Yes."

Sir Clinton looked thoughtfully at the car for a moment or two, and then tested the throttle-lever gingerly with his finger.

"It's quite tight, you'll find, sergeant, if you test it. The shock of the smash wouldn't shift it over, so far as one can guess. So apparently the car was on full throttle when the smash happened. If he'd been driving on the accelerator, the throttle would have been right back— just giving enough gas to let the engine tick over when the clutch was out."

"I see that, sir, though I don't drive a car of my own."

He looked doubtfully at Sir Clinton.

"I suppose I ought to make a note of that, sir ? "

"Wait a bit. There's something else to couple on to

it. You don't drive a car, you say. Well, this is a four-speeds-forward gear-box. And the gear-lever's in the notch for the third speed—the car's not on top gear. You'd better jot that down in connection with the full throttle."

Ledbury's little eyes brightened.

" I think I see what you mean, sir. It's a flat road, so he wouldn't have been changing gear between here and the village. And he wouldn't be driving full throttle on third speed when he might have been getting more out of the machine by putting his gear on top and closing the throttle a bit ? "

Sir Clinton seemed in no mood to encourage premature theorising.

" All you know, sergeant, is the position of the two levers. That's a matter of fact. Let's leave the pretty hypotheses out of it at present."

He turned from the car to the spot where the body of Quevedo lay under the waterproof sheet.

" We'll have a look at him now, sergeant," he suggested.

" He's a bit ugly, sir," the sergeant suggested. " The glass of the windscreen cut him all about the face and neck—ghastly."

" I'm not sensitive," Sir Clinton explained curtly. " Let's see what damage was done."

Ledbury lifted the sheet and exposed the body. It was clear at a glance that the sergeant had not overstated the case. Quevedo's face had apparently been driven across a sharp edge of the broken windscreen, and hardly a feature had escaped intact. Even the neck, where it was unprotected by his collar, had been cut deeply here and there.

" I told you, sir," the sergeant pointed out. " He's not a pretty sight. Nothing much to be seen but blood and cuts. Even if he hadn't been hurt in the smash-up, the glass would have finished him. His jugular vein's

severed. He'd have bled to death in no time. You can
see the amount of blood there is round about him on
the grass."

Sir Clinton nodded absently in reply and continued
his examination.

" Funny what a clean cut you get from a piece of
glass," Constable Peel communicated to the world in
general. " Just like a razor, it is."

" Or a piece of paper," the sergeant amplified. " I've
had a finger cut with the edge of a bit of paper once—
deep. You'd hardly believe it unless you saw it."

He seemed anxious to soothe Peel's feelings after the
rough handling that Sir Clinton had given the constable.
Ledbury was not the man to bear a grudge too long.

" A thread'll bite deep enough, too," Peel pursued.
" If you pull a fine bit of thread through your fingers
too quick, it'll give you a nasty sort of wound—just like
a glass-cut. It's so clean that it doesn't bleed on the
surface for quite a while."

Sir Clinton rose to his feet.

" You can cover him up again for the present," he
said. " I've seen all I want to see just now."

He moved over to the car and stood examining it
while the two officials covered the body with the
sheet again.

" I suppose you've taken a note of the appearance of
the face and so forth ? " he asked, as Ledbury came to
his side.

" Yes, sir. But of course there'll be a P.M. and the
surgeon will get all the details then."

Sir Clinton leaned on the side of the car and examined
the litter of broken glass on the floor of the driving-seat.

" Lot of blood there," he pointed out. " Better make
a note of that, sergeant. By the way, did you note anything about blood on his clothes ? "

" There was a lot down the front, sir. I suppose it
soaked him pretty well when the jugular began to bleed.

60

He was lying partly on his side ; and it would flow all over the place when it gushed out."

" I'd make a note of that too, if I were you. Now we'll have a look at these car-tracks. It's lucky the tyre-marks seem to be different. Makes it easy to pick out one from another."

He stepped along the road beyond the body.

" This is the mark of Barford's car, I take it ? " he asked Peel. " He overran the spot where the smash was, and then pulled up sharp, if one can trust the marks."

Peel followed his gesture, and saw where the regular marking of the tyre merged into a long clean stroke in the mud.

" You mean these'll be his back wheels with the brakes on and the wheels locked—just sliding on the road instead of rolling, sir ? "

Peel stopped abruptly, realising that he was on the forbidden ground of theory. Sir Clinton's smile reassured him slightly.

" This mark here, sir," he went on, rather encouraged, " is where Teddy Barford reversed his car after I'd told him he'd have to come along with me."

" Did he start off with a jerk ? " Sir Clinton inquired, pointing to the place where the back wheels had evidently spun and slipped as the clutch was let in.

" He did, sir. He always does."

Sir Clinton accepted the information as though it were fresh to him.

" Now, I think, we'll have a look at the track of the wrecked car," he suggested. " We may as well be thorough when we're at it."

Accompanied by the two officials, he started at the point where the two-seater had gone into the ditch and worked back along the trail without haste.

" One of you had better make a diagram of this, before the marks get obliterated," he suggested. " It's an easy enough job for you—the track's almost perfectly straight. All you have to do is to measure the near wheel's distance from the edge of the road, here and there, along the track at fixed distances apart."

They had come to the lodge gate as he spoke ; and a glance showed him that the lodge itself was unoccupied. The gate was slightly set back from the road, and the avenue from the house broadened out like a delta so as to round off the turns at the sides. Sir Clinton left the track of the wrecked car and moved into the end of the avenue.

" H'm ! " he said. " See that ? Here's the track of another car. Down on the road, its track's crossed by the track of the wrecked car, so this one was here before Quevedo came along."

They studied the fresh track for a short time ; and at last Constable Peel could restrain himself no longer.

" Here's a funny thing, sir ! " he pointed out eagerly. " This car turned in to the mouth of the avenue and then reversed out again. Funny thing to turn back at this point on the road. He must have missed his way, or something, and only noticed it when he reached this length."

Ledbury had examined the track even more minutely.

" Another funny thing," he contributed, with an expression on his face which showed he was not ill-pleased to wipe the eye of his colleague. " This fellow's track coming in is overlaid by Quevedo's car-track, just as you said, sir. But the track he made after he reversed out is on top of Quevedo's track. And, what's more," he added, " this fellow seems to have been manœuvring about a bit. He came in here ; then he reversed till he was half across the road ; then he drove in again ; and finally he reversed out a second time for his turn homewards. The two tracks of his wheels are almost on top of each other, but I can see the double trail in the blur all right."

" That's a sound bit of observation, sergeant," Sir

Clinton complimented him. " I'll add two further points ; and then I think we've got the lot. First, the bed of the avenue's fairly soft ; and if you look at the point where the car rested when it came in first, you'll find the marks are deep compared with the ones made when it came to a standstill a second time. Evidently it stood for quite a while the first time, and only a short time afterwards. Second, this car wasn't here when I passed along the road last night ; and I may tell you I met Quevedo's car just outside Raynham Parva. So this fellow must have come along a side road and turned into this road after I'd passed. Otherwise, I'd have met him. And I met no one but Quevedo."

He seemed to consider carefully before he continued :

" You've seen Barford's clothes by daylight, I suppose. Any blood on them, did you notice ? "

Ledbury looked at the constable, and both shook their heads. Sir Clinton's expression seemed to suggest that he was relieved by this negative evidence.

" I'd like to have another look at that car," he said, turning back along the road in the direction of the wreckage. " We'd better do the thing thoroughly, sergeant ; and search the floor in case there's something to be picked up amongst the litter."

Under his directions, the sergeant began to collect the broken glass which strewed the seats and floor of the car, each fragment being handed to Sir Clinton for examination as it came to hand. Most of those on the floor were moist with blood. At last it seemed as though only a few minor fragments remained to be secured.

" Nothing that looks important so far," Sir Clinton confessed. " Still, stick to it, sergeant. Let's have every scrap you can find."

Ledbury obediently grubbed on the floor ; and, after fishing out one or two fresh samples of glass, he came upon one which Sir Clinton evidently regarded as of more interest than the rest.

" Have a good look at this, sergeant," he suggested, holding the fragment out for inspection. " Would you say that was plate glass from the windscreen ? "

Ledbury and Peel bent over it.

" That's not plate glass," Peel declared. " It's far too thin ; and you can see a rounded sort of edge at one side—a ground edge, isn't it ? "

" That describes it well enough," Sir Clinton admitted.

" I know what that is, sir," Ledbury broke in. " It's a bit of a spectacle lens."

" Have a good look at it," Sir Clinton repeated, offering it to the sergeant.

Ledbury scrutinised the fragment for some seconds.

" It's a spectacle lens, sir, right enough."

" Hold it up and look through it, sergeant. It's not a lens, you'll see. There's no curvature. It's plain on both sides."

" So it is, sir," Ledbury admitted, handing it over to Peel so that he also might examine it.

" Hunt around a bit more, sergeant. This looks as if we might find something else worth having."

Ledbury returned to his task, handing out his discoveries as he made them. Three or four small pieces of glass were dismissed by Sir Clinton without comment ; but at last he seemed to find something which interested him.

" What do you make of that ? " he inquired, handing the last chip back to the sergeant.

" It's too thin for plate glass, so it isn't a bit of the windscreen. There's no other broken glass on the car that I can see ; for the lamp lenses wouldn't get in here ; and the clock and speedometer faces aren't smashed— nor the dashboard light." Ledbury held the fragment up and peered through it. " It's got a curve on it."

He fished out a pocket-lens and scrutinised the chip.

" Looks like cheap glass, sir, so far as I can see. One

or two bubbles in it ; and there's a faintish tinge in it. What do you make of it ? "

" A bit of broken bottle, perhaps ? "

" I believe you're right, sir. It looks like something of the sort.".

" Well, keep it carefully, sergeant. It may turn out to be important. One never can tell. By the way, where's the other thing—the flat bit with the round edge. Oh, here it is."

Sir Clinton drew a few coins from his pocket and compared the curves of their edges with the arc of the ground rim of the glass fragment.

" The complete thing's been a shade larger than a half-crown," he pointed out, handing the glass and the coin to Ledbury for comparison. " You'd better preserve that carefully also. It might have a bearing on the case, once things are pieced together. Is there anything left on the floor of the car or on the seats ? Nothing ? "

" Just some bits so small that they're almost powder, sir."

" I'd sweep them up before the car's shifted. One never can tell what may be useful. And now, I think, we might have a look at the contents of Quevedo's pockets."

" I've got all the stuff parcelled up, sir," Ledbury explained. " I was able to get at the pockets without disturbing the body."

He produced a brown-paper parcel from a recess in the car, where he had placed it for safety ; and unrolled it on the grass for Sir Clinton's inspection.

" H'm ! Not much here of interest. Cigarette-case, match-box, fountain-pen, and so forth. Just what a normal man carries. What about this letter, sergeant ? "

" We didn't make much out of it, sir. What with the blood that had soaked it, and the fact that it's in some foreign language, it left both Peel and me standing. Perhaps you'd glance at it, sir, and see if it suggests anything."

Sir Clinton unfolded the blood-stained paper gingerly and examined it thoughtfully. Ledbury, scanning his face, saw his brows contract sharply for a moment ; but immediately afterwards his expression relaxed again.

" I can't make much of it out," he admitted frankly. " It's almost illegible, with all this blood on it. You'll need to get it cleaned up by an expert before you'll be able to decipher the whole of it. All I can read are one or two isolated phrases. Here they are : ' A bouquet . . . aboard *Mihanovich* . . . four packages, 21, 22, 23, 25 kilos . . . remount service . . . Martigue . . . Le Grec . . . your beefsteak . . . *atorrante*.' H'm ! The *Mihanovich* appears to be a boat, sergeant. A kilo is a two-pound weight, roughly. If I'm not mistaken, Martigue is a slang term for a Marseillais. *Atorrante* means a low-down cuss of some sort—it looks abusive. Not very illuminating, altogether, at first sight, is it ? "

Ledbury shook his head rather disconsolately, and held out his hand for the paper. As Sir Clinton returned it, the sergeant glanced over it before putting it away.

" Here's some initials at the bottom, sir, under this splotch of blood. I believe one might read 'em if one held it up to the sun." He suited the action to the word. " It looks like a V. and an F., so far as I can make it out, sir. V. F. Aren't these the initials of Mr. Francia, sir ? "

" I believe so," Sir Clinton confirmed.

" Just so," Ledbury agreed. " This'll perhaps be one of his business letters."

Sir Clinton glanced along the road as the sergeant repacked his parcel.

" Let's have a last look round," he suggested, moving off towards the lodge gate.

From that point he followed the tracks of Quevedo's car a few yards in the direction of Raynham Parva and then halted suddenly.

" Make anything of that ? " he demanded, indicating one particular point on the trail.

Ledbury and Peel knelt down and examined the place carefully.

" Looks like the scrape of a wheel starting, sir ; but it's very slight. There's just the faintest change in the track."

Peel confirmed the sergeant's suggestion with a nod, but refrained from any verbal comment.

" That's what I'd take it to be myself," Sir Clinton agreed. " Well, that seems to be all I want to see, sergeant. And, now, what about giving you a lift into Raynham Parva, if you've any business in that direction —fetching up a cart to remove the body, or what not ? "

" You haven't given us that expert opinion yet, sir," Ledbury reminded him slyly.

" Oh, my opinion ? Well, here it is, for what it's worth. You're both wrong."

The sergeant was evidently quite unprepared for this verdict.

" I'm not quite sure what you mean, sir," he blurted out.

" Simple enough," Sir Clinton answered. " You said it was an accident pure and simple. It wasn't. Constable Peel said that Mr. Teddy Barford was a murderer. He isn't. If the coroner sees things as I do, I think you'll find the jury persuaded to give the verdict, Murder by some person unknown. And a remarkably clever person, too, I can tell you, sergeant. He's struck a new line in murders—at this late stage in the game."

The two officials were completely taken aback by this bold statement.

" There's just one other thing," Sir Clinton continued. " Go over that car with a small-toothed comb if necessary ; but see that you don't miss a piece of the rim of a pair of horn-rimmed spectacles. That would come in very handy, if you can lay your hands on it. But I doubt if it's there. One can't expect to have all the possible luck."

Ledbury recovered quickly enough from this second surprise.

" You read all that from the things you saw, sir ? " he asked.

" Yes, you've seen everything for yourself. I know no more than you do. I'll explain it, if you like."

The sergeant hurriedly put up his hand to check the impending revelation.

" No, sir. Just wait a moment, if you please. If it's a murder case—you're not having a joke, I take it ?— then it's the first murder case that's come my way. I've often wondered how I'd shape, if anything of that sort did happen hereabouts. Now, if you were to tell me all about it, there wouldn't be much for me in it, would there ? I mean, I'd like to feel I hadn't just been led by the nose, you see ? If it's all there, I'd like to have a chance of thinking it out for myself and comparing notes with you later on, if I may. There'd be more of what you might call intellectual satisfaction that way."

Sir Clinton felt more convinced than before that Ledbury was a man after his own heart. He liked independence of mind when it was coupled with efficiency.

" Quite right, sergeant. I'd feel the same myself."

Ledbury's face showed that he took this as a compliment.

" But remember, sergeant," Sir Clinton added, " one can't afford to lose time in a murder case. If you find you don't tumble to it quickly, then ring me up and I'll give you my notions for what they're worth. In any case, I'd like to hear your interpretation."

Ledbury was evidently pleased by this.

" I'd like to talk it over with you, sir. You think there's no reason why we shouldn't let Teddy Barford out now ? If we've really made a mistake in locking him up, then the sooner he's let out, the less fuss he's likely to make."

Sir Clinton gave Ledbury a good mark for that " we," since the detention of Barford had been contrary to his own wishes. The sergeant might not like Peel, but he had refrained from shuffling the burden of the mistake on to the constable's shoulders, as he might have done.

" Well, I think that's all we have to do here," he said, by way of closing the affair. " If you happen to have a camera handy you might photograph the smash-up before you shift things. It's as well to have a permanent record. And, now, if you'll get aboard, I'll run you into Raynham Parva so that you can get a cart or something to fetch away the body as soon as possible. There's no need to leave it here any longer."

CHAPTER VI

A NEW LINE IN MURDERS

A few minutes sufficed to take Ledbury into Raynham Parva and drop him at the entrance to the police station. So long as the sergeant was with him, Sir Clinton showed no sign that he had anything on his mind ; but as he drove back through the village again towards Fern Lodge, he was free to concentrate on a problem which the Quevedo affair had suggested to him ; and it was evident that he found it but little to his liking.

Ledbury would, of course, release Teddy Barford at the earliest possible moment ; and Sir Clinton felt that he could relieve Staffin's anxiety on this score as soon as an opportunity presented itself. He had seen enough, on the scene of the disaster, to feel sure that Barford could be exculpated. Only the ill-controlled zeal of Constable Peel had thrown suspicion on the man ; and, on the facts of the case, no jury would feel justified in bringing in a verdict against him. That side of the affair was as good as closed.

When Sir Clinton drove up the approach from the gate of Fern Lodge, he noticed that Francia had returned to the lawn and that two girls were there also, along with Elsie. As he passed them on his way to the garage, his niece made a gesture inviting him to join them ; and as soon as he had put his car under cover, he strolled across the grass towards the group.

Francia had a newspaper in his hand, from which he appeared to have been reading aloud to the girls ; and

Sir Clinton saw that he had a pair of large, tortoiseshell-rimmed spectacles on his nose, which markedly altered his appearance. Catching sight of Sir Clinton, he put down the newspaper and folded up his glasses, storing them away in his pocket. As her uncle came up, Elsie introduced him to the two strangers.

" My uncle. This is Miss Anstruther, uncle . . . and Miss Noreen Anstruther."

Sir Clinton's glance passed from the grey eyes of the elder girl to the brown ones of her sister ; and the impression he got was one which pleased him. Frankness and naturalness were two qualities which he rated highly ; and both girls seemed to have them in full measure.

" A nice, straight pair," was his mental verdict. " Not much cash to spend on their clothes, evidently ; but they've got good taste and they've done the best with what they have. No cheap shoes and stockings to ruin the effect."

He looked round, and was about to seat himself when his niece cautioned him.

" Mind that chair, uncle. It's the rickety one, so don't drop into it with a thud."

Sir Clinton inspected the camp-chair dubiously, tested it, and then seated himself gingerly.

" Don't let me interrupt," he suggested to Francia, with a glance at the dropped newspaper.

Francia waved the matter aside.

" It is only a copy of *El Diario* which I got by the post this morning," he explained. " I was translating some of the news for the ladies. As they are going out to my country, I thought it might amuse them to hear something of what is going on there at present."

He dismissed the matter with a shrug of his shoulders which accentuated that foreign appearance to which Mrs. Thornaby took exception.

" Going out to the Argentine, are you ? " Sir Clinton

71

asked lazily, turning to the two girls. " May I smoke ?
. . . Thanks. . . . Funny thing, everybody I meet nowadays seems to be going out to the Argentine."

He lighted a cigarette, after offering his case.

" My niece nearly persuaded me to go myself," he
added.

" My uncle's promised to come out later on," Elsie
told the two girls. " Miss Anstruther and her sister are
going to stay with us at first, uncle. Vincent thought it
would be more comfortable for them. They're going out
to take an engagement that Vincent's arranged for them."

" I'm a fiddler," Linda Anstruther explained, " and
my sister plays the piano. Mr. Francia very kindly
secured some engagements for us over there. It's so hard
to get anything in this country, nowadays, when one
isn't first-class."

" You don't sound like a misunderstood genius," Sir
Clinton interjected with a smile. " I've met very few
musical people who would admit frankly that they
weren't worth a place at the top if they had their rights."

" Miss Anstruther's very good indeed, uncle. Wait
till you hear her play," Elsie put in. " He's not really a
Philistine," she added, turning to the girls, " but he's
got a cold, hard mind, and all that sort of thing,
you know. See-things-as-they-are-and-draw-the-proper-
inferences."

" Just so, as my friend Sergeant Ledbury would say.
Get hold of the right end of the stick, no matter who's
at the other end. It's his look-out."

" He can't keep away from it," Elsie complained in
mock vexation. " I haven't seen him for months and
months, you know ; and we'd just settled down to have
a talk this morning when this sergeant-person put his
nose in at the gate. Off you went, uncle, without a
second thought for your affectionate niece. No, you
needn't apologise, really. No afterthoughts, by request.
You can tell us about it, if you like, though."

Sir Clinton threw a glance at Francia, but the Argentiner chanced to be looking in another direction. Evidently he had not thought it necessary to tell Elsie any details of the sergeant's visit.

"There was nothing much in it," Sir Clinton explained. "A motor-smash, and the sergeant wanted some help over a minor point."

With the tail of his eye he saw Francia glance sharply across, as though he had been taken by surprise.

"It was our car that has been damaged," Francia explained smoothly to Elsie. "I lent it to a—to an acquaintance ; and he has unfortunately come to grief with it. I am afraid it will not be fit to use for some time?"

His interrogation was evidently addressed to Sir Clinton.

"No, not for a while, I'm afraid. You can use mine any time you want to, Elsie," Sir Clinton suggested.

If Francia wished to spare the girls the news of Quevedo's death, there seemed no reason for bringing it out. They were sure to hear of it sooner or later ; but there was no need to speak of it just then.

"Oh, yours will do quite as well," Elsie assured her uncle. "It's lucky you're here just now."

"Yes, isn't it ?" Sir Clinton retorted ironically. "As the owner of a spare car, I'm a positive asset."

Before his niece could reply, Johnnie appeared at the front door and, espying his uncle, ran to them across the lawn.

"I say, uncle ! I've got the box all unpacked. Some of the things are just what I wanted. And thanks ever so much for them. But, I say, uncle, one of the motors has got a plug for the electric power, and the plug won't fit our plug-holes. Mother said I wasn't to go fiddling about with it myself. I was to bring it to you and see if you would do something with it. Will you come now ? I want to see the motor working."

Sir Clinton rose with a gesture of apology to his companions.

"We'll have a dash at it, Johnnie. I daresay there will be a spare plug somewhere about the house which will work all right. Come along."

Johnnie, delighted at his success in cutting out his prize under the very guns of the enemy, carried off Sir Clinton in triumph to the house.

"I've got all my stuff in the smoke-room, uncle," he explained. "Nobody uses the place much, you see ; and it's got a big table in it that's just right for setting things up. I can build up what I want, there, without people coming fussing round and telling me to clear my things away. Here's the place."

He ushered Sir Clinton into a big, light, airy room furnished with comfortably cushioned cane chairs, which lent a summery aspect to the place. Opposite the door, a broad window overlooked the lawns before the house ; to the right, the wall was broken by a French window giving access to a verandah, and by a second window. Between the windows stood Johnnie's table, littered with Meccano parts and tools.

Sir Clinton crossed the room and, glancing from the window on the verandah side, found that it overlooked a little lake with wooded sides.

"That's the lake I told you about, uncle," Johnnie informed him, rather unnecessarily. "Down on the left there, you can just see the roof of the boat-house. There's a roller-slip for putting the boats into the water, and a lot of pulleys and tackle for hauling them up again. It's as easy as anything. I can bring my boat up myself."

Sir Clinton seemed interested in the view for a moment. Then he glanced absently at a row of books which stood rather untidily on the sill of the window, and mechanically he shifted one or two of them so as to bring them into order. Johnnie failed to notice his uncle's preoccupation.

" Here's that motor, uncle. Look, it's got a plug on the wire like these ones they put on electric irons. It won't fit our wall-plugs."

Sir Clinton's introspection came to an end abruptly. He glanced at the plug which Johnnie held up.

" There's bound to be a spare plug lying about the house somewhere. Let's see . . ."

He moved across the room to the bell and rang.

" If we can't find one on the premises, I daresay we can pick one up in the village," he suggested. " If not we'll take out the car later on and hunt one up some-where."

Staffin appeared in answer to the bell's summons, and Sir Clinton turned to her with a glance which warned her that he wished to speak to her alone.

" I need a spare plug for the power-circuit. Where do they keep them ? " he asked.

Staffin evidently understood what he wanted.

" I think there are some in a drawer in the pantry next the wine-cellar, sir. Or else they're kept in a box of odds and ends up in one of the attics. I'm not sure."

" Cut along, Johnnie, and see if you can fish one out," Sir Clinton ordered.

When his nephew had disappeared, Sir Clinton turned to Staffin.

" I don't think you need worry about Mr. Teddy Barford," he said kindly. " Probably by this time he's back home again."

Staffin was evidently about to break out in gratitude when he stopped her.

" I may want to hear more about this affair later on. In the meantime, take my advice and say nothing about last night's business to anyone. If Barford keeps quiet, it's quite on the cards that you'll not be dragged into it after all. But remember, if I have to ask you any ques-tions, I want the plain truth and the whole truth. You understand ? "

75

Staffin flushed.

" There was nothing in it that I can't tell you, sir. Now I look at it, I see what a fool I was. Mr. Quevedo had such a smooth way of putting things, that half the time I just took what he said without really thinking about it. It looks different now—quite different."

" I expect so. If any points happen to strike you, keep them in mind. Nothing but the whole truth's any use to me. And now you'd better go, in case people find us talking together."

Staffin made another effort to thank him for his help ; but he cut her short and dismissed her, just as Johnnie's footsteps sounded along the corridor.

" Got it ? " Sir Clinton demanded as his nephew re-appeared. " All right. Give me a screw-driver."

" I can do it myself," Johnnie asserted, rather resentfully. " I could have fixed it up myself easily enough, only Mother won't let me meddle with the electric connections the least little bit. She's so beastly nervous, you know. Just you see how I can fix it."

He went over to the table, selected a screw-driver, and attacked the plugs. Sir Clinton kept a watchful eye on him as he exchanged the wiring.

" Tuck in the end of that wire," he ordered, when the work was half-done. " You'll have a short if you leave that tail floating round loose like that. Attention to details, young man, is half the secret of success in the police, if you're really aspiring to a job with them in the future."

Johnnie grinned at the rebuke ; but he took pains to see that there were no further slips in his work.

" There, that's done," he said, at last, putting down his screw-driver.

Sir Clinton took the plug from him, tested the grip of the screws on the wire, and then slipped the plug into the socket of the power-circuit. Johnnie bent lovingly over the humming motor and tested the spin of the pulley with his finger.

" That's the very thing I needed," he exclaimed. " It's far stronger than the one I've been using. I'm going to build a big crane, next ; and this will be the motor of the travelling carriage, you know."

Sir Clinton bent over the table, with its litter of bars, wheels, springs, and bolts.

" All right for a wet day," he suggested, " but I shouldn't waste the sunshine indoors, if I were you, Johnnie. What about taking me out on this lake of yours ? Only, you'll be good enough to keep your breath for your rowing, if you don't mind. I have some things to think about and I don't want to be bothered answering questions just now. Come along. Which is the way to the boat-house ? "

Johnnie, overjoyed to learn that he was to have his uncle's company for longer yet, led the way through the French window and down the path to the little landing-stage at the edge of the lake. The prohibition which accompanied the invitation did not trouble him much. He had been trained to keep quiet when his uncle was in an uncommunicative mood. Merely to have Sir Clinton's company was a treat in itself.

Though it was of no great extent, the lake was not without variety ; and Johnnie managed to display most of its features in the course of his row. Sometimes the boat explored a cool inlet overhung with trees, where Johnnie shipped his oars and, leaning perilously over-side, studied the bottom in search of trout. Farther on, they coasted banks where the green turf ran clear to the water's edge ; or again they slid into forests of high swishing reeds among which Johnnie entangled his oars. Very occasionally Sir Clinton dropped a remark which showed that his eyes were alert ; but Johnnie was not tempted to prolong any conversation which sprang up. He knew the symptoms of his uncle's mood, and he suppressed his desire for talk.

An ordinary oarsman would have made the circuit

of the lake in a very short time ; but Johnnie's rowing-technique was in the elementary stage ; and when he had completed his somewhat leisurely exploration it was lunch-time. They tied up the boat at the tiny landing-stage and went back to the house. Sir Clinton was still in his uncommunicative mood ; and Johnnie could see that the problem, whatever it was, had not been solved. During luncheon, Sir Clinton roused himself, as polite-ness required, and seemed to shake off his concentration. Without showing it, he studied Francia and attempted to draw him out. But the Argentiner had the knack of bringing other people into a conversation instead of talking himself ; and Sir Clinton learned little more about him than he already knew.

Late in the afternoon, Sergeant Ledbury presented himself again ; and from his expression it seemed clear that he was not ill-pleased with the way in which he had spent the day. Sir Clinton took him to the smoke-room, which offered the best chance of privacy.

" Well, sergeant, got to the bottom of it yet ? " he asked, with obvious interest.

Ledbury shook his head cautiously. It was clear that he did not propose to boast of his results.

" I think I see my way through some of it, sir. That's as far as I'd care to go."

" Suppose we go that length together, then ? " Sir Clinton suggested. " Let's compare notes. You let me have your theory of the business, and I'll tell you if we happen to differ on any point."

The sergeant seated himself in response to a gesture from his host, pulled out a notebook, and glanced over some entries.

" Well, sir," he explained, looking up again at Sir Clinton, " I started with the car tracks."

" So did I," Sir Clinton admitted.

" There were five of them altogether," the sergeant continued after a nod of acknowledgment. " First of all there was the trail of the car that passed while Peel was on guard over the smash-up this morning. We can disregard that, seeing that Peel saw it go by without doing anything."

He glanced at Sir Clinton as though seeking confirmation of this before continuing.

" Its tyres were different from all the rest," Sir Clinton interjected, " so it's reasonable to leave it out of the case. It wasn't one of the other cars coming back, or anything of that sort. We needn't bother about it."

" That leaves four tracks," the sergeant proceeded. " One of them was your own track, made when you arrived here last night. A bit along the road, near the village, the track of Quevedo's car crosses your track. That confirms what you said this morning—that you met Quevedo coming out of the village."

Sir Clinton's expression showed that he was in no way offended by this.

" That's very sound, sergeant. You were quite right to check everything and take nobody's word for any point. I'd have been glad to have had you under me when I was in the police myself. Nothing like testing things and taking nothing for granted. Next ? "

" That leaves three tracks : Barford's, Quevedo's, and the track of the man who reversed into the avenue. I took Barford's trail next, sir. Now you'll remember that Barford's track went straight on without a check until he pulled up sharp just beyond the site of the smash. That meant that he'd never got out of his car until the smash was over—that's obvious, isn't it ? "

" Quite, I think," Sir Clinton conceded willingly.

" Just so," Ledbury continued. " But it struck me that one man in a motor mightn't need to get out of his car if he wanted to kill another man in a second car. He might do it either of two ways."

Sir Clinton became obviously alert.

" You're getting interesting, sergeant. This is good stuff. Go on."

" The way I look at it," Ledbury pursued, with obvious pleasure at the compliment, " is this. Barford might have driven up level with Quevedo and hit him a bat on the head in passing. That's not outside the possibilities. But there's two things against that notion, as I found when I went into things. First of all, I know enough about first aid and ambulance work to find out for myself whether a man's skull's gone. I looked carefully ; and there's nothing wrong with Quevedo's skull. What he died from was loss of blood from the glass cuts so far as I can see. Besides, if you were driving a car and someone hit you a bat on the head, you'd lose control of the wheel and your car would swerve."

He glanced interrogatively at Sir Clinton, who nodded in confirmation.

" Just so," Ledbury went on. " Now there wasn't a sign of a swerve in Quevedo's track, so far as I could see —not a big swerve, anyhow. The track wasn't dead straight ; but no motor track ever is dead straight, anyhow. It was as near straight as one usually sees 'em. So that put out of court any notion that Quevedo was killed at the wheel from a passing car."

" I'm quite with you there," Sir Clinton commented. " Now what about your second possibility about Barford's behaviour ? "

" Well, it's this way, sir. Suppose, I thought, that Barford had been coming along full tilt behind Quevedo and had made up on him. Wouldn't it have been possible, with both of them travelling at a fair lick, for Barford just to draw level and then begin scrounging, so to speak. I mean edging in towards Quevedo's car until he forced him into the ditch. That would fit the long, smooth curve of Quevedo's track, edging in and in towards his own side of the road until he got his near wheel into the ditch, wouldn't it ? "

" Undoubtedly it would," Sir Clinton admitted. " But I'll tell you what it won't fit. I noticed that Teddy Barford's track overlay Quevedo's track for most of the way. I mean that Barford's near wheels were running between the tracks of Quevedo's wheels. Whence it's obvious that Barford came along almost in Quevedo's track, and that he only passed him, as the crossing of the tracks shows, after Quevedo had gone to smash."

" Oh, you noticed that, did you, sir ? I thought it was a bit of a discovery of my own. Things are as you say, and that put the lid on any notion that Teddy Barford killed Quevedo without getting out of the car."

" You've been very thorough, sergeant, I see. Go on."

" Well, if Teddy didn't kill Quevedo up to that stage, there's no case against Teddy. He didn't knock him on the head, like Peel wants to make out ; for I've examined Quevedo's skull and there's no sign of any knock on it heavy enough to finish him. And Teddy didn't cut Quevedo's throat or anything of that sort, while he was lying on the ground ; for there isn't a trace of blood on his hands or his clothes. Lucky for him he hated Quevedo, sir. If it had been an ordinary man, Teddy would have been trying to lend a hand and got all mucked up with blood in doing it. It wouldn't have been as clear a case."

" So Barford's cleared, in your opinion ? "

" Quite cleared, sir. I'm glad of it. And now, sir, we come to the track of the man who reversed into the avenue entrance. The way I reasoned it out was this. He arrived there, coming from Raynham Parva direction. I've traced his tracks and they turn off into a side-road a bit along the main road. I can't trace 'em farther than that, for there's been a lot of new metal laid down thereabouts lately and the surface is bad for tracks. I've followed him up as far as I could go on a bicycle ; but in the end the tracks disappeared, and when I tried the side-roads I found nothing. He turned off somewhere or other and got clear away."

81

Sir Clinton nodded without speaking.

" Well, I had to give it up," Ledbury went on. " All I had to go on was the tracks round about the avenue gate. Here's what I made of them."

" Wait a bit," Sir Clinton interrupted. " It'll be easier if we give this man a name. Call him Mr. Jones for the present. It saves words."

" Jones, sir ? Very well," Ledbury acquiesced, with a broad smile. " This Jones, then, came along the road before Quevedo, but after you'd passed last night. I checked that up by the overlaying of the tracks when they happened to cross. It was clear enough in one or two places. And that confirmed your statement, sir, that this Jones wasn't at the avenue gate with his car when you passed there yourself."

He glanced slyly at Sir Clinton to see if this hit was acknowledged.

" Go on," Sir Clinton suggested. " Truth-telling at the right time is one of my accomplishments, sergeant. It hardly calls for comment."

Slightly damped, Ledbury continued his exposition.

" The way I look at it is this. The Jones man came along the road in front of Quevedo. For some reason or other, he decided to turn back, and he drove into the end of the avenue. Then he began to reverse out. Just as he'd got his car broadside across the road, Quevedo came along in his car. This Jones, seeing Quevedo's lights, started to drive back into the avenue entrance so as to clear the road. Meanwhile, Quevedo had seen the obstruction and pulled up. After the Jones man had got his car back into the avenue out of the road, Quevedo started up and drove on again."

Ledbury paused, as though awaiting comments, but Sir Clinton failed to use the opportunity.

" Now, that helps to account for one thing you pointed out, sir. It explains how Quevedo's gear-lever was in third speed and not in top. He'd gone off from a standing start and was changing up. He just got into third when the smash happened—before he'd had time to reach top gear."

" And the full-open throttle, sergeant ? "

" I can't somehow fit that in," Ledbury admitted, rubbing his hair the wrong way at the back of his head in a perplexed fashion. " I'm almost inclined to think, sir, that that lever may have got jolted over in the smash."

" Well, we part company there," Sir Clinton said bluntly. " You can take it from me, sergeant, that the smash didn't shift the lever. It was on the stiff side, if anything. I tested it to make sure. Now nobody drives a car on the throttle if the throttle-lever's stiff. The accelerator's far easier. So I inferred that Quevedo was most likely driving on the accelerator. Most people do as a matter of fact. I don't know anyone who doesn't."

" Well, I can't sort of fit that in, I admit," Ledbury confessed. " I don't profess to know more than the ordinary about cars. Perhaps I've missed something or other that I ought to have seen ; but I don't see it, sir."

" We'll come back to it later on," Sir Clinton suggested. " Go ahead."

Ledbury's little eyes betrayed something of his discomfiture.

" To tell you the truth, sir, that's about as far as I got," he confessed. " I don't somehow seem able to fit anything more into place. I'd like to hear how you worked it out yourself. If it's really a murder, then there's no time to be lost, I know, and it doesn't seem quite straight to go muddling along myself when you've got something up your sleeve that might help."

Sir Clinton could appreciate Ledbury's position.

" I daresay if you'd had a little more time, sergeant, you'd have worked things out a bit further. We've been much on the same lines of thought so far, apparently ; and at one or two points you've been more thorough than I was."

" I had more time, sir."

" Well," Sir Clinton continued, brushing this aside, " what you haven't fitted in yet, so far as I remember, are three things at any rate, or perhaps four : the open throttle, the two bits of glass we found amongst the *débris*, and the blood on the inside of the car."

Ledbury's sudden gesture betrayed his vexation as this last item was mentioned.

" Now I see it, sir. I *was* a bit of an ass," he added ruefully.

Then his face, which had cleared for a moment, became puzzled again.

" I'm not sure I see it rightly yet, sir," he confessed. " You mean, don't you, that if Quevedo got cut by being thrown through the windscreen, then he'd have bled outside the car and not inside ? His blood would have been on the grass and not on the floor and seats of the car ? That's right enough, now I come to see it ; but it doesn't seem to get us much forrarder, does it ? "

" Perhaps not," Sir Clinton conceded. " It certainly doesn't get me so far that I can tell you much about the murderer. You won't be able to arrest him without a good deal more trouble, I'm afraid. All I can give you is a story which fits all the facts. Whether it's the right story or not, I don't profess to know, naturally. That's a matter for further investigation. Not my job, sergeant."

" I'd like to hear it now, sir, if you don't mind."

" Here it is, then, for what it's worth."

Sir Clinton lighted a cigarette before continuing. He seemed to use the pause to fit his narrative together.

" Suppose this is the sequence of events," he began at length. " This Mr. Jones has a grudge against Quevedo —a grudge big enough to make murder a possible way of squaring the account. I assume that ; I can't prove it. Mr. Jones discovers something about Quevedo's movements. I don't know how he managed that. He was known to Quevedo and he wanted to keep Quevedo in ignorance of his pursuit of him. I suspect he must have had a confederate or confederates who watched Quevedo. However it was done, Jones knew that Quevedo was leaving Raynham Parva last night by motor, and he even knew the approximate time. He believed that Quevedo would be driving alone ; and he knew the car was an open touring one. All that's implicit in my theory. I can't prove it."

Ledbury made a movement as though to jot down something in his notebook ; but an obviously disapproving glance from Sir Clinton checked him in the act.

" There's nothing there that you need put down. It's the purest surmise. I've nothing to back it. Well, Mr. Jones starts off in his car ahead of Quevedo and he halts at the avenue gate. He couldn't afford to be late, so probably he was a bit early. He swings his car into the entrance to the avenue, and he waits. He waits a good few minutes, evidently ; for the tracks of his wheels were deep where he stood the first time, as I pointed out to you."

Ledbury made a gesture of acknowledgment.

" I'd forgotten that point, sir. Stupid of me."

" From that spot, Mr. Jones could see down the road towards Raynham Parva. It's a straight, level stretch, you remember. By and by, he sees the lights of a motor coming along ; and at once he lets his car run out, blocking the road. If it turns out to be a stranger, there's no harm done. All Mr. Jones needed to do was to apologise for blocking the road, and drive his car back into the avenue to clear the way for the other man. No one would think twice about a thing of that sort. The other driver would see Mr. Jones was turning his car. Quite an innocent thing to do. The blocking of the road would look quite accidental."

" I see," Ledbury hastened to interject. " Go on, sir. What happened next ? "

" As it chanced, there was no hitch of that sort. The

85

first car that came along was Quevedo's. Everything happened according to plan : Mr. Jones ran his car out, blocked Quevedo's car, and made Quevedo pull up. That was what he wanted. He left his own car still blocking the road, got out, and walked over to Quevedo's car as if he wanted to ask something. There would be no great difficulty in keeping out of the direct line of Quevedo's headlights—at any rate, he could keep his face from being thrown up clear by the glare. He walked over, then, quite naturally ; and Quevedo would suspect nothing. Mr. Jones, I think, had in his hand the bottom of a bottle with the upper part broken away to leave a cutting edge."

Sergeant Ledbury brought his open hand down on his knee with a slap.

" That's it ! " he exclaimed. " But I never came near seeing it till you pointed it out, sir."

" This is only a bit of fiction, remember, sergeant. I can't guarantee that it's accurate. I think I ought to have mentioned that Mr. Jones had taken some trouble to avoid being recognised by Quevedo. That's a very shaky bit of theorising, however, so don't lay too much stress on it. Some people have normal sight in one eye and weak sight in the other ; and consequently they wear spectacles with a lens on one side and a plain glass on the other. Possibly the murderer was like that. But horn-rimmed spectacles change a man's appearance markedly, specially if you shave off a moustache as well ; and, on the facts of the case, I'm inclined to think that the spectacles were a bit of disguise. The murderer wanted to be able to pass muster as a stranger for a few seconds—all the time that he needed for his work."

" You mean Quevedo knew him well, sir ? "

" It might be a case of a homicidal maniac, of course," Sir Clinton admitted. " If it were, then the first motorist who came along would have served as a victim and there would be no point in disguise. But, on the facts of the case, I think it's safer to leave the homicidal maniac as a last resource and to assume that it was a case of Mr. Jones paying off a score. In that case, it's most probable that Quevedo knew him and would be on his guard if he recognised Mr. Jones at the first glance. Hence the need for a disguise which would pass muster for just a a few seconds, even if it wasn't good enough to stand lengthy examination."

Ledbury showed his agreement by a nod.

" And what happened next, sir ? I think I can guess."

" It's pretty obvious, isn't it, provided you swallow the initial hypothesis ? Mr. Jones walked up to the side of Quevedo's car, bent over as if to say something—and then a single slash of the sharpened edge of the broken bottle opened Quevedo's jugular neatly. A glass-cut, you see."

" A razor would have done the job just as well, and it'd be a handier thing to use, sir," the sergeant objected.

" Yes," Sir Clinton conceded, " but a razor has a nasty knack of keeping blood-stains round about the handle—round about the pivot of the blade, where you can't clean them away without breaking the whole thing to bits. A microscopic examination would show up the blood corpuscles. So, if you happened to be caught with that kind of razor in your possession, you'd be in Queer Street. And if you threw it away immediately, a razor lying by the roadside is a thing that might attract notice. Mr. Jones was cleverer than that, I think. He meant the whole affair to look like an accident, pure and simple ; and he wasn't going to leave any link with himself, such as a weapon."

" I see your point, sir. By the way, I think I'll have a look round about the lodge gate and see if I can't pick up that broken bottle. It ought to have blood on it."

Sir Clinton interjected a caution.

" Don't under-estimate your man, sergeant. Would you yourself just pitch a blood-stained bit of bottle over the hedge at the very point where people would look for it ? "

Ledbury's face fell.

" No, I wouldn't," he admitted. " But there's no harm in being thorough, is there ? "

" Of course not. But, if I'd been Mr. Jones, I'd have had a thermos flask in my car, and I'd have washed the bottle before throwing it away, say, a mile or so up the road. As it was, poor Mr. Jones had hard luck with his bottle."

" You mean it broke when he was cutting Quevedo's throat, sir, and that chip with the bubbles in it got snapped off—the bit I found on the floor-boards ? "

" I don't profess to know exactly how the chip got split off. It may have been as you say ; or Quevedo may have struggled and the bottle got knocked against the side of the car. The certain thing is that the chip was left behind. You must remember, sergeant, that Mr. Jones was in a hurry. That's obvious, or he wouldn't have left part of his spectacle glass lying about. But when you're standing on a public road with a murdered victim beside you, and a chance that someone may come along any moment, I don't suppose you can spare time to do everything you'd like to."

" That's so, sir. He must have been a smart lad, even with these little slips in his scheme."

" Very smart indeed to invent a new line in murders," Sir Clinton agreed, with something suspiciously like admiration in his tone. " I expect Quevedo struggled a bit and accidentally knocked the spectacles off Mr. Jones's nose. In falling, they must have hit the gear-lever, or something ; and the plain glass got smashed. Mr. Jones was hurried. He had to get the rest of his little play staged before anyone came along. So he grabbed the spectacle-frame, felt one of the glasses intact, and perhaps hadn't time to bother about the rest. It was going to be covered up and lost in a pile of smashed glass anyhow, later on ; and I expect he just let it go at that, rather than waste time hunting about. By the way, did anything occur to you about the wound, sergeant ? "

" The wound ? You mean the cut in the jugular ? No, sir. Nothing particular."

" Do you think the man in the street could put his finger on his own jugular vein straight away ? "

" Well, no, sir, perhaps not. You mean Mr. Jones was an expert ? He certainly got straight on to the right place."

" One can't lay too much stress on it, I'm afraid. Mr. Jones may have been Dr. Jones with a good knowledge of anatomy ; or he may merely have been someone who took the trouble to find out exactly where the jugular could be cut with least fear of bungling. One can't say."

" It does look like expert work, now I come to think of it," Ledbury admitted doubtfully. " But, as you say, sir, this Jones might have studied it up beforehand. He's taken great pains in other things, apparently. And what happened after that ? "

" I don't *know*, sergeant. I'm only telling you a pretty story, remember. Don't take it too seriously. Here's the final instalment. Once Quevedo was done for—and, by the way, the blood inside the car was an unfortunate item, though I don't see how it could have been helped —once Quevedo was done for, Mr. Jones set about staging the accident. He ran his own car back out of the way, up the avenue as we saw. Then he stood on the footboard of Quevedo's car—no, he must have got inside to get the clutch out and in—and he started. The engine would be running, of course. Quevedo wouldn't have switched off. Once the car started, Mr. Jones got on to the running-board and closed the door—if he'd opened it to get in, that is. He leaned over and steered, and at the same time he changed gear. He got up to third, and by that time the car was travelling at a fair rate. He couldn't afford to get on to top, because he had to jump off ; and he wasn't going to risk a tumble at high speed. So he put in the third speed, opened the throttle full, so as to brisk up the car during the rest of its run and ensure a fine smash at the end. Then he put the wheel as straight as he could, jumped off, and left the car flying up the road at increasing speed. It was bound to take the ditch on one side of the road or other before long ; and there was a stone wall on each side which would ensure a good smash-up of the windscreen. I expect he'd counted on Quevedo being left in the driving-seat instead of being thrown out. Then the blood on the floor-boards would have been neatly accounted for."

" He must have been a bit mucked up with the blood when he got into the car beside Quevedo's body," the sergeant reflected unpleasantly.

" I expect he was wearing a light driving-coat or one of these linen overall things. That would shield his own clothes, and when he got well away in his own car he could get out and burn the blood-stained coat with the help of a little petrol. And he could wash his hands in some stream or other. Now, I think that finishes my effort in fiction, sergeant. What do you make of the villain of the piece ? "

Ledbury pondered for a full half-minute before taking up the challenge.

" If you're right, sir, then I'd say he was very likely something like this. He was somebody who knew Quevedo before. That might mean a foreigner. Or again it mightn't. H'm ! That's not much help, is it ? "

" Not if you put it that 'way," Sir Clinton admitted, with a broad smile. " But go on, sergeant."

" He must have known Quevedo was going to London last night, so he must have had some sort of information about Quevedo's movements. If he had a grudge against Quevedo, he'd hardly have shown up much before the murder for fear of putting Quevedo on his guard. That means there's a confederate somewhere, perhaps. This Jones must have had pretty up-to-date news."

Sir Clinton hesitated a moment as though about to interrupt. He was not quite sure whether he should divulge the facts about Staffin and Teddy Barford to the sergeant. One point which might be of importance later was involved ; but, at the moment, a knowledge of it would hardly help Ledbury, so Sir Clinton decided to say nothing about it at that juncture.

" Yes ? " he prompted the sergeant.

" He might be wearing horn-rimmed glasses with one plain glass and one lens," Ledbury pursued. " Or, again," he added regretfully, " he mightn't wear glasses at all."

" True," Sir Clinton confirmed solemnly.

" Then he might be a medical man. But perhaps he wasn't. Really, sir," Ledbury commented in an aggrieved voice, " these notions of yours sound all right, but they don't somehow seem to lead anywhere particular, do they ? "

" He has a car," Sir Clinton suggested.

" Yes, he has a car all right," Ledbury admitted, " but its tyres are worn smooth and that doesn't help much, does it ? How many people in this country are running round in cars with well-worn tyres, sir ? "

" Quite a lot, I suppose," Sir Clinton said, laughing at the sergeant's expression. " Poor Mr. Jones ! He's had hard luck. If it hadn't been for Peel's grudge against Barford, no one would have dreamed for a moment that it was a case of murder. Mr. Jones would have got clear away with it. Everyone would have put it down as a purely accidental smash. Hard lines on poor Mr. Jones."

" I wasn't suggesting you hadn't cleared things up a lot, sir," Ledbury hastened to explain. " As you say, it'd have passed as a plain motor-smash easily enough. But I don't somehow seem to have much to take hold of, with it all. I get no sort of notion of what this Jones

91

was like, if you understand me. If this is the sort of thing one finds in a murder case, then I hope this one'll be my last. I don't seem to make much of a fist of it, and that's the truth."

" You're under-estimating yourself, sergeant. You didn't expect to lay hands on Mr. Jones in ten minutes, surely ? "

" Well, sir, they say that if a murderer gets twenty-four hours start, it's mighty difficult to prevent him getting away with it."

" It depends on what you mean by ' twenty-four hours start,' sergeant. That might mean one thing to some people and quite a different thing to other people. Don't get discouraged. You've gone the right way to work, so far, if that's any satisfaction to you. It's more than a good many people can say for themselves."

Ledbury seemed slightly cheered by this compliment.

" Well, sir," he said, as he rose to leave the room, " I suppose something may turn up that'll suggest something, perhaps. I'll have a hunt round for that broken bottle, anyhow ; and I'll see if I can get word of any burnt place where this Jones man could have been destroying his coat. That might point to which road he took when he went off, at any rate ; and that would always be something done."

He moved over towards the door, but suddenly came back again.

" It slipped my memory, sir," he explained. " There's a young gentleman staying at the Black Bull just now. A Mr. Brandon. He was talking to me—very pleasant-spoken, he is—and it seems he knows you. He asked me to let you know he was in the village when I saw you."

" Tall, clean-shaven, fair-haired, blue eyes ? " Sir Clinton inquired, making certain of the identity.

" Yes, sir. That's him."

" Thanks, sergeant. I'll ring him up and leave a message if he's out."

" Then that's all, sir," Ledbury said, turning again towards the door. " I've just got to see Mr. Francia again, to make sure of one or two little points."

Sir Clinton nodded ; and, as Ledbury left the room, he walked across to where the telephone stood on a small table close to the door.

CHAPTER VII

THE AGENT 7-DH

The freshness of the air tempted Sir Clinton to halt under the porch of Fern Lodge when he came out of the house next morning on his way to keep an appointment with Rex Brandon at the Black Bull Hotel. For a moment his glance swept over the lawns, from which a heavy dew had just been lifted by the sun ; then he turned towards the water. The surface of the little lake was untroubled in that still air, save where Johnnie's boat left its long ripple-track ; and, as Sir Clinton watched, even this died away. Johnnie shipped his oars. fitted a rod together, and began to fish.

Sir Clinton watched his nephew's efforts for a while with sympathetic interest, making mental notes for some hints for improvement in the boy's technique. The minutes slipped past unnoticed, for Sir Clinton lingered on in the hope that Johnnie might fluke a catch while he was watching. At last, however, a glance at his watch showed him that he had idled longer than he had meant to do ; by that time it was too late to walk into Raynham Parva if he meant to keep his appointment. He had still time enough in hand to be punctual if he took his car ; so, abandoning his original plan, he turned towards the garage.

Rex Brandon was evidently on the *qui vive* ; for, as the car slowed down at the entrance to the Black Bull, he was standing on the steps of the hotel in conversation with a dark, clean-shaven stranger. Catching sight of Sir Clinton, Rex parted from his acquaintance with a hurried apology, to which the stranger responded with a punctilious gesture of farewell.

" Jump in, Rex," Sir Clinton invited, opening the door of the car. " I'd meant to stroll down and take you for a healthy walk ; but I was a bit late in starting and had to drive. It'll always give you a breath of fresh air. By the way, who's your foreign friend ? "

" Referring to his flamboyant style of taking farewell, sir ? I can give you the life-history of our friendship in a few words, because I met him for the first time last night and for the second time this morning," Rex explained, settling himself comfortably in his seat.

" We'll go along this road and see where we get to," Sir Clinton suggested, as he started the car. " So he isn't your long-lost Uncle Jeremiah from Australia, or anything of that sort ? "

" No, sir. The only kindness he's done me was to introduce me to a new cocktail and to give me his card. His name's Roca—Dr. E. Roca. My Spanish was grossly neglected at school, so I can't say definitely whether he calls himself Esteeban or Esty-ban, but he spells his first name E-s-t-e-b-a-n on his card, I remember."

Sir Clinton nodded with apparent indifference.

" A stranger in a strange land ? Decent sort, or other-wise ? " he inquired.

" Oh, quite decent, sir. I rather took to him, in fact. Except in gestures, he's not the overflowing kind of foreigner."

Sir Clinton seemed favourably impressed by this verdict.

" If we happen to run across him on the way back you might introduce me," he suggested. " He must feel rather a fish out of water in a place like this."

Rex acquiesced with a gesture ; and for a time Sir Clinton drove on in silence. It was too early to think of drawing any inferences yet ; but the presence of a third foreigner in a tiny place like Raynham Parva seemed

95

to furnish food for thought. There would be no harm in cultivating Dr. Roca's acquaintance, since chance had thrown him into Sir Clinton's way.

For some minutes, Rex Brandon seemed to have fallen into a taciturnity which was foreign to his normal character ; but at last, with an obvious pretence of indifference, he threw out a question.

" Elsie's at Fern Lodge, sir ? "

Sir Clinton had no particular desire to guide the conversation in this field. He contented himself with a confirmatory nod. Rex relapsed again into silence for a while.

" What sort of a man is her husband, sir ? " he asked at length, in a casual tone which seemed to cost him something of an effort.

" About your height, dark, brown eyes, rather suave voice," Sir Clinton answered, with a deliberate avoidance of the real purport of the question.

" H'm ! "

Rex seemed doubtful whether to regard Sir Clinton's answer as a snub or not. He gazed down the road in front of the car, evidently hesitating about pursuing the subject. Sir Clinton examined him with a swift sideglance and felt a twinge of discomfort. Rex Brandon was so obviously the sort of man Elsie ought to have married, instead of picking out that foreign fellow with his feline softness and his expertness in handling women. Rex, possibly, was not a deep person ; his character had few reserves. But at least he could be trusted to pick a sound line of behaviour and stick to it through thick and thin. He had tenacity of the comprehensible kind. Sir Clinton had known him before he was in his teens and had tested him, as he tested most people. Sound stuff. Somehow, compared with him, Francia came out of it badly. His air of reticence contrasted so markedly with Rex's frankness.

Sir Clinton's reflections were broken by Rex's voice.

From his tone, it was evident that he knew he was venturing on thin ice.

" I mean, is he good enough for her and that sort of thing ? "

This was the very question which Sir Clinton had been asking himself for the last twenty-four hours, and it flicked him on the raw to have it put into audible words.

" How should I know ? " he demanded brusquely. " I've only seen him a couple of times or so."

Rex was sharp enough to see the reservation in the answer, but he evidently felt that he was overstepping the bounds.

" I just wanted to know," he said, half-apologetically. " Elsie's a good sort and . . ."

His voice trailed off into silence.

" It's done now," Sir Clinton pointed out.

If he meant to close the subject, he had chosen the wrong line.

" I suppose it is," Rex admitted. " Didn't it come as a bit of a surprise, sir ? To me, it did. I'd never dreamed of anything of the sort until I heard about it. Some shock."

He watched Sir Clinton's face as he spoke, but the late Chief Constable had too much command over his muscles to betray anything on his features. Rex, by some sixth sense, seemed to read what was going on behind the mask.

" Well, I hope she's happy, sir," he added, giving in all innocence the final stab to Sir Clinton's feelings.

" She seems to be," Sir Clinton answered brutally.

Rex's questions were acting as irritants to his own misgivings about Elsie's marriage ; and in his reaction he could not help rasping the feelings of the youngster beside him.

" That's always something," Rex replied in the tone of a man talking in order to conceal the fact that he has had a severe shock. " In fact, I suppose, it's the main thing. So long as she's happy, and he's a decent sort . . ."

Sir Clinton felt the probe inserted clumsily into his private feelings ; but he had no grudge against Rex for doing it. He knew the boy was torturing himself as well as his listener when he put questions like that. Rex had always wanted Elsie ; and he wasn't the sort of person to forget in a hurry or console himself at once with the next best. This business would ruin his life for years. Sir Clinton thought rapidly and came to a decision. One might as well bring things to a head at once and let the boy see the state of affairs with his own eyes. Since Elsie was now out of his reach, the sooner he recognised that the better. It would be a radical cure ; and it would save any further questions.

"Johnnie's taken to fishing nowadays, Rex," Sir Clinton began after a pause. " It's the first real chance he's had, and he seems to be keen. I haven't done any-thing in that line myself for years now, and I'm so hope-lessly out of practice that I can't teach him properly. Could you drop your own fishing for a morning now and again and give him a bit of tutoring ? I hate to see him flogging the water as if he meant to hurt it. He hasn't a notion of throwing a cast decently."

Rex looked doubtful, as Sir Clinton had expected.

" Well," he began grudgingly, " I daresay he wouldn't be the worse of some help, or he'll get into bad habits."

A fresh idea seemed to strike him, and his face cleared.

" Send him down to the Black Bull and I'll take him out with me this afternoon. I'm going to fish a stream quite near the village. It won't be far for him to walk."

But this arrangement did not suit Sir Clinton's pur-pose. He meant to bring Rex up to Fern Lodge.

" I think you'd better try the lake instead. It's not so much a matter of catching anything : I want him taught how to cast properly. When he rowed me round the lake, I spotted the very place for that : a little promon-tory near a stream. No trees or undergrowth, deepish water close inshore, and just enough current from a stream that comes in near by. The fly will float down as nicely as you could wish. And, if he catches nothing there, you can always give him a point or two about trawling from the boat. There are plenty of trout, though I don't suppose you'll find a salmon, naturally. I'll fetch you in the car this afternoon. The sun will be just about right then."

For a moment or two Rex hesitated, evidently torn between conflicting desires. He wanted to keep away from Fern Lodge and its might-have-beens ; and yet something was pulling him in the opposite direction. Even if Elsie was out of his reach now, still he wanted to see her again. Facts were facts, of course. His romance had gone down the drain, as he phrased it bitterly to himself. Still, it would be interesting to see what sort of man had beaten him. This thought gave him the excuse which he felt he required in order to justify his decision to himself. No harm in paying a visit to the place. He had a good pretext, and he could keep his feelings below the surface easily enough. To Sir Clinton, Rex's face was an open book ; and he carefully refrained from an interruption which might have influenced the conflict. At last the balance swayed definitely to one side.

" All right, then," Rex agreed. " I'll take Johnnie on, if you think it'll be any help to him."

Then, as though to avoid the risk of changing his mind if he dwelt further on the matter, Rex broke abruptly into a fresh subject.

" You've been abroad lately, sir, haven't you ? "

" Just back," Sir Clinton confirmed.

" Hope you had a good time ? " Rex inquired perfunctorily.

" Not bad."

Once again Sir Clinton's habitual reticence about his own affairs was of good service. Not even his sister had suspected that his so-called " holiday " had really been spent in a confidential mission for the Government. But the subject was one best avoided, and Sir Clinton bestirred himself to draw Rex off to other topics. He succeeded so well that they were nearing Raynham Parva again before Rex realised how quickly the time had passed. As the village spire came in sight round the shoulder of a hill, Sir Clinton thought it well to give his companion a reminder.

" When we get back to the Black Bull, Rex, you might hunt up your foreign friend and introduce me."

Rex, apparently, had not taken the earlier suggestion on this point very seriously. He looked a little surprised.

" You really want it, sir ? H'm ! I don't guarantee the lad. He may be a cough-drop for all I can tell. Know him from Adam by the costume, of course, but otherwise not."

" I'll take the risk ; you do the rest," Sir Clinton reassured him.

At the Black Bull, Rex was fortunate enough to run up against Dr. Roca in such a way as to make the introduction of Sir Clinton seem a matter of mere chance. When they came face to face, Sir Clinton was surprised to find something familiar in the features of his new acquaintance.

" Surely we must have met before ? " he suggested. " I'm almost certain I've seen your face somewhere, Dr. Roca."

Roca smiled as though he saw some jest which was concealed from the others.

" In bad company, perhaps ? " he inquired innocently. " I understand you are in the police, Sir Clinton."

But his remark had given the late Chief Constable the clue for which he was searching in his memory.

" It was in *bad* company," he confirmed, in an indifferent tone. " You had a moustache then, hadn't you ? Shaving it off has made a lot of difference."

Roca smiled again.

" Sometimes a white sheep gets mixed up with a flock of black ones."

A flash of comprehension passed over Sir Clinton's face.

" League of Nations, you mean, perhaps ? " he demanded.

" Exactly," Roca admitted. " I go by the name of 7-DH at headquarters."

" H'm ! That explains it, then."

Sir Clinton's tone was non-committal.

" Rather an unpleasant job, I should think," he added, as though to keep the conversation going.

Roca nodded apathetically.

" A labour of love, in my case."

Then seeing Sir Clinton's brows twitch ever so faintly, he hastened to make his meaning clearer.

" I see I've made what you English call a pun, I think."

" Something of the sort," Sir Clinton agreed coldly.

Roca's face cleared.

" That was not what I meant at all. With me, the business is a sort of mission, you understand—a kind of crusade. I feel strongly . . ." He pulled himself up for a moment, then went on with an assumption of indifference. " You know the Centre, Sir Clinton. Now, I am what you would call ' a decent sort of person '—like most people. Which side am I likely to be on : for the Centre or against it ? "

Sir Clinton shrugged his shoulders as though dismissing the subject. Rex had listened to the conversation with growing astonishment, which betrayed itself on his face. He was evidently completely out of his depth, and was about to put a question when Sir Clinton spoke again.

" I think you and I might have a talk later on, Dr. Roca," he suggested, in a tone which definitely excluded Rex from the matter.

Roca acquiesced with a gesture, and, as though recognising that this particular subject was closed, he began to speak of Raynham Parva and its surroundings.

" I suppose you're merely a bird of passage here ? " Sir Clinton inquired a short time later. " Drove past in a car and happened to like the look of the place ? "

" No," Roca explained. " I came by train from Micheldean Abbas, some stations down the line. I am looking for someone, as it happens ; and I got word that he might be in this neighbourhood."

Sir Clinton nodded, and glanced at his watch.

" Well, I must be going. I'll ring you up, Dr. Roca." Then a thought seemed to strike him.

" I think, if I were you, I'd be inclined to say nothing about the Centre in the meantime—to anyone."

Roca acquiesced with a gesture.

" I mentioned it to you merely to explain my position, since you evidently knew me and might have got wrong impressions."

" I understand," Sir Clinton admitted.

Then, with a nod of farewell to Rex, he went down to his car.

CHAPTER VIII

THE CENTRE AND MARCELLE BARRÈRE

Sir Clinton had no intention of letting the grass grow under his feet before he learned more about his latest acquaintance. The telephone put him in touch with Dr. Roca that evening ; and on the following morning he drove to the Black Bull Hotel to keep the appointment they had made. While Roca was being informed of his arrival, Sir Clinton went to the desk ; and, learning that Rex Brandon had gone out fishing earlier in the day, he left a note telling him that Johnnie expected his first lesson that afternoon.

When Dr. Roca appeared, Sir Clinton admitted to himself that the doctor's personality made a favourable impression. He succeeded in being cordial without effusiveness ; and there was nothing furtive in the reserve which underlay his outward affability. It suggested, rather, the normal mental poise of the medical man accustomed to deal with grave situations as they arise.

" Any particular part of the country you'd like to see ? " Sir Clinton inquired perfunctorily as they went out to the motor.

He had brought the car mainly because it offered the best chance of completely private conversation ; and his question had been put merely out of politeness. Much to his surprise, Roca apparently had a clear preference ; and the nature of his choice was rather unexpected.

" That's very good of you," the doctor hastened to

103

say. " I've been looking at a map of the district in the hotel smoke-room, and I noticed, marked on it, a thing I'd like to see, if it's all the same to you. It's called the Bale Stones."

" Then we'll look it up," Sir Clinton agreed readily.

He opened the door-pocket and was extracting a map when Roca stopped him with a gesture.

" It's all right," he explained. " I memorised the map. I had meant to make the thing an excuse for a longish promenade. If it suits you, I'll give you directions at the turns in the road. The place is about seven miles out from the village. I suppose that's not taking you too far ? "

" Not at all ! " Sir Clinton replied as he started the engine. " What sort of thing is it ? I don't know much about this district, since I only arrived a couple of nights ago."

" I bought a guide-book and looked it up," Roca answered, taking a cigar-case from his pocket. " It's quite a landmark in this part of the country—a sort of miniature Stonehenge. When I was already so near it, I thought it might be worth the walk. But this is a much easier way, thanks to your kindness."

" You're interested in archæology ? " Sir Clinton inquired.

" I find it interesting to compare your ancient monuments with those in my own country."

" South America ? " asked Sir Clinton at a venture.

" Yes, I was born in Las Flores, but I've been in the north also."

Sir Clinton relaxed his pressure on the accelerator and let the car slow down a trifle. He did not intend to reach the Bale Stones until he had got some information out of the doctor. Dropping archæology abruptly, he made a frontal attack.

" You said you were known as 7-DH, doctor. I didn't care about discussing that sort of thing before young

Brandon ; but I'm curious to know how a man of your type got mixed up in a business of that kind. You don't seem to fit in, if I may pay you the compliment."

Roca smiled, as though his mind had been relieved by Sir Clinton's words.

" I think you have changed your mind about me a little, Sir Clinton. Otherwise, I cannot quite understand how you come to have, in your car with you, the . . . the pot-companion, shall we say ? of Noel le Bosco, La Pioche, and Angiola la Grecque, those distinguished ornaments of the White Slave Trade."

Sir Clinton neither confirmed nor denied Roca's assertion.

" One of my hobbies is an interest in humanity in general," he said, rather drily. " It puzzles me that a man of your stamp should turn out to be 7-DH."

Roca's amusement seemed to have vanished.

. " My employers tell me that the reports of 7-DH have been very useful," he said indifferently. " They are, at any rate, cheap. I pay my own expenses."

" Indeed ? "

Sir Clinton's tone betrayed a mild surprise at this rather unlooked-for piece of information. Roca pulled at his cigar for a moment or two without speaking ; but at last he seemed to make up his mind on some question.

" You have the knack of generating confidence in a stranger, Sir Clinton," he began, turning to the ex-Chief Constable. " In a small way, I have that gift myself ; otherwise 7-DH would have secured much less information. But that is beside the point."

Sir Clinton nodded. He began to wonder if Roca really meant to allow himself to be drawn so easily. The doctor's next words relieved his anxiety.

" I speak entirely in confidence, of course, as one official to another. In a way, I can hardly help myself ; for already you have penetrated so far into my affairs

105

by a mere chance. Unless I tell you something more, you will be inclined to be suspicious ; and I cannot afford to have people speculating at large round the links between 7-DH and Dr. Esteban Roca. That might destroy the usefulness of 7-DH ; and it might also hamper Esteban Roca in his private affairs, which would be a much more serious state of things from my point of view. Much more serious."

He broke off to direct Sir Clinton into a side-road which appeared at this point.

" We go along here for about a couple of miles," he explained. " The next turn-off is at a cottage beside a plantation."

Sir Clinton glanced at the milometer dial.

" I studied medicine at Cordoba," Roca continued, " and for a time I was in practice. I did not need the money—I was an orphan left with more than sufficient for my needs ; but I had an idea that I was doing humanity a little service by giving it good advice and a few drugs for next to nothing. Perhaps I was. Who knows ? "

Sir Clinton disregarded the rhetorical question and waited patiently for Roca to come to business. The doctor evidently guessed what was in his companion's mind, for he laughed shortly.

" You think this very unimportant, Sir Clinton ? But it has a bearing on the rest of the story, so I tell it to you. I had my illusions, you see. And, by and by, I had a desire to increase my knowledge. I suppose most young medical men—the ambitious ones, at any rate—have, at the back of their minds, a picture of themselves standing beside the sick-bed of some King or President and drawing a valuable life back from the grave by their supreme skill. A pretty conceit, isn't that true ? It was mine, once."

There was a faint undertone of irony in his voice, as though he were himself sneering at his youthful visions.

" I determined to become a specialist—a great specialist, naturally. That comes cheap enough in dreams, of course. The price for all seats is the same, in that theatre. So I threw up my little practice and set out for Paris—slipping from one dream into the next."

He glanced at Sir Clinton's face.

" I fear I bore you," he said apologetically. " Nothing is so tiresome as other people's dreams. But I am coming to the point. I landed in Paris and set about a post-graduate course. I was, to be sure, much older than the ordinary *carabin*—the medical student—but I was not too old to enjoy myself ; and I had plenty of work—work which I enjoyed. And always there was the dream, you understand."

He sighed almost imperceptibly, and paused for a moment, though with a complete absence of theatricality.

" Then I met a girl—Marcelle Barrère. And by and by I found that a second dream had fused itself upon the older one. I fell in love, you understand ? It happens to most of us. Marcelle fell in love with me. That happens to most of us also. Like myself, she was an orphan. It was all plain sailing, as you English say. I had enough money to make things smooth ; I had the dream of a career, you understand ? and now I had someone else to share my dream and make it seem more real. And I had my little Marcelle, and yet other dreams. Most auspicious. I think we turn to the left here."

Sir Clinton swung the car into the by-road which Roca indicated.

" And then, by some little accident, the dream turned into a nightmare. Curious, is it not ? "

His voice had gradually taken on a tone of irony, as though he wished to guard himself from ridicule by sharing in the jest himself.

" Even now I cannot recall precisely what led up to it. It seems strange, doesn't it ? that one can't remember

107

the beginning of an affair which changed one's life. Things happen like that, it appears. Anyhow, Marcelle and I quarrelled over some trifle, some little thing or other. We were both over-sensitive, probably. You know how it is. She broke off our engagement and I was too proud to give in. Things slipped out in anger, of course. They always do. It's quite common. I must have hurt her feelings badly. She refused to speak to me again— a very ordinary lover's tiff, as you see. It happens every day."

He paused again and examined the landscape.

" I think those must be the Bale Stones just round the turn of the road," he pointed out. " Yes, there they are, on the other side of the hedge. That's most convenient."

Sir Clinton pulled up the car and waited for a cue. He was quite prepared to listen to the rest of Roca's story. A certain stoicism in the man's voice had touched him during the narrative. No Englishman would have told such a tale to a stranger ; but Roca had managed to tell it without alienating sympathy. There was something more than a little pathetic in his attempt to cover his real feelings with a mask of irony ; and that saved him from any appearance of lachrymosity.

Roca seemed to overlook Sir Clinton's tacit offer to hear the rest of the tale immediately. Instead of continuing, he opened the door and stepped out of the car ; so Sir Clinton had no choice but to follow him. The doctor walked over to the hedge and inspected the megaliths in what seemed a very casual manner.

" Very interesting," he commented in a tone which almost suggested boredom.

" I think we can get into the field," Sir Clinton pointed out. " There's a gap in the hedge farther down."

He moved off along the road, and Roca followed him perforce. But when they reached the standing stones, it was evident that Roca's interest in them was entirely superficial. Sir Clinton, who was always thorough, made

a careful inspection of the relic ; and, for his own amusement, endeavoured to guess at the uses to which the
temple had been put. Roca watched him taking rough
bearings of the temple axis and examining the whorl
markings on the altar-stone ; but the whole affair was
obviously of no direct interest to the doctor. When Sir
Clinton had satisfied his curiosity, Roca showed no
reluctance to return to the car ; and soon they were on
the road again.

" Suppose we go a bit farther out ? " Sir Clinton proposed. " It's rather early to turn home again."

He started the engine and then turned to Roca.

" And the rest of your story ? "

The doctor nodded, waited till the car was on top
gear, and then took up the thread of his narrative where
he had dropped it.

" Where was I ? " he began. " Oh, yes : I was telling
you about that lovers' quarrel. It was the first we had
ever had—and it was the last. She never spoke to me
again. She wrote once, but that comes later. I met her
in the street and she refused to recognise me. So very
ordinary, wasn't it ? "

He glanced at his cigar and, after deliberate consideration, threw away the stub and drew his case from his
pocket.

" I forgot to tell you, I think," he continued, " that
Marcelle was a pretty girl—beautiful, in fact. Of course
every lover thinks that of his Dulcinea, else why should
he desire her ? It is by no means remarkable. But it was
not to me only that my little Marcelle was beautiful.
When we walked together, I saw other men admiring
her, and—what is perhaps more significant—I saw
admiration in other women's glances. She was, in fact,
what you English call ' rather out of the common.' Very
pretty, very gentle, and so forth, you understand ?

" We quarrelled, and she refused to see me. Both of
us were deeply wounded over this trifle which I have

109

forgotten ; and each of us was proud. Then another man appeared, a compatriot of my own. It was all so ordinary. She was hurt and angry over our quarrel ; her self-respect must have been ruffled by the things I said without meaning to say them. I suppose the other man was cleverer than I, and he caught her ' on the rebound ' as I have heard it called. It happens so often.

" At last I was worn out with the ache of my longing for her. As you say in your language, I put my pride in my pocket and went to the place where she stayed. I was very full of penitence and ready to do anything if I could only get her back once more. It must have happened thousands of times last year to different people.

" You can imagine me climbing the stairs—she lived on the third floor—and how I felt that each step was bringing me nearer to my dreams again. Very funny, indeed. I rang the bell, and her landlady came to the door. ' Mademoiselle Marcelle has left here. She was married on Tuesday and has gone away.'

" One does not describe these things, you know. If one's audience cannot picture them for itself, no description would make them clear. I went away like a man in a nightmare, praying that I might wake up to real life again. I tried to throw myself into my other dream—the great career of usefulness, you remember —but now that dream seemed very faint and small, like a picture away down a long dim gallery. The reality had gone out of it. It never came back.

" I made inquiries in a dull sort of way. One cannot help being curious to know what has happened, after one has been badly shattered. She had, of course, married this compatriot of mine—Ramon Zarrilla was his name ; and they had sailed almost immediately for my country. And that was all.

" Time passed. Most men have the strength of mind to get over these things, but I suppose I have less tenacity

than the usual run. Or perhaps more tenacity—it's difficult to say. You are a very good listener, Sir Clinton."

The late Chief Constable refrained from comment.
He could see that it was a case of now or never, and he
kept silent lest he should break the chain of thought in
Roca's mind. The doctor glanced at his face, and seemed
to be encouraged by its expression.

"Time passed," Roca went on. "I turned back to
my work, but it had now become a mere mechanical
task. All the joy had gone out of it. That also is a fairly
common experience, I think. Then, at last, there came
a letter from Marcelle. There was no address, and from
the writing I could see that she was very ill.

"It was another common story—though less common
than the rest. After her marriage she and her husband
had sailed for the Argentine. They had touched at Montevideo and transhipped there to the *Mihanovich*. You do
not know the *Mihanovich*, Sir Clinton ? She starts about
ten o'clock at night. Very gay indeed, the *Mihanovich*,
decked out with illuminations like an Eastern bride with
her jewels. She is well known on the Rio del Plata,
steaming through the night..

"I have often imagined what happened. It was not
in the letter, of course, except for a hint or two. The
Mihanovich gets in at eight in the morning. The illuminations have all gone out. It is time to think of everyday
life, to plunge into business and leave romance behind.
Bread and butter, as you English would say. I picture
my little Marcelle there at the rail, beside this husband
whom she has taken in a fit of pique, watching Buenos
Ayres coming closer and closer. Then the disembarka-
tion on a strange soil, the people about her speaking an
unknown tongue, the loneliness creeping on her and
making her more and more dependent upon this husband. A drive to a station, tickets procured, which she
never sees and which would mean nothing to her even
if she had been permitted a glimpse of the name of the

111

station on them. Then a long train journey, another station crowded with an alien people, another taxi, a house. Home at last ! "

Roca bit savagely at his cigar, and waited until he could recover control over his voice.

" Home ? " he continued. " Well, hardly that, perhaps, unless one calls a prison ' home.' You can guess the rest, Sir Clinton. The awakening, the revolt, refusals —then the ' discipline treatment.' My little Marcelle learned it all. She was not an easy case for them ; she caused them a lot of trouble. But of course the system wins in the end. She was much too valuable a consignment to waste. And so, at last, a shameful surrender. Then, months of the life you know about . . ."

He broke off with a gesture which left the rest to Sir Clinton's imagination.

" Typhoid released her in the end. She wrote to me from the hospital. I sailed by the next boat, but of course I was too late. She died very soon after she had written her letter to me."

Roca glanced again at Sir Clinton's profile, and as he continued his voice took on again the tinge of irony which had faded out during the later part of his narrative.

" I arrived too late. Naturally I made some inquiries, but one learns little. The Centre can afford to pay for people's silence when it requires it. I made very little fuss—in fact, I posed as an acquaintance of some relation of hers, someone who had only a casual interest in the case at all. I had been thinking hard on the boat, you see. I had nothing else to do, during the voyage.

" There was nothing to be done from the outside. The Centre talks freely enough when you get inside ; but it keeps quiet so far as outsiders are concerned. I could pick up nothing of any value. And I meant to get my information by hook or by crook. I owed this Ramon Zarrilla—and others—a debt, and I hoped to pay it in time. Of course he had vanished from the scene almost as soon as he had delivered the article, handed over the Franchucha to her new owners. I could not get on his track from the outside.

" That was how I became 7-DH, Sir Clinton. I knew that the League of Nations was taking a hand in the game. They had an organisation for procuring information—a set of spies, if you like to call it that. Playing a lone hand, I did not see much chance of tracking down the men I wanted to find ; but, if I enrolled with the League, I would have the help of their machinery when I wanted it. I would have access to the information which they were gathering together from all quarters. A man working single-handed can do very little with the Centre ; but it was different when I came into touch with the League's people. A bit of news here, a scrap of information picked up yonder : they all began to fit together and help me to work back along the trail which led from the hospital to Paris. The agent 7-DH proved invaluable to Dr. Esteban Roca, I can assure you.

" That was how you happened to come across me in Paris. You see, 7-DH was especially useful because he was a medical man. People will talk to a doctor more freely than to any other kind of man—except a priest, perhaps. And 7-DH was known to be a broken-down doctor who had just missed prison for some affair or other. He'd been just a shade too clever for the police, it appeared. Everyone knew that on the best authority, because 7-DH made rather a boast of it himself. Of course, that case had finished his practice in decent circles ; so he had come down a bit in the world and gone among people who weren't so particular—and so on."

" You took me in completely when I saw you," Sir Clinton admitted frankly.

Roca acknowledged this with a gesture.

" I must have been successful," he said, without a trace

113

of boasting in his manner. " I became quite a valuable character among the group of the Centre. There's no general organisation of the Centre ; but they play into each other's hands ; and with my reputation I got myself passed on from one *caftane* to another. Who would suspect the broken-down doctor, who was so useful when he wasn't drunk ? Sometimes it was handy for a *souteneur* or a *madame* to have a medical who could be called in and who wouldn't chatter. After my experiences, I can quite imagine that doctors may be useful even in hell. And, of course, through the other people I scraped acquaintance with the group of *commissionnaires*. They interested me most, naturally. A false marriage is one of their habitual methods for procuring a beefsteak . . ."

" Beefsteak ? " Sir Clinton demanded. " Slang, I suppose ? "

" Yes. Same thing as ' article,' or ' package ' or ' remount.' Argot of that kind is useful when it comes to writing or telegraphing, you understand. I continue. I supposed that I should find my friend Zarrilla among the *commissionnaires* eventually ; but by and by I got on a fresh track. Behind the main machinery of the Centre stood a handful of men—prosperous fellows who seldom take a direct part in the business itself. They do the planning and supply the capital, mainly. My information, bit by bit, began to point in that direction. It was very difficult to get evidence without exciting suspicion ; and I took pains to avoid that. It was very slow. These fellows, you understand ? are quite well camouflaged. They all have some ostensible business to account for their existence—they are importers, or something of that sort —and their positions would stand a fair amount of examination if it were carried through without definite suspicion at the back of it. My friend Zarrilla was one of that group, apparently.

" It was very slow, oh, so slow. But the other day, quite by chance, I got some information which seemed worth looking into. And, of all places, it pointed to this little village here as the spot where I might learn more. Someone here knew the facts that I wanted to know—after all that time ! So I have come across to look for him. And now I run across you, Sir Clinton. It is really a very restricted world."

" It wasn't by any chance this man Quevedo who was killed in a motor-smash the other day ? " Sir Clinton demanded.

" Quevedo ? No, I never knew anyone with that name," Roca replied.

Sir Clinton scrutinised the doctor's face, but Roca seemed to attach no importance to the question or the answer. For a few moments there was silence. Then Sir Clinton took the bull by the horns.

" Frankly," he said, " I can see your point of view. It would be no great loss to the world if your friends of the Centre were quietly put out of it. But bear in mind, Dr. Roca, that the English law has a very long arm and a very firm hand. It doesn't recognise private revenges. I shouldn't advise you to run the risk of executing justice on British soil if I thought—well, that the police would catch you at it. Think that over."

Roca's smile did not include the expression in his eyes when he acknowledged the advice.

" I take it that our talk has been confidential. Your recognition of me forced my hand, isn't that true ? Otherwise I should hardly have wearied you with my story."

Sir Clinton had given his warning and saw no reason to labour the point. He was about to dismiss the subject, when a thought struck him.

" Have you any friends in this neighbourhood, Dr. Roca ? "

Roca shook his head.

" None among the population, at any rate," he said. " One of my friends . . ."

He broke off abruptly, as though he had made a slip.

" Is it not time that we were returning to Raynham Parva ? " he inquired, as if to cover his mistake.

Sir Clinton had sized up Roca and was quite sure that there was nothing further to be gained by fishing for information. In a short time, he dropped his companion at the Black Bull and turned his car towards Fern Lodge. But as he drove along the street, he was evidently perplexed. An obvious suspicion had lodged itself in his mind, despite the doctor's denials ; and it had grown stronger during the interview.

The murderer of Quevedo had known where to find the jugular vein without fumbling ; and Roca was a medical man. The incident by the roadside on the night of his own arrival at Raynham Parva suggested more than a little when it was connected up with the operations of 7-DH. And Roca's one mistake in the course of the interview threw some light on the possibilities in the case. If Roca had a confederate who nosed out information for him, then the doctor himself need not have appeared at Raynham Parva in order to secure previous knowledge of Quevedo's movements on that fatal night. And Roca had admitted the existence of a friend whom no one had identified.

" H'm ! " Sir Clinton mused. " That doctor's a cool card ; and I can't say I'd blame him much if he's taken the law into his own hands. Any man gets outside the normal decencies when he utilises a girl's trustfulness in order to trap her and send her down into that hell ; and if Roca was keen on this girl, I can't pretend to condemn his methods too much. Something with boiling oil in it wouldn't be too harsh treatment for gentry of that sort. All the same, I wish Roca hadn't made that slip. It's going to give me a pretty little moral problem to solve in the near future, I'm afraid."

But a more immediate puzzle was in his mind just

then. He could not understand Roca's behaviour at the Bale Stones. Why had the doctor been so manifestly anxious to visit the monument ; and yet, when he reached it, shown not the slightest interest in it ? Sir Clinton had no key to the riddle.

CHAPTER IX

THE CYPHER TELEGRAM

As he drove along the main street of Raynham Parva,
Sir Clinton caught sight of Constable Peel on the pavement ; and something tempted him to pull up.

" Well, Peel," he demanded as the constable came to
the side of the car. " How's the investigation going ?
Got on the track of your homicidal friend yet ? "

Constable Peel seemed uncertain as to how he should
take this remark. He glanced dubiously at Sir Clinton,
as though not very sure of his ground ; but his love of
hearing his own voice evidently overcame his scruples
almost immediately.

" The sergeant's working away, sir," he confided in
a slightly acid tone. " But I haven't seen much in the
way of results—and that's a fact. He's been out on several
wild-goose chases, so far as I know ; and that's about
all. This new foreigner here, the one at the Black Bull,
he gave him a fine set back, from all I've heard."

" Dr. Roca, you mean ? "

" That's him. Ledbury, he went off to see this doctor ;
and he came back with a flea in his ear, he did. I saw
that for myself. Ledbury didn't report *that* conversation
in full to me, you may take your oath—I beg pardon,
sir ! I mean he said nothing about it. But I heard a few
things from the Black Bull people. There's one or two
of them that hears a lot more than visitors think."

" So Sergeant Ledbury found he'd made a mistake ? "

" He did so, sir. This Roca has no car—I could've
told Ledbury that myself if he'd taken the bother to ask

118

me. I was at the station when he arrived by the train. He'd got no luggage bar a suitcase with him. When Ledbury asked him where he been staying before he came here, he was quite open about it. He came up from Micheldean Abbas. He'd been there for the best part of a week, it seems, staying at the inn."

" Micheldean Abbas is just down the line, isn't it ? "

" Yes, sir. Fourth station. Then Ledbury asked Roca about Quevedo, and he said he'd never heard of any-one of that name. Then he hesitated a bit, or something ; and Ledbury pressed him a bit harder. Then he admitted that he did know somebody called Quevedo, and the sergeant he thought he'd got on to something good. But it turned out that Roca was thinking of some fellow Quevedo that wrote books in the time of Shakespeare. That was a bit of a leg-pull for the sergeant ! I did laugh when I heard it."

" So it turned out a blank end ? "

" Dead blank, sir. Ledbury, of course, he believes in being thorough ; and I heard him ring up Micheldean Abbas later on in the day. The inn people confirmed the story about Roca's movements. When the murder was being done, he was in bed and asleep."

He hesitated for a moment.

" You'd see what the coroner's jury brought in, sir ? Death by misadventure ! That's a good 'un, knowing what we know. But Ledbury, he must have squared the coroner or something ; for none of the real stuff came out in the evidence he gave ; and I got the tip not to give the show away, either."

Sir Clinton disliked the constable's tone ; but he refrained from checking him for fear of drying up what might easily prove a fluent source of private information.

" Well, good luck ! " he said in a hopeful tone, as he let the car move off.

Just outside the village, his eye was caught by a

119

familiar slim figure on the road before him ; and as he came up to the girl he stopped his car.

" Hullo, Estelle ! This is a surprise. Taken to walking, nowadays, for a change ? " he hailed her as he opened the door for her.

" Daddy's using our car this afternoon, so I couldn't bring it over," Estelle explained, as she slipped into the seat beside him and laid her tennis racquet on her knee. " Parents are getting a bit selfish in these days, aren't they ? "

" Hungry look in your eye, I notice. Coming to lunch with us, I suppose ? "

" According to plan. Elsie rang me up this morning. It seems she's got two young Peris she wants me to take under my wing. What sort of people are they ? "

" Very nice girls, from all I've seen of them ; so you can set your mind at ease."

" Right ! By the way, you've been on holiday, haven't you ? Nice trip ? "

" Not bad," Sir Clinton admitted, unscrupulously plagiarising himself.

" Don't rave, dear. It makes one so uncomfortable when you break loose like that."

Sir Clinton grinned youthfully.

" Right ! as you say," he promised. " I'll restrain my transports. Loquacity's always been my failing in company manners."

" Like your new nephew-in-law ? " Estelle demanded carelessly.

" I haven't seen much of him yet," Sir Clinton confessed. " I'll take your opinion till I get more experience."

" Oh, he's all right. A bit swalmy, you know."

" Swalmy ? "

" Oh, you know what I mean. Rather . . ."

A vague gesture completed her description.

" Thanks. My own thought put neatly into words," Sir Clinton interjected.

It was curious, he reflected, that Estelle seemed to have the same difficulty as himself in defining the impression left by Francia. Perhaps she, like himself, was influenced by a tinge of jealousy, now that a fresh figure had supplanted her to some extent in Elsie's affections. Whatever was at the root of it, Estelle evidently did not take whole-heartedly to Francia.

" A case of ' I do not like thee, Dr. Fell ' ? " he inquired jestingly.

" Something of the sort," Estelle answered, with a touch of seriousness in her voice which made Sir Clinton prick up his ears. " But it's rather mean to say that," she added quickly, " after he's been so decent in inviting me to take a trip out to the Argentine with them."

" You're going, then ? "

Estelle nodded.

" Daddy's been rather hard to persuade—can't lose his dear daughter, you know. But Elsie turned him round her finger in the end ; so it's all fixed up. If these girls are really good sorts, it'll be quite a happy party. I'm looking forward to it."

Sir Clinton seemed to think that this called for no comment, and in a few minutes they reached Fern Lodge.

During lunch, Sir Clinton found himself fully occupied in listening to a detailed account of Johnnie's fishing experiences in the morning ; and he took little part in the general conversation at the table. Francia, he noted, seemed to be exerting himself to please Estelle ; but it was difficult to see whether he was making much progress or not. She seemed much more interested in the Anstruther girls ; and Sir Clinton was not ill-pleased to find that she evidently liked them.

When the meal was over, Francia excused himself almost at once, pleading that he had to attend to some business correspondence. The rest of the party went out to the lawn before the house ; but Johnnie soon detached himself to return to his fishing.

" I'll take a walk down to the lake later on and see what you're doing," Sir Clinton promised. " Rex will be here shortly, Johnnie. I'll send him on as soon as he turns up. See that you pay attention to what he tells you. He's a first-class fisherman and you'll learn a lot."

He watched the boy take the path down to the boat-house, and then turned his attention to the conversation which was going on around him.

" How's the play getting on ? " he heard Elsie ask, addressing her question to the two sisters.

Linda Anstruther shook her head in mock despair.

" We seem to spend half our time in tearing up what we've written. Noreen suffers from too many ideas, and she hates to see any of them left out ; so we go back and back over it again and again to see if we can't fit them in."

She glanced at Sir Clinton, and apparently guessed that he had not heard of the matter before.

" We thought it would be a good idea to supplement the musical part of our show with a sketch or two," she explained to him shyly. " So we've been trying to work up two or three dialogues. It's not so easy as we thought."

" I sympathise with you," Sir Clinton condoled. " I've always hated paper-work of any description. Chronic paralysis in the pen is one of my troubles."

" It's so difficult to be downright colloquial when one has a pen in one's hand, I find," Noreen Anstruther put in. " I used to think one just sat down and wrote ; but somehow everything comes out as if it was on stilts —not a bit natural."

" Why not try over one or two of your sketches ? " Sir Clinton suggested. " You've got a ready-made audience here. When you came to act the things, you'd soon see any weak points."

Linda Anstruther seemed to shrink a little from the idea.

" Mr. Francia very kindly offered to look over the

things some time and let us know whether they would do. He knows the type of stuff that would suit, you see. What we really ought to do is to get them translated into Spanish and learn them up so that we could patter them off, even if we didn't really understand what we were saying. The accent would be dreadful, of course ; but no one expects much in that way from a foreigner."

" You don't speak Spanish, then ? " Sir Clinton inquired.

" Not a word of it, either of us. That's what makes it difficult."

" Rather awkward, going out to a strange country without knowing the language, isn't it ? " Sir Clinton suggested.

" Of course. But Mr. Francia's very kind. He's promised to look after us until we find our feet out there. He'll do all the interviewing and so forth, at first ; and he says we'll soon pick up all the Spanish we need for our work."

Sir Clinton did not pursue the subject ; and the girls fell upon a fresh topic which allowed him to drop out of the conversation.

" What about some tennis ? " he heard Elsie suggest a little later on. " We'll leave you here, uncle. You're too much of a handicap for the partner that gets you."

Sir Clinton acquiesced in his exclusion.

" What I like about you, Elsie, is that your remarks give one so much to think over. The ambiguity of that last sentence will keep me busy till tea-time, and even then I won't be too sure of the exact meaning."

" We'll leave you to ponder, then. Come on, Estelle. You brought your racquet, didn't you ? "

The four girls rose and went off towards the tennis-court, leaving Sir Clinton and Mrs. Thornaby together on the lawn.

" I've asked young Rex Brandon to come across this

afternoon," Sir Clinton intimated to his sister. " He'll be here any minute now."

Mrs. Thornaby glanced across at her brother with a certain doubt in her face.

" Do you think that was the kindest thing to do ? " she inquired.

" I should think so," Sir Clinton retorted in a careless tone. " The thing's done now. He may as well swallow his dose at once and get it over. Nothing like seeing with your own eyes. I asked him on purpose, just to bring things home to him bluntly."

" It seems rather a brutal cure, doesn't it ? Rex was very fond of her, Clinton."

" He's still fond of her ; that's the trouble. He's not the changeable sort."

" And yet you think you'll cure him by showing him the two of them together ? Sometimes I doubt if you know so much about human nature after all, Clinton."

Sir Clinton shrugged his shoulders as though argument were useless.

" Ask him to tea, anyhow," he said, as he dismissed the subject. " He's going down to the lake first of all to give Johnnie a few hints."

Just as he spoke, the figure of Rex Brandon appeared round a bend in the approach to Fern Lodge. He seemed to be coming reluctantly ; but when he caught sight of Sir Clinton and Mrs. Thornaby, he pulled himself together, waved to them, and quickened his steps.

" Your pupil's down by the lake," Sir Clinton explained, after they had talked together for a few minutes. " He's in a great state of excitement, so you'd better cut along and not keep him waiting."

Mrs. Thornaby obeyed her brother's instructions ; and after a very obvious hesitation Rex accepted her invitation ; then he set off in search of Johnnie.

" Sound stuff, Rex," Sir Clinton commented, with a

tinge of regret in his voice, as he watched the athletic figure disappear among the bushes which fringed the boat-house path. " H'm ! I seem to have finished my cigarettes. I'll go and get some more."

He moved across the lawn and entered the house. His stock of cigarettes was in the smoke-room ; and he went there to refill his case. But just as he entered the door, the telephone bell rang and he picked up the receiver.

" Yes ? Fern Lodge speaking."

" Can I speak to Mr. Francia ? " a voice demanded over the wire.

" Is that you, Dr. Roca ? " Sir Clinton asked, since he thought he recognised the voice.

Rather to his surprise, the wire suddenly went dead and there was no answer. He rang several times, and finally the girl at the exchange intervened to tell him that his interlocutor had rung off. Quite evidently Roca had been taken aback by having his voice recognised at Fern Lodge ; but, though he puzzled over the matter for a time, Sir Clinton could not hit upon any reason for this behaviour. It was plain enough that Francia was the man of whom Roca had spoken, the man from whom he expected to get the information for which he had come to Raynham Parva ; for otherwise the telephone call was unaccountable. Without fathoming the matter, Sir Clinton felt uncomfortable. Francia was becoming rather too much of an enigma to him ; and some of the possible solutions raised disquieting thoughts in his mind.

He put down the telephone and crossed the room to the window which looked across the verandah towards the lake. He soon picked up the figures of Rex and Johnnie, evidently absorbed in the study of the art of casting. Sir Clinton found the sight reassuring. Rex was obviously taking his post as instructor very seriously ; and that meant that his mind would be occupied until tea-time. He would have no time to brood over the might-have-beens ; and that was a clear gain.

Sir Clinton leisurely filled his cigarette-case and went out to rejoin his sister. As he reached the front door, he saw a telegraph-boy approaching on a bicycle, and he strolled down the avenue to meet him.

" Telegram for Sir Clinton Driffield, sir," the messenger announced in answer to an inquiry. " You, sir ? "

He fumbled in his pouch, handed over the wire, made a gesture of thanks for the tip Sir Clinton handed over, and then waited for the envelope to be opened. Sir Clinton unfolded the sheets of a long telegram and glanced at the opening words.

" *Planisphere, transit, equatorial, right ascension, asteroid, ecliptic* . . ."

Sir Clinton folded the sheets and put them into his pocket.

" All right. There's no answer," he told the boy, who remounted his bicycle and rode off again.

Sir Clinton had recognised the code, which was one that had been supplied to him for use while he was on the Continent recently ; but without the key it was impossible for him to decipher the message. Re-entering the house, he went up to his own room, locked the door, and set to work with the help of a small volume. The communication, he found, dealt with some details of a report which he had sent in after his return from the Continent. Apparently some amplifications of one or two points were desired. He drafted a reply which he put into cypher with the help of his book and copied out on some telegram forms which he took from an attaché-case. Then, after burning his rough drafts, he placed his answer in his pocket and went downstairs again. There was no particular need to get his wire off immediately. Any time that evening would do quite well.

Mrs. Thornaby had left the lawn ; and, after a glance in search of her, Sir Clinton moved off towards the lakeside. He was not unwilling to take the opportunity of uninterrupted thinking which had been presented to him. Since his arrival at Fern Lodge, he had been irritated by uncertainty. With the best will in the world, he could not bring himself to like Francia ; and the thought of Elsie in the hands of a man whom he distrusted was a continual irritant to his mind. No doubt the fellow had succeeded in attracting her ; one had only to see them together to be sure of that. But often a girl takes a fancy to a " wrong 'un." Her insight counts for very little in such things, as Sir Clinton knew. A man can cover up a lot of his deficiencies if he can make love to a girl in the way she expects ; and the bigger experience a man has had in that field, the more likely he will be to go the right way about it in a particular case, especially if he starts with the advantage of a certain attitude towards women.

That was the basic factor in the problem which presented itself to Sir Clinton ; and the other features of the situation naturally attached themselves to it in the mind of the late Chief Constable.

First of all, there was Quevedo. He was an associate of Francia, and hence anything connected with Quevedo had its value as an aid to assessing Elsie's husband. There seemed to be little doubt about Quevedo, so far as Sir Clinton could see. To the ordinary mind, the affair with Staffin and Teddy Barford pointed to one conclusion and one only : Quevedo had been planning to get control of the girl. He had temporarily disarmed her suspicions, quite cleverly ; and she had been fool enough not to see through him : but the facts of the case could hardly be twisted in a way which would evade the obvious inference. If Quevedo was free from the taint of White Slave traffic, then the whole business was inexplicable.

As to Quevedo's death, Sir Clinton had no doubts on

127

the matter at all. Roca and his confederate were at the back of that affair ; for nothing else seemed capable of fitting the facts which he knew. One or other of them had done the murder.

And, as he followed this line of thought, Sir Clinton came again to a problem which had been exercising his mind since the morning. What was his own position in the case ? Since he had resigned, he was no longer an official and could look on the affair from a more aloof standpoint ; but that hardly covered the whole ground. He had been drawn into assisting Ledbury in the Quevedo case and had uncovered the neatly concealed tracks of Roca and his accomplice, which would never have been detected except for his intervention. Could he draw back now, if he were asked to go further with his assistance ? If he did, would his refusal not lead to Ledbury suspecting something ? Ledbury was by no means a fool ; and he was hardly likely to turn off from a track merely because Sir Clinton declined to go any further along it with him. Sir Clinton recalled the fact that Ledbury had checked even his own statements about his doings on the night of the Quevedo murder, although on the face of things there could be no connection between the two.

Then there was Roca himself, whether he was the actual murderer or not. Sir Clinton had only one interview with the doctor, and yet Roca had established something which almost amounted to sympathy between them. Despite his acquaintance with the seamy side of human nature, Sir Clinton had retained a certain protective attitude of mind when women came into a case. He hated the thought of a woman being ill-used ; and he had every sympathy with the feelings of Roca when he thought of the sufferings of an unwilling girl in the Argentine infernos. This was hardly a case in which one could stand above the battle on a platform and deprecate the employment of crude methods to square the account.

If Quevedo had really been mixed up in the White Slave traffic, Sir Clinton was enough of a realist to waste no energy in censuring the final act in the business. At the same time, as a member of the general public, he had a moral duty imposed upon him : he ought not to become an accessory after the fact by suppressing information which had come into his possession. That was where the shoe pinched.

A man with a deep and genuine grievance might well be tempted to take the law into his own hands and run the risks involved in a private act of vengeance. But had an outsider the right to shield a murderer merely on the strength of a pathetic story which might, after all, be the merest pack of plausible lies ? Sir Clinton did not think that Roca had told him a false tale ; but nevertheless he recognised well enough that no proof whatever had been advanced in support of Roca's story. All that he had to go upon was his own impression of the doctor.

Then, again, he had really very little against Roca except the merest suspicion. Possibly if he dropped a hint to Ledbury, something might come out of it—though Ledbury seemed to have made very little of his inquiry into the doctor's affairs already. It would probably take a smarter man than Ledbury to carry the thing through against a man of Roca's calibre ; and, if Sir Clinton intervened at all, he would be almost morally bound to see the business through by giving the sergeant his assistance. Could he decently go so far as that, on the strength of mere suspicion ?

Worst of all, he recognised that this matter was one which would admit of no delay in the decision. Roca might vanish from Raynham Parva at any moment ; and, if he once got away, the chance of laying hands on him would shrink considerably.

" This is a damned difficult business," Sir Clinton admitted to himself as he walked by the lakeside. " I wish I'd never touched it. And the worst is that this is only the first link in a chain. I wish I could be sure where the other end of the chain's lying. There'll be a lot of dirty water stirred up before it all comes to the surface : that's certain."

He continued his review of the case until his watch told him it was time to go up to the house for tea.

CHAPTER X

THE RESPONSIBILITY

When Sir Clinton made his way back to Fern Lodge, he found Elsie, the two Anstruther girls, Estelle, and Mrs. Thornaby on the lawn.

" Find a chair, Clinton," his sister suggested. " These girls don't want to go into the house, so I've ordered tea to be sent out here."

" Rex and Johnnie will be here in a moment," Sir Clinton explained. " They were just coming in when I left the lake. Don't let me interrupt your conversation," he added, turning to Linda Anstruther.

" Miss Scotswood was just telling us about an evening dress she's been making," Linda explained. " It sounds a lovely thing."

" I'll lend you the pattern, if you like," Estelle proposed. " But these waters are a bit too deep for that honorary uncle of mine, you know. He's not æsthetic. In fact, there are times when I could kill him, if it weren't for subsequent bothers. I've taken him out to the theatre often, put on a split-new dress in honour of the occasion, and really been a credit to him. And what do you think he says ? ' H'm ! I don't think I've seen you in that before.' You don't somehow seem to have the knack of rising to the occasion in your remarks, Uncle Clinton."

Before Sir Clinton had time to defend himself, Johnnie appeared at the head of the path leading to the boathouse, and Rex Brandon followed him.

" What do you think of these ? " Johnnie demanded

131

proudly as he came up to the group. " That was the
first one I caught ; then that one ; and the last two I got
just one after another."

He waved four diminutive trout strung together by
grass threaded through their gills.

" They seem to have been young and inexperienced,"
Sir Clinton commented, examining Johnnie's catch.
" But I can distinctly see the difference between them
and minnows. First-class, Johnnie ! You'll soon be able
to grapple with the old and wily ones. I'll give you
half a crown for the first one you get that's over four
ounces."

Johnnie turned to his mother.

" May I have these cooked for me ? Rex says it makes
all the difference if you eat 'em at once, fresh out of the
water."

Mrs. Thornaby, with a smile at her son's eagerness,
gave the required permission ; and Johnnie set off immediately to interview the cook, swinging his catch as
he went. Rex Brandon, having greeted the company
and been introduced to the Anstruther girls, took a chair
among the others ; but he showed little desire to force
himself into the general conversation. Sir Clinton, with
the tail of his eye, could see him covertly examining
Elsie's face as though he hoped to read something in its
expression.

Staffin brought out the tea-table and set it up beside
Mrs. Thornaby.

" Tell Mr. Francia that we're out here, Staffin,"
Elsie said, as the maid was turning to go back to
the house.

Rex showed no sign of having heard, but he swung
round very slightly in his chair, so as to command a
view of the front door. When Francia appeared under
the porch, Sir Clinton was puzzled to see something in
Rex's face which suggested recognition ; but, when the
two men were introduced to each other, Rex betrayed

no previous knowledge of the man who had supplanted him. Sir Clinton was on the alert to read Rex's thoughts, if possible ; but Rex kept control of his features, and it was hard to say whether or not he disliked his successful rival more now that he had seen him in the flesh.

They had hardly finished handing round the cups when Staffin appeared again.

" There's somebody ringing you up on the telephone, sir," she intimated to Francia. " He didn't give any name—just asked to speak to you."

Quite obviously, this took Francia by surprise. He seemed puzzled, as though he could not understand why anyone should call him up. He excused himself hastily and went off to the house.

" Roca again," Sir Clinton inferred ; and his brow darkened slightly as his earlier perplexities thrust themselves up in his mind once more.

When the Argentiner returned after a short interval, Sir Clinton scanned his face with interest ; but Francia betrayed nothing very marked in his expression. It was clear enough that the message, whatever it was, had given him something to think over ; for, although, he joined in the conversation, it was always with an almost absent-minded air, as though he were trying to keep two lines of thought in his mind at one time.

" Some more tennis ? " Elsie suggested when they had finished tea. " Care to play, Rex ? "

Rex Brandon glanced down at his well-worn tweeds and shook his head.

" Don't feel in the dress for it, somehow, Elsie. I'll umpire for you, if you like."

" I'll come too," Sir Clinton said lazily, getting up from his chair as he spoke. " My comments are always appreciated in the best circles."

" If you'd teach me that service of yours, instead of telling me all the things I shouldn't do, you'd be more of a help, Uncle Clinton," Estelle pointed out. " I can't catch the knack of it, somehow ; and it would be worth a good deal to me if you could put me up to it."

"Another time," Sir Clinton decided. "Come along. I'll run you home in my car afterwards, so you can exhaust yourself as much as you like on the courts."

Rex Brandon folded up some camp-chairs and prepared to carry them round the house ; Sir Clinton collected a number of cushions ; and the group moved away towards the tennis-courts. Sir Clinton sat down beside his sister, while the girls went down to play ; Rex took up his position ; whilst Francia, a little way off, seemed to be divided between watching the game and puzzling over the problem which had been sprung upon him. Sir Clinton could see his appraising glances following the girls' movements almost mechanically whilst he evidently was cudgelling his brain in search of some idea which evaded him.

"Roca's given him something to think over, evidently," was Sir Clinton's silent conclusion. "But what it is one can't make out. I wish I knew."

He glanced at Rex Brandon's face and found it rather tired. Rex was endeavouring to play the part he had assigned to himself, but his eyes were following Elsie more than they should have done ; and once Sir Clinton found him giving a wrong decision because his attention had obviously been elsewhere at the critical moment. It was impossible to tell from his features whether Sir Clinton's experiment had been successful or not ; but once a stray glance in the direction of Francia, aloof and self-absorbed, betrayed clearly enough that Rex felt no attraction for his supplanter. It was so charged with dislike—or something even stronger—that Sir Clinton began to wonder whether, after all, he had been quite wise in forcing the two men into contact.

The players were so evenly matched that time passed without anyone realising how quickly it had gone ; and when at last Estelle came up and glanced at her wrist-watch, which she had left in Sir Clinton's charge, she made an exclamation of dismay.

" I'd no notion it was so late. I've got some letters to write which *must* catch to-night's post. I'll need to fly."

" I'll have the car round for you immediately," Sir Clinton assured her. He glanced at his own watch. " You've heaps of time to write letters and still catch the post, if you don't hang about too much."

" Hurry, then," Estelle urged him, beginning to put her racquet into its case.

" I'll give you a lift to the Black Bull, Rex," Sir Clinton said, as he rose to his feet.

Linda Anstruther suddenly remembered something which had slipped her memory.

" Don't forget you promised to lend me that dress-pattern, Miss Scotswood."

Estelle made a mental calculation before replying.

" I've just got time for it, I think. Suppose you come over with me in the car now. Then I can show you the thing itself as well as give you the pattern. You'd better see what it looks like when it's finished."

" That's ever so nice. I'd love to see it."

When Sir Clinton brought the car round, he found Francia waiting with the others.

" I've just remembered I want something in the village," the Argentiner said half-apologetically. " Your car's a five-seater, isn't it ? Would you mind giving me a lift ? I'll walk back."

Sir Clinton nodded, and his four passengers got on board ; Estelle and Linda Anstruther eagerly discussing some point in the dress-pattern, whilst Francia remained silent, as though he were still perplexed by his mysterious problem. Rex, in the front seat with Sir Clinton, seemed disinclined to talk.

In a few minutes the car reached the outskirts of

Raynham Parva ; and Francia, leaning forward, touched
Sir Clinton on the shoulder and asked to be let out.
Sir Clinton put on his brakes at once and allowed his
guest to alight ; but as he drove on again he could not
help speculating on Francia's errand.

" He might as well have let me put him down at the
door of the place he wanted," he mused. " Funny idea,
asking for a lift and then getting me to drop him a
quarter of a mile from the shops. Didn't want me to see
where he was going, evidently ; and banked on the fact
that I'd have to go straight on with the girls."

He leaned back and inquired from Estelle where she
was staying.

" First on the right, once you're past the church," she
directed him. " Then it's the fourth house on the left.
You'll know it by the sundial on the lawn. Daddy's not
at all pleased about it. You see, I persuaded him to come
here—against his better judgment, he says—because
Elsie was coming to Raynham Parva this summer. And
now Elsie's going off to foreign parts and taking me
with her. So poor old Daddy is left marooned in this
place. ' Not a decent golf-course within fifteen miles,'
as he says tragically."

" You youngsters have very little thought for your
elders," Sir Clinton observed, knowing that he would
get a rise.

" Our elders have a way of evening things up, any-
way," Estelle retorted. " They seem to spend all their
time thinking about us—mostly with disapproval. If
you knew what a fuss there was before I was permitted
—*permitted*, if you please !—to take this trip to Buenos
Ayres, you'd have some notion of the waste of good
grey matter that goes on nowadays. However, it's all
fixed up. I said to Daddy : ' Well, I'm going out with a
proper chaperon and all that sort of thing ; and you've
known Elsie, and Mrs. Thornaby, and Uncle Clinton all
your life ; so you can't start getting the squakes about

respectability, and so on and so forth.' So he gave in, at that, not having a leg to stand on."

Sir Clinton laughed shortly.

" You young parasites give a lot of trouble."

" Parasite ? Me ? " Estelle demanded indignantly. " Who's a parasite ? "

" Everyone's a parasite who doesn't do something for the rest of the world."

" Indeed ? " Estelle produced a sound like a suppressed snort of indignation. " Well, if I *am* a parasite, at least I'm a polite one, so I won't say what I think of that remark."

" Quite right." Sir Clinton turned to Rex. " Sorry I passed the Black Bull in the heat of that argument. I'll drop you on the way back."

Rex nodded his acquiescence in this suggestion, and Sir Clinton, once past the church, turned as he had been directed and pulled up in front of an old garden, beyond which could be seen an ivy-covered house. Estelle stepped out of the car and turned to Sir Clinton.

" You can run away and play, if you like. I'm highly displeased with you, if it's any joy to you to know it. Parasite, indeed ! If you noticed the way people glare after me in the street, you'd realise the amount of æsthetic pleasure I bring into folks' drab lives—same as any other great artist. Doesn't that justify my existence ? "

" There may be something in it," Sir Clinton conceded, though in a sceptical tone. " Now I'll come back in a quarter of an hour for Miss Anstruther, so don't waste time."

As the car passed down the main street of Raynham Parva on its way to the Black Bull, Rex raised himself slightly in his seat.

" There's Francia," he pointed out. " Are you going to pick him up ? "

Sir Clinton saw the figure of the Argentiner emerge

137

from the druggist's shop and turn towards Fern Lodge. Evidently he had not caught sight of the car.

" No, I think I'll leave him to get home on his ten toes," Sir Clinton decided.

Rex seemed to hesitate for a moment before speaking again.

" You seem to have become great pals with my ceremonious friend," he said at last.

" Roca ? "

" Yes. By the way, I happened to be talking to Roca outside the hotel this morning when a fellow passed up the street. I could see by Roca's expression that he recognised the bird, so quoth I : ' I thought you knew nobody round about here, doctor.' To which sez 'e, very boldly and in a tone intended to convince : ' No more I do '—or words to that effect. But he knew that bird all right, none the less and notwithstanding. So I drew in my feelers, not wishing to seem intrusive. When I got to the tea-table this afternoon, there was my bird sitting at it : Francia. What do you make of that ? "

Rex's hostility to Francia was almost unconcealed now ; and his attempt to cover it with his mask of flippancy failed completely. Quite obviously he suspected something, he knew not exactly what. Sir Clinton had not quite bargained for this development in his game.

" Roca's a decent sort of person, so far as I know," he pointed out, leaving Rex to draw any conclusions he chose from this testimonial. " By the way, Rex, I wish you'd come up to Fern Lodge this evening after dinner. You've nothing to do down here at the hotel ; and you'll be an asset with us. There's an odd girl in the party ; and, if you come, we can always fill in some time with dancing. They've a portable wireless, I know."

" Girls are no treat to me," said Rex grudgingly.

" Well, say you're doing me a favour, then."

" Oh, if you put it that way," Rex consented with marked reluctance.

Sir Clinton, having got his way, refrained from labouring the point.

" Seen Roca to-day ? " he asked casually, as though merely seeking a fresh subject for conversation.

" He's flitted," Rex explained. " I saw his suitcase going down the street towards the station this afternoon. He was carrying it."

" You're sure he's gone ? " Sir Clinton demanded, rather taken by surprise at the news.

" Fresh woods, etc." Rex replied. " As a matter of fact, he bade me adieu—or *adios*, it may have been, perhaps—at the close of our morning interview. We'll knock up against him on the steppes of Uranus or some other likely place when the weather's favourable. Till then . . . "

Sir Clinton had drawn up the car before the Black Bull, and now his eye wandered to the clock on the dashboard.

" Well, ta-ta," he said. " I've got to call at the post office before I go back for that girl."

He drove away before Rex had time to reconsider the question of the visit to Fern Lodge later in the day. At the post office he despatched the wire which he had already written out in cypher, and then he took the car back to Estelle's house and blew his horn at the gate. Linda Anstruther did not keep him waiting long. Almost immediately, the two girls appeared at the door and Estelle accompanied her new friend to the gate.

" You're forgiven," she announced graciously. " At least, I'll overlook it if you'll admit I'm not a parasite and that I do some good in the world. I've put on my new evening dress to prove my æsthetic value. At least, I put it on to show it to Miss Anstruther, and you're getting the benefit. Isn't it pretty ? "

" Beautiful," said Sir Clinton half jestingly, though in reality he admired both the dress and its wearer.

" Oh, raving again, of course ! " Estelle complained in a mock-weary voice. " It's quite embarrassing when you let yourself go like that. Get the habit of moderation, dear, especially before third parties."

" Time you went off to your correspondence," Sir Clinton reminded her.

He opened the door of the front seat for Linda and she took her place beside him. Estelle stood at the gate and watched them as they drove down the road ; and Sir Clinton, glancing back, admitted to himself that she was certainly justified in her boast about her æsthetic effect.

" It's a shade early to go back to Fern Lodge," he suggested to the girl at his side. " There's nothing to do there except hang about until the dressing-gong goes. Suppose we take a short run round ? You haven't seen the country hereabouts, have you ? "

" I'd like to," Linda agreed, " if it's not going to bore you."

" Not a bit. We'll go up this road and see what it looks like farther on."

He turned into a side-road and soon passed beyond the outskirts of Raynham Parva. For a time, neither of them spoke. Linda Anstruther was apparently of the type which does not think it necessary to chatter continuously in order to pretend interest. At last, however, she broke the silence ; and her subject proved an unexpected one to Sir Clinton.

" I've been feeling just a shade ashamed of myself since I came down here," she volunteered shyly, as though she realised she was overstepping the normal bounds and yet felt herself forced to risk a snub.

Sir Clinton's method was always to allow people to talk without interjecting leading questions. Linda glanced at his face and apparently was encouraged by its expression.

" The fact is, Sir Clinton, I came down here feeling

more than a bit distrustful, so I owe all of you an apology.
I suppose I ought to be content to do my apologising
inside ; but somehow . . . well, you've all been so nice
to me, and I felt a bit of a little beast over the business.
So I'm clearing my conscience, if you understand what
I mean."

" I don't," Sir Clinton admitted with a smile. " But
perhaps it'll become clearer as the story unfolds."

" Well, this is what I mean," Linda hurried on, as
though anxious to finish her self-appointed task as
quickly as possible. " When we came in touch with Mr.
Francia first of all, we knew nothing about him except
that he knew some friends of ours. And when he offered
to fix up this engagement for us, I felt in a bit of a hole.
Noreen and I simply *must* find something to do, you
understand ? But still, one's heard a good deal about
things in South America ; and it seemed a bit of a risk
to plunge on the strength of what we knew about Mr.
Francia—which was next to nothing. Noreen's the
optimist of the party, and I feel a bit responsible for her,
you see ? She's always been in my charge, in a sort of
way."

Sir Clinton's nod expressed his interest, but his features
stiffened almost imperceptibly. Here was another side
to his problem looming not too obscurely ahead, it
seemed. Things were growing very complex.

" Frankly," Linda went on, " I had half a mind to
chuck up the whole affair. Something seemed to suggest
that . . . well, that it wasn't the sort of thing that we ought
to go in for, considering how little we knew about Mr.
Francia. It needs no brains to see that a couple of girls
might get into difficulties in a foreign country, if their
money ran short. And we wouldn't have much to come
and go on. I was very worried about it, between that
side and the throwing up of what might be a good
engagement.

" Then Mrs. Francia invited us down here to Fern

141

Lodge ; and I made up my mind I'd come down simply to see what sort of people you were. A spy on you, in fact. It seemed all right from my point of view."

" Quite sound," Sir Clinton reassured her. " What's wrong with that ? I'd do the same myself. "

" So I felt when I came down. I just wanted to see what sort of people Mr. Francia's friends were. One can judge him by that. And when I got here, everyone was so kind. Mrs. Thornaby's a dear. And no one could have been nicer to us than Mrs. Francia. One can't help getting to like her more and more. And, of course, when I heard her uncle was a retired Chief Constable, I knew everything was all right, and that I'd been misjudging Mr. Francia in the most awful way. And, naturally, I felt beastly uncomfortable at having been so suspicious about him when he was only going out of his way to do us a good turn. In fact, I felt like a worm over it all. Do you see how I felt ? "

"Most likely I'd have felt something of the sort myself," Sir Clinton assured her, " though I doubt if I'd have had the courage to own up to it as you've done."

He turned away from that aspect of the subject.

" So it seems that my sister, my niece, and myself are the guarantors in this business ? " he inquired in a faintly quizzical tone.

" If you like to put it that way," Linda answered. " I know you'd never let your niece—and Miss Scotswood— go off out there . . . "

She broke off, evidently feeling she was getting back on to thin ice. Sir Clinton made no attempt to force her into clarity. He dismissed the whole subject.

" What about those sketches you and your sister were putting together ? " he asked.

" We've written a few. They sound quite good ; but I expect that's just because we wrote them ourselves. Once we've got one or two more finished, we're going to give them to Mr. Francia to look over and see if they'd be suitable."

Sir Clinton did not press the conversation further ; and at last he turned the car towards Fern Lodge. Occasionally Linda made a remark ; but neither of them talked for talking's sake. As the car entered the Fern Lodge grounds, Linda's eye fell upon the trip-dial of the milometer.

" Two hundred and seventeen miles ! " she said. " You haven't done all that to-day, surely ? "

Sir Clinton leaned forward and pressed the stud which brought the figures back to zero.

" No, I must have forgotten to reset it," he explained. " That mileage includes my trip up from town as well as the running round I've done since I got here."

He drew up at the house door, allowed Linda to alight, and then took the car round to the garage. Now that he was alone, his face showed much more clearly the traces of the anxious thoughts which his problems were raising in his mind. With his resignation from the Chief Constableship, he had looked forward to complete freedom from responsibility ; but now he began to wonder whether in his official career he had ever been faced with a moral responsibility such as had been thrust on his shoulders in the last few days.

First had come the Quevedo murder and his suspicions of the part which Roca might have played in that affair. Already he had delayed over-long in making up his mind in the matter ; for Roca had left Raynham Parva now, and the chance of tracing him was growing less as the hours went by. Sir Clinton had few illusions, and he recognised that he was already falling into the category of an accessory after the fact, if Roca was really the murderer. That problem brooked no delay.

Then a more personal matter demanded attention, one which was hedged round with even sharper thorns. Roca and Quevedo were linked through the White

143

Slave traffic ; Quevedo and Francia were confessedly business associates, and it was no use burking the fact that this " business " might be the traffic itself. Roca's communication with Francia on the telephone would hardly admit of any other interpretation. And, through Elsie's marriage to this foreigner, Sir Clinton and his sister had been drawn into that shameful ambit.

Putting things at their worst, the whole affair was clear enough. Francia had gone through a ceremony of marriage with Elsie. Whether that ceremony was genuine or not, Sir Clinton had no means of guessing. Francia might be a bigamist for all one knew. In any case, he had established himself as Elsie's husband, and had gained sufficient influence over her to control her move-ments. There was nothing unwarranted in a husband going back to his own country and taking his wife with him.

But, still putting things at the worst, other steps had followed. Francia had manœuvred matters so as to get Estelle invited out to Buenos Ayres. It had been done cleverly enough ; the young bride had been used as a lure to bring the other girl into the net ; no one would be likely to suspect anything. And the affair had not stopped there. The two Anstruther girls had also been involved and their suspicions calmed by putting Elsie to the front. Nothing could be more respectable or less likely to seem underhand.

At that point, Sir Clinton himself had been drawn directly into the toils. As Linda Anstruther had told him bluntly, it was his position which had been one of the governing factors in her decision to rely on Francia. He had, quite unconsciously, become a guarantor of the whole scheme. And, now that he knew this, he could hardly stand aside and wash his hands of any responsi-bility.

What could be done ? Francia's guilt was no more than a matter of suspicion as yet. The whole thing might be quite above-board. In that case, to raise open trouble would mean losing Elsie for good ; she would never forgive him for throwing such a charge at her husband unless he had evidence in support, and strong evidence, too. Investigation ? But, as Roca had told him, people of Francia's type had ostensible businesses which would stand examination. And an investigation which broke down would ruin him with Elsie just as effectually as a baseless charge. It was no good thinking of cabling inquiries to Buenos Ayres, evidently.

Yet if he allowed the party to leave the country, what guarantee had he against disaster ? What had happened to Marcelle Barrère in the same case ? It would be merely the landing of four " articles " instead of one. Sir Clinton set his teeth as he recalled Roca's picture of the landing of Marcelle and her transfer to an up-country inferno. Suppose that happened to Elsie and Estelle ?

There was very little time left in which to act, even if he could determine his course of procedure immediately. On the one hand there was the obvious disaster if his suspicions were correct ; on the other stood the unforgivable offence which he would commit in the eyes of Elsie if he happened to be mistaken.

" What's needed here is a *deus ex machina*," he reflected ; and at that the thought of Roca and his confederate crossed his mind. Roca had possibly squared an account with Quevedo ; but was that the whole of the bill ? After Quevedo was dead, Roca had admitted that he was expecting further information about the people who had wronged him. That certainly suggested that he had more debts to pay ; and his telephone calls furnished further evidence in the matter. When he first rang up, he had recognised Sir Clinton's voice answering, and at once, hoping that his own voice had not been identified, he had rung off. That meant that he did not wish his communication with Francia to be known, if this could be avoided. He had rung up again later and had given

145

his message to the maid, who was not likely to interrogate him as Sir Clinton might have done.

Then Sir Clinton recalled Rex's news. Roca must have left Raynham Parva before he telephoned at all, since Rex had seen him leaving the village early in the afternoon and the telephone message had been much later in the day. For a while Sir Clinton pondered over this sequence of incidents, and before long he evolved an hypothesis which might fit the facts when they came to light. A grim smile crossed his face as he forecast one possible chain of events.

Prophecy with only half the facts on the table had never appealed to Sir Clinton ; so, rejecting his hypothesis for the time being, he considered his personal problem from a fresh angle. It would be extremely awkward to drop his affairs in England at that juncture ; but there was really no vital objection to his leaving the country for a short time. So long as he could book a passage on Elsie's boat, no harm could come to her or her companions. If Francia was above-board, Sir Clinton would find all correct when the party reached its destination ; whilst, if anything underhand was in prospect, his presence would make the scheme impossible.

" It's too big a risk to let these girls run," he reflected finally. " I'll have to change my mind and go with them ; and I'd better see about booking my passage at once. But in the meantime, I ought to get on Roca's track if it's possible. I think I could induce him to be a bit franker about things now."

He shook off his preoccupation and set himself during the evening to keep the Anstruther girls amused. Rex appeared later, and had evidently made up his mind to present an indifferent aspect as well as he could. He attached himself to Noreen Anstruther almost exclusively ; and it was only now and again that Sir Clinton's sharp eyes detected glances which Rex turned on Francia and Elsie. Estelle's arrival seemed to brighten up the party ; and by half-past ten Sir Clinton's suggestion of some dancing met with approval. He went in search of the portable wireless, and was about to fix it up in the hall, where there was room for three couples to dance, when he heard Francia complaining of thirst.

" A cocktail ? " the Argentiner proposed. " I have the recipe for an excellent one for just such an occasion. May I prepare it ? "

He turned to Mrs. Thornaby, and, receiving her permission, rang for one of the servants and gave instructions as to the ingredients which he required.

" It should be made with tamarinds," he explained regretfully. " And of course we have no tamarinds. But I think I can make it good enough without that."

He set to work when the maid had brought the requisites, and, when he had completed his task, he brought each of the party a glass in turn. Sir Clinton sipped his doubtfully and put it down. Francia drank his own with evident enjoyment ; and Rex seemed to find the mixture to his taste also. The girls speculated vaguely on the ingredients, and Francia wrote out his recipe for Estelle's benefit.

" Now I really feel inclined to dance," Francia declared with a gesture of invitation to Elsie.

Sir Clinton switched on the portable set, and, finding on his return that Estelle and the younger Anstruther girl were without partners, he invited the stranger, with a jesting apology to Estelle for leaving her out.

For the best part of an hour they danced, exchanging partners from time to time so that all the girls had their turn. Suddenly Sir Clinton noticed that his niece looked pale.

147

" What's wrong, Elsie ? " he demanded, as she stopped dancing and went to sit down beside her mother.

" Nothing much," was the reply. " I feel a bit sickish. Perhaps it's the heat of the night."

Her gesture indicated that she wished to be left in quietness ; so Sir Clinton abstained from worrying her with questions. But after a few minutes she seemed to feel worse rather than better. She called her husband over to her side, and Sir Clinton, without intending it, chanced to catch her words.

" I think I'll go to bed now, Vincent. I feel beastly seedy all of a sudden ; I can't think why. Would you mind taking the dressing-room to-night and leaving me to myself ? "

Francia gave a nod of agreement, though his face suggested that he was none too well pleased with the arrangement. He murmured a few words in a caressing tone ; but Elsie was evidently in no mood for verbal comfort.

" I'll get off upstairs, then," she said, rising from her chair as she spoke. " I feel dizzy, somehow. I can't think what's come over me."

She moved rather unsteadily into one of the adjoining rooms and rang the bell there. Then, on her way back, she bent over her mother and spoke to her in a low voice, apparently asking Mrs. Thornaby to give the necessary directions about the dressing-room to the maid who had been summoned. Reassuring her mother with a faint smile, Elsie crossed over to the stair.

" Good night, everybody," she called. " I'll be all right—just a bit out of sorts. You needn't worry. Don't stop dancing."

She seemed more than a little giddy ; and Francia, excusing himself to his partner, ran up the steps and gave her his arm. Together they disappeared round the turn of the stair. Almost as they did so, the fox-trot music stopped ; and the loud-speaker remarked suddenly : " That was a cough-drop from the Savoy Dance Band."

Sir Clinton took advantage of the pause. By a skilful move he engaged his partner in conversation with Mrs. Thornaby whilst he unobtrusively secured the cocktail glass which Elsie had used, and concealed it behind one of the palms which stood in the hall. He had suspicions about his niece's sudden sick turn ; and it seemed worth while to preserve any evidence which the glass might yield.

" Just one more," Estelle proposed. " After that I'll have to get home. You haven't got a car, Rex ? All right, I'll give you a lift down to the village."

Francia came downstairs as they were dancing ; and immediately afterwards Estelle and Rex took their departure. As he stood on the steps at the front door, watching them drive away, Sir Clinton suddenly recollected something which he had forgotten. Johnnie had come to him that morning with a cheap air-gun. The spring had collapsed, and Johnnie had turned to his uncle in the hope that he might be able to patch up the toy ; but the thing had been put aside in the smoke-room and had passed out of Sir Clinton's mind. Having nothing further to do, since the Anstruther girls were saying good night, he bethought himself of the air-gun and made his way to the smoke-room.

With the help of a screwdriver which he found on the Meccano table, Sir Clinton dismantled the gun easily enough and extracted the broken spring. Since only a small section had been broken off, he had some hopes that the remainder might still be long enough to serve ; but, when he tested it, he found that it would not work smoothly.

" Nothing for it but to get a new one," he decided, leaning the useless gun against the Meccano table. " It's such a cheap make that it's not worth while buying a fresh spring to replace this one. I'll send off an order for a new gun to-morrow."

He replaced the screwdriver on the Meccano table along with the fragment of broken spring, switched off the lights, and then, finding that everyone else had preceded him, went upstairs to bed.

CHAPTER XI

AN OLD LINE IN MURDERS

When Sir Clinton came downstairs next morning, he found his sister at breakfast.

" How's Elsie feeling now ? " he inquired, as he helped himself from the side-table.

" She seems to be all right again," Mrs. Thornaby replied, " I've persuaded her to stay in bed till after breakfast ; but there was really no need even for that. She's been sick, though ; and there's no use in her getting up and running about until she's had a rest."

Sir Clinton was obviously relieved.

" Queer turn she took," he commented briefly. " Must have swallowed something that disagreed with her."

He had hardly finished breakfast when the telephone bell rang in the smoke-room and Staffin brought word that someone wanted to speak to him. Sir Clinton put down his unlighted cigarette and went to the instrument.

" Is that you, Sir Clinton ? " inquired a voice which he recognised as Sergeant Ledbury's. " I'm sorry to trouble you, sir, but I'd take it as a favour if you'd spare me a short time. I've got another motor case on my hands this morning—a suicide, it might be, this time."

Sir Clinton considered for some seconds before answering. It was hardly his business now to spend his time in assisting the police in affairs which did not directly concern himself ; and he felt more than a little inclined to refuse point-blank to give his help.

Ledbury, at the other end of the wire, evidently noted the hesitation and feared a refusal.

" I know it's a good deal to ask, sir," he went on. " I've no claim on your time ; but I'd take it as a personal favour if you'd spare an hour. We found the car at the Bale Stones. It's no distance away ; you'd get there and back in your car under an hour, sir. I wish you'd come."

At the other end of the line, Sir Clinton started slightly.

" The Bale Stones, you say ? " he demanded.

Ledbury seemed to take this inquiry as a sign of awakening interest ; and his voice betrayed a tinge of relief.

" Yes, sir. Anyone'll direct you to them—a lot of old standing stones on the road to Stant-in-the-Vale."

Sir Clinton's mind had gone back to the peculiar interest which Roca had shown in the Bale Stones ; and this association was sufficient to overcome his scruples.

" All right," he said. " I'll come over at once."

Ledbury was effusive in his thanks, but Sir Clinton cut him short by laying down the receiver. He sought out Mrs. Thornaby, explained to her that he might be late for lunch perhaps, and then took his way to the garage. As he leaned forward to press the knob of the self-starter, his glance fell on the face of his speedometer ; and his eyebrows lifted slightly as he read on the trip-dial of the milometer the figures 17. He recalled that when he brought the car home the night before, Linda Anstruther had called his attention to the dial, and he remembered quite clearly that he had re-set the trip-meter to zero. And now it read 17. Someone else had been using his car during the night, clearly enough. Who could it have been ?

Sir Clinton stepped out of his car and made a careful examination of the lock on the door of the garage. There were no signs to show that it had been forced in any way. Whoever opened it must have used the proper key or else must have picked the lock. The key, Sir Clinton knew, was left at night in a drawer in the hall, so that it was available to anyone in the house. He made a rapid review of the people at Fern Lodge ; his sister, Francia, Johnnie, Elsie, Staffin . . .

The convergence of two apparently isolated trains of events in the past twenty-four hours led him to a conclusion which made his brow darken. Now he felt that he could make a shrewd guess at what lay behind Elsie's sudden sick turn ; and as the possible developments of the situation unfolded themselves in his mind, his face showed how black he feared they might be. This was going to be something very much worse than anything he had anticipated, unless the whole idea turned out to be moonshine. And that, he felt, was hardly likely, though it was still on the cards.

Sir Clinton stepped back into his car, re-set the trip-dial of the speedometer to zero, and drove out of the garage. He had no need to inquire his way to the Bale Stones ; his trip thither in Roca's company was still fresh in his mind, and he took the route which they had followed on that occasion. As he drew near the last turn-off before actually reaching the Stones, a policeman stepped from the side of the road and signalled him to pull up.

" Sir Clinton Driffield, sir ? " the man inquired, as Sir Clinton brought the car to a standstill. " That's all right, sir. Just drive on. The sergeant's waiting for you. I've orders to keep wheeled traffic off this road, sir. That's why I stopped you, not being sure it was you."

He saluted and fell back to the roadside, whilst Sir Clinton let his car move on. A glance at the dry surface of the road was enough to show that there was but little to be hoped in the way of tracing the tracks of motor-wheels on it ; but evidently the sergeant was taking no chances of having a possible clue destroyed by cars passing along that particular stretch of highway.

When he approached the neighbourhood of the Bale Stones, Sir Clinton pulled up his car and got out, so as not to superpose his wheel-tracks on any which might have been left on the road. As he walked on towards the corner round which he knew the Bale Stones lay, Sergeant Ledbury made his appearance and came forward to greet him.

" Glad you've come, sir," he said, with obvious gratefulness. " It's an ugly business, this one—uglier even than the other affair. The look of the body . . . ugh ! "

" No use being squeamish, sergeant. It's all in the day's work, for you, you know. But if you think it's going to upset my high-strung nerves, I suppose I'd better wish you good day now and go home again."

" Wait till you see him," the sergeant advised gloomily. " It's no treat."

" Most encouraging mood you seem to be in, now you've got me here," Sir Clinton commented. " If you'd breathed something like that over the 'phone, I might have thought twice about it. However, since I'm on the spot, suppose we waste no time. What's happened ? "

Ledbury pulled out a notebook ; but it seemed merely a reserve in case of need, for he was able to give his account of the affair without reference to his jottings.

" First thing we heard about it, sir, was from the driver of a post office mail van that takes this road with the early morning mail. When he came along, he found the wreck of a car standing by the roadside—just round the corner there—all burned and still smoking in places. He got down from his seat and went over to have a look at it. One look did him, it seems. I don't wonder much, either. It must have been a rum start to come up against a corpse like that, all on one's lonesome in the early morning."

Sir Clinton's face showed that he preferred facts to psychological imaginings, and the sergeant hastily dropped the gruesome and returned to plain narrative.

" The van-driver scuttled back to his motor and drove hell-for-leather into Raynham Parva to give us the news, since we are in charge of this district. He was considerably shaken up by what he'd seen. That was about half-past seven this morning."

Sir Clinton nodded to show that he had noted the time.

" As soon as I could," Ledbury went on, " I got hold of some constables and we all came out here on our bicycles. I suppose I've no authority to close a road ; but I chanced it, and posted men to turn anyone off until we'd finished with things and got the place cleared up a bit. You probably met one of 'em down the road ? "

" Yes, go on."

" We borrowed a big weather-proof sheet from the nearest farm to cover the thing up ; and then we had time to get down to business. When we reached the wreck of the car, it was quite hot still ; so I take it that it must have been set alight in the late small hours, sir. If the blaze had gone up earlier, someone would've seen it and come to find out what it was."

" Say three, or four o'clock, then, at a guess ? "

" Round about there," Ledbury agreed. " Well, I'll go on. To start with, it looked as if it might have been an accident, like the Quevedo business. Car catching fire and burning the driver, you see, sir. But two seconds' thinking knocked that on the head. No live man would sit still in an open car and let himself be burned to death, when he could jump over the side in a tick. If it had been a saloon, he might have been choked by fumes all of a sudden—but not in an open car."

" Unless he was a cripple ? " Sir Clinton suggested slyly.

" Well, he wasn't a cripple, so that finishes that," Ledbury retorted. " I'm giving you things just as they came to hand, sir, if you don't mind. The next thing we did was to lift the body out of the driving-seat—a nice job that was !—and go over the remains of the car. Uncomfortable, we found it. The metal was still pretty hot, here and there."

He exhibited a large burn on his hand by way of proof.

" We didn't get much of interest for a while. You see, sir, the fire had destroyed practically everything that would burn. Clothes, papers, anything of that sort : all gone up the flue. But at last, as I was grubbing round in the bottom of the wreck, I picked up this pistol."

He produced from his pocket a tarnished Colt automatic.

" You can handle it if you like, sir," he said, as he offered it to Sir Clinton. " After it had been through that fire, there wasn't much good looking for finger-prints on it."

Sir Clinton took the weapon into his own hands and turned it over cautiously. The blue-black finish was all discoloured by the heat through which it had passed ; and the cartridges in the magazine had evidently been ignited by the rise in temperature, for the stock of the pistol was badly wrenched and the end of the magazine had been blown away in the explosion.

" What do you make of it ? " Sir Clinton inquired as he finished his initial scrutiny.

" Not much, except that he was carrying arms—which isn't over common in this country. I expect he set fire to the car and then shot himself, thinking that the fire would destroy the traces of what he'd done."

Sir Clinton subjected the pistol to a more minute examination.

" The safety-catch is on," he pointed out. " Do you think a man who had just shot himself fatally would take the trouble to snick that into place ? "

Ledbury looked doubtful when this piece of evidence was brought to his notice.

" It hardly sounds likely," he had to admit.

Sir Clinton gripped the pistol and endeavoured to pull back the slide ; but the fire had caused a jam, and he was only able to force the breech open to the extent of about half an inch. He peered down into the cavity which was thus exposed and then turned the weapon so that the sergeant could see into the hole.

" No cartridge-case there, sergeant."

156

" Quite so," Ledbury confirmed. " It would be ejected when he fired the shot."

" And another cartridge would have been forced up into the breech immediately," Sir Clinton completed the description.

" That's so," Ledbury conceded. " There ought to be a cartridge-case there."

" Obviously, since the safety-catch is on. With that in position, the breech couldn't open to eject the cartridge-case even if the cartridge in the barrel had been exploded by the heat of the fire. Whence it's pretty clear that there wasn't a cartridge in the barrel at all."

" Just let me think that out, sir," Ledbury interjected. " You mean that what happened was this. He had his pistol in his pocket, with a loaded magazine. He hadn't pulled back the slide to bring the first cartridge out of the magazine into the breech of the pistol, ready for firing ? So when the fire got to the pistol, it exploded the magazine ; but there was nothing in the breech, so there's no empty case left there. That's it, isn't it ? "

" That's what I infer," Sir Clinton confirmed. " We'll just count the stuff in the magazine now ; and, if we're in luck, none of the cartridges has escaped in the explosion."

He drew a *multum-in-parvo* knife from his pocket, selected the tool required, and attacked with it the jammed material in the butt of the pistol. For a time nothing came loose ; but all at once his efforts were successful ; and, on shaking the pistol, he was able to extract the distorted cartridge-cases and bullets from the cavity.

" A full magazine," he reported, after counting the articles. " I'm afraid that finishes your idea about a suicide by shooting, sergeant. It's pretty evident that he never had this pistol in a condition to shoot. He still had to pull back the slide and bring his first cartridge up into the breech."

157

Sergeant Ledbury grudgingly admitted the force of this.

" What I had in my mind," he confessed, " was the case I read in the papers a while back—the fellow who poisoned himself in a burning car. I've been a bit too previous, it seems."

" Let's keep clear of preconceptions," Sir Clinton suggested. " Now what about the rest of the facts ? Anything left of the car that might be useful ? "

" Yes, sir, there's one point. The car's burned to bits, except for the metal parts ; but I noticed that it's been carrying what looks like a pair of false number-plates screwed on top of the ordinary ones. The fire's licked all the lettering off, of course, but the metal plates are there, right enough. He must have wanted to conceal something, or he wouldn't have been playing that game."

" He couldn't have foreseen this state of affairs, then," Sir Clinton speculated. " First, because in any case the numbers would be burned off by the fire. Second, because the identity of the car will be easy enough to establish from the number stamped on the engine. It won't have been effaced with the heat."

" You mean that he was using false number plates to cover up something he was doing with the car and that he never meant to commit suicide at all, sir ? "

Sir Clinton turned an expressionless face on the sergeant.

" I haven't seen any evidence for suicide yet," he pointed out mildly.

" Then you think it's another murder case, sir ? "

" I haven't seen any evidence for murder, yet," Sir Clinton varied his phrase. " Your brain's too swift for me, sergeant. I simply can't follow these leaps of intuition. Give me the facts first. We haven't even got the length of the body, and you expect me to give an opinion about the cause of death."

The sergeant's face showed that here he thought he had a surprise in store.

" We've examined the body, sir." He made a wry grimace at the recollection. " Everything was burned off it except some ash and a few bits of cloth which might have been the seat of his breeches. Protected from the main flames for a good while, you see, sir. And of course we picked up the clips of his suspenders and things like that. But anything in the way of papers had been burned completely ; and he didn't seem to have any identifiable metal stuff in his pockets. One or two coins we found—that was all. But amongst the stuff in the car we picked up his wrist-watch, with the strap burned through ; and on the back of that his name was engraved."

" Ah ! Very fortunate, that."

" His name, sir, was Roca—that Dr. Roca who was staying at the Black Bull the other day."

" Indeed ? "

Sir Clinton seemed hardly so surprised as the sergeant had anticipated.

" You'll be able to tell us something about him, sir ? " Ledbury inquired, with an air of innocence which was rather overdone. His little eyes were fastened on Sir Clinton's face as though he suspected something.

" I met him twice, sergeant. He was a medical man, a South American . . ."

" Like Quevedo, sir ? " the sergeant interjected. " You do seem to have a knack of running up against these South Americans, don't you ? It was you that met Quevedo on the road that night he was murdered, I remember."

Sir Clinton laughed unaffectedly.

" Two South Americans meet with violent deaths. Driffield has met these two South Americans. Therefore Driffield is a suspicious character. Is that the chain of reasoning, sergeant ? It seems a bit weak in some links."

Ledbury joined shamefacedly in Sir Clinton's laugh ; but he did not take his gimlet eyes from the face of the late Chief Constable ; nor did he disclaim the suspicions in words.

" I'd like to hear some more about this Roca," he reminded Sir Clinton.

" You're quite right to suspect everybody," Sir Clinton admitted. " But it must make investigation a bit complex when you cast your net as wide as all that, sergeant. About Roca, now. He had private means, I believe. I didn't know he had a car. He was interested in archæology—to some slight extent, I gathered. From some things he let fall, as from one official to another, it appeared that he was a secret agent investigating the White Slave traffic."

" Oh, indeed ? Was he ? " the sergeant inquired with a slight start. " Now that might be a useful bit of news."

" He had some grudge against the traders," Sir Clinton added, to complete his summary of his conversation with Roca.

" He had ? That's interesting."

The tone of the sergeant's voice suggested something different from the actual words ; and he still kept his eyes fixed on Sir Clinton, as though he expected to detect a sign of uneasiness in his manner. Sir Clinton suppressed a desire to laugh. It was evident that Ledbury really had at the back of his mind a vague suspicion, based on the coincidence that Sir Clinton had come across the two dead men since he arrived in the village. It was apparently part of the sergeant's policy to suspect everyone who had the slightest connection with the case in hand—an interpretation of " thoroughness " from the Ledbury standpoint.

" Well, let's see what we've done so far," Sir Clinton suggested. " The pistol, the body, the car : nothing more about them, is there ? Suppose we have a look

160

round about, now. Have you examined anything except the road ? "

The sergeant seemed to wake up suddenly from his reflections.

" No, sir," he admitted, with a slight increase of politeness in his tone. " Since it seemed to be a suicide business, I haven't bothered about that part of the thing yet. But we could do it now, if you like."

Sir Clinton had been racking his brains to recall the exact sequence of events on the day when he had brought Roca to the place before. It was now clear enough to him why Roca had been interested in the prehistoric monument. It was a landmark in the country-side ; and quite obviously Roca had picked it out as a meeting-place which a stranger could readily identify. He had come up to see if it would suit his purpose ; and, after inspecting it, had evidently found that it would do. Then he had made an appointment with someone—and that appointment had resulted in his death. The telephone call to Francia fitted neatly into that series of events, if Francia was the man whom Roca desired to meet. Sir Clinton had hazarded this hypothesis to himself in the garage. Now it seemed on a firmer basis ; and the prospect was a gloomy one. If Francia were detected, Elsie would be stamped as the wife of a murderer.

He put aside this grim picture for the moment, and turned back to his earlier visit to the Bale Stones. Suppose Roca had summoned Francia to a settlement of their account, was it likely that he would meet him on the public road ? Hardly, since they would be liable to interruption from any passing car. And if one went off the road, what easily described place was there in the neighbourhood except the stone circle itself ? That was the obvious spot for two strangers to meet, an unmistakable rendezvous. Sir Clinton paused for a moment before answering Ledbury. He reflected that

161

Ledbury prided himself on thoroughness ; and that sooner or later the sergeant would examine the stone circle in the course of his general policy. It would be just as well to direct his attention to it now, and see what he made of it.

" Let's try this field first of all, then," Sir Clinton suggested, leading the way to the gap in the hedge which gave access to the Bale Stones.

Ledbury followed him without demur ; and in a few moments they had reached the circle of monoliths. As the sergeant came into the ring, he uttered a suppressed exclamation and pointed to the altar stone, on the upper surface of which a brownish mark stood out. Ledbury ran forward and bent over the slab.

". Here you are, sir ! " he ejaculated, beckoning to Sir Clinton. " See ! there's been a patch of blood on this stone and somebody's wiped it away. You can see the trace of the scrubbing he gave it. But he didn't do the job thoroughly ; and some of the blood's trickled into these little grooves—these spirals in the slab, sir— so he didn't go deep enough to swab the liquid away."

Again the look of suspicion came into his face.

" It's wonderful how you manage to suggest things that turn out to be right, sir," he added, with something in his tone that hinted at more than irony.

" Meaning that ' He who hides knows where to seek,' sergeant ? " Sir Clinton replied, rather to Ledbury's discomfort.

" You're putting words into my mouth, sir," he answered rather grumpily. " I didn't say anything like that."

" No ? Language is a queer thing."

Sir Clinton waved the matter aside. He had not quite made up his mind what line to follow.

" The way I look at it," Ledbury said, in a reflective tone, " is this way. This is where Roca was shot, clear enough. Then he was carried down to his car—I expect

162

we'll be able to find some blood on the trail when we get to work on it. Then he was bundled into the car, petrol was spilled over everything, a match sent the whole thing up in a blaze, and that was that. Then the murderer came back here and cleaned up things as well as he could. It wasn't a bright moonlight night, last night, so he most likely couldn't see very well what he was doing, and so he left these traces behind him. Then he hopped into his own car and cleared off. Or most likely he didn't set fire to the car until he was ready to leave himself. Or something like that, anyhow."

" He had a car, then ? " Sir Clinton asked.

" Oh, yes, he had a car. I've found bits of its track here and there down the road," Ledbury explained. " That's why I put the pickets on—to keep other wheels off the road till I'd time to photograph this track."

He shouted to one of his constables to bring a sheet ; and, when the man arrived, Ledbury rigged up a rough protection over the blood patches on the altar stone.

" I think that's all we need do here," he suggested, as he finished his task. " Is there anything else you'd like to see, sir ? "

" Nothing in particular," Sir Clinton replied, rather absent-mindedly. " What do you propose to do next ? "

" I've telephoned round the country already, asking for information from all the hotels and garages about a car of this make that Roca was driving. It must have been garaged somewhere for the last week. One bit of paint had escaped bad damage, so I was able to give its colour ; and the make's recognisable even after the fire. Perhaps we'll get some news soon. And I'm going to ask the doctor who does the P.M.—I wish him joy of his job, I do—to look out for any smashed bones. There's no real proof yet that he was shot, you know."

Sir Clinton recognised Ledbury's acuteness in this last proposal. The sergeant was by no means a negligible factor in the affair.

" Well, I think I'll get off now," he intimated, getting up from the altar stone on which he had seated himself. " I've given you all the help I can."

" Very suggestive your visit's been, sir," Ledbury assured him, with the plainest intimation of a double meaning in his tone, " It's wonderful how much you've given me to think about."

He accompanied Sir Clinton towards his motor.

" These are the tracks the murderer left, sir," he pointed out. " Very faint, they are ; but quite unmistakable, you see. They'll be a useful clue, perhaps."

Sir Clinton, glancing at the tracks on the road, suppressed a start only with difficulty. He recognised the markings well enough.

" Good luck, sergeant ! " he said carelessly, as he opened the door of his car and settled himself in the driving-seat. " Mind standing back a bit while I turn ? Thanks."

When he had gone some twenty yards on his way, he turned round. The sergeant was stooping over the road, evidently comparing the traces on it with one another.

" H'm ! So he's spotted that ? And now he knows it was my car that was here last night. This is getting a bit complicated," Sir Clinton commented inwardly. " I wonder what his next move will be."

Feeling more than a little disquieted, he drove to the post office in Raynham Parva, entered the telephone box, and called up a reliable friend who lived in the next county.

" Will you send me a wire immediately," he requested, giving his address. " Word it this way : ' Meet me in main street Micheldean Abbas about four o'clock this afternoon.' Sign it with your own name. . . . You'll get it off at once ? Thanks."

He rang off, and immediately called up Estelle.

" That you, Estelle ? "

" Yes, Uncle Clinton."

164

" I want you to do me a favour and to keep quiet about it, please."

" Right ! No words of mine shall betray your guilty secret, etc., etc. What is it you want ? "

Despite her flippant tone, Sir Clinton knew that he could trust her to carry out his orders.

" Nothing much. Will you ring up at once and invite the whole lot of us, even Johnnie, over to your house for the afternoon. The whole lot, remember, myself included. And don't take any excuses. We've simply got to come. You understand ? You'll easily be able to fake up some sort of excuse. I leave that to you."

Estelle's voice betrayed severely suppressed curiosity as she replied ; but she asked no direct question, and agreed at once to do as he wished. Sir Clinton gave her no time to press for explanations, but, urging her to ring up Fern Lodge immediately, he put down his receiver and left the box.

His next call was at the druggist's shop out of which he had seen Francia come on the previous afternoon.

" A friend of mine asked me to get him a second dose of something he got from you yesterday," he explained to the proprietor. " He's staying with us at Fern Lodge —I'm Sir Clinton Driffield."

The guess that his title would prove helpful was not unwarranted.

" I know you by sight, Sir Clinton," the druggist hastened to explain. " What was it your friend got, can you tell me ? "

" A mild emetic, I think it was," Sir Clinton suggested. " You'll be able to look it up ? The name's Francia, if he handed in a prescription."

" Ah, yes. Now I remember," the druggist said. " Didn't it act ? That's curious."

He bustled away to fill the order. When he brought back the bottle and was preparing to wrap it up, Sir Clinton leaned over the counter and lifted it.

" I seem to recognise the smell," he remarked, as he casually uncorked it and put it to his nostrils. " Funny how one can't put a name to a thing that one knows quite well, really."

" It's a preparation of ipecacuanha," the druggist explained helpfully.

" Of course ! " Sir Clinton exclaimed. " I knew I'd smelt it some time ; but I couldn't have named it, all the same. Thanks."

He returned the bottle ; and when the druggist had wrapped it up, Sir Clinton bought a phial of chlorate of potash tabloids before wishing him good day.

A few minutes later, when Sir Clinton stopped his car at Fern Lodge, a glance at the trip-dial of the speedometer showed seventeen miles as the reading. Quite obviously, it was Sir Clinton's car which, on the previous night, had gone out to the Bale Stones and played its part in the events leading up to Roca's death.

CHAPTER XII

FRANCIA'S ATTACHÉ-CASE

When Sir Clinton made his appearance at the lunch-table, he found that his confederate had not failed him.

" Where have you been ? " Elsie demanded. " I've been hunting for you all round the place."

" Oh, just out and about," Sir Clinton answered vaguely.

He had no desire to give a more definite account of his morning's doings. Murders, and especially murders of a gruesome type, were subjects which he preferred to deal with in their proper environment. Certainly the lunch-table was the last place for the discussion of such matters. He glanced casually at Francia, who was seated on the other side of the table ; but, except for a certain heavy-eyed look, the Argentiner showed no sign of anything abnormal.

" Feeling all right again, Elsie ? " Sir Clinton demanded in order to change the subject completely.

" Quite all right, thanks. It was just a sick turn, and I can't make out how I got it."

" Good ! And what's this stop-press news you're burning to distribute ? "

" Cross my hand with silver, kind sir, and I'll tell you who'll pour out your tea for you this afternoon."

" Oh, no, you won't," was Sir Clinton's unspoken comment. Aloud, he asked : " Well, who is it ? "

" It's Estelle. She rang up a few minutes ago and invited the whole lot of us over there this afternoon.

Johnnie's to go too ; he can flog the stream at the end of their garden."

" I'm going to catch something there," Johnnie broke in excitedly. " I've seen trout in it—great big ones. Mr. Scotswood told me he once saw a two-pounder in one of the pools."

Elsie ignored her brother completely.

" I told Estelle it was a futile notion to drag seven people across the country to visit one girl—especially as I'm sure Mr. Scotswood would far rather go off and play golf—and I advised her to come here instead. But you know she's always been pig-headed. She said her tennis-courts were better than ours . . . "

" So they are," Johnnie interjected, only to be suppressed at once.

" Then at last she broke down and admitted that she'd ordered dozens and dozens of cream cakes for tea. Of course, unless they're eaten, the cream will go wrong. So that finished it. She got her own way. But I'll see those cream cakes even if I can't eat them. I believe they were just an excuse she thought of at the last moment."

Sir Clinton gave Estelle a good mark for her fertility in expedients. She had certainly managed to carry out orders well.

" So we're all going off there in the afternoon ? " he inquired, secure in the knowledge that his spurious telegram would arrive in time to let him escape the expedition. " We're going to play tennis, you said ? "

" There'll be eight of us, counting mother and Mr. Scotswood. You'll play, of course, mother ? "

Before his sister could reply, Sir Clinton bethought himself of the effect his abstention would have.

" A bit short on the male side, aren't you ? " he suggested. " Johnnie doesn't count ; and that leaves old Scotswood and two of us from here. Why not ring up Rex and take him along. Estelle will be quite pleased, if she hasn't thought of it already herself."

168

" I'm not particularly keen to play," Mrs. Thornaby admitted, " and that arrangement would give each of you girls a man for a partner."

She was evidently resigned to following her brother's lead in the matter, though he could see that she was not entirely whole-hearted in her proposal. Clearly, she had doubts about dragging Rex Brandon into too intimate contact with Francia and Elsie.

" Very well, then," Elsie said, taking the arrangement as settled. " I'll ring up Rex as soon as lunch is over. He'll put off his miserable fishing if I ask him, even if he's planned anything for the afternoon.'.'

Sir Clinton wondered whether that attitude of hers had not been the root of the whole trouble. Rex had always been ready to fall in with her wishes ; and perhaps he had made himself cheap while hoping to become indispensable. If he had stood up to her more, she might have taken a different kind of interest in him.

Just as they were finishing lunch, Staffin came in with the familiar brown envelope for Sir Clinton. He opened it, made a pretence of reading the message, and then frowned.

" You'll have to give Estelle my excuses," he explained, handing the telegram form to Elsie. " I must get across to Micheldean Abbas and see this man. It's important, or he wouldn't have wired me at the last moment like this."

" Not very polite, breaking your engagement like that, uncle. Estelle will be disappointed."

" Theoretically, that's so. Practically, she couldn't be sure I was coming, since you didn't get hold of me when she telephoned her invitation," Sir Clinton pointed out. " Use your tact, and simply say I'm sorry I can't join you."

" Why not say it yourself ? " Elsie demanded. " You'll have to drive over. It's too big a party to cram into one car, so we'll need yours to take half of us."

"I hadn't thought of that," Sir Clinton confessed. "It's all right, though. I don't need to be in Micheldean Abbas until four o'clock. I'll take you over to Estelle's before that."

He paused for a moment ; then a fresh thought seemed to strike him.

"You'd better scurry off and get hold of Rex at once," he suggested to his niece. "You'll need him now, since I'm dropping out, because even with him you'll be a man short."

Elsie nodded ; and, as they rose from the table, she went into the smoke-room to telephone to the Black Bull. Sir Clinton detained his sister by a sign while the remainder of the party quitted the dining-room.

"By the way, Anne, I shan't be back here until I come to pick up you people on my way home. It's a pity to keep the maids hanging about on a fine day like this. Suppose you let them all off for the afternoon ? "

"So long as they get back in time to look after our dinner, I don't mind," his sister acquiesced.

She shot an inquiring glance at him.

"You're getting very soft-hearted, these days, Clinton."

"I've always believed in treating subordinates well," he defended himself ; but he examined his sister's face closely to see if there was anything behind her remark.

Apparently, however, Mrs. Thornaby had merely thrown out her suggestion at random, for she failed to follow up the subject. Before any more was said, Elsie passed along the hall.

"It's all right," she said, catching sight of her uncle. "I persuaded him—after he'd made a bit of a fuss, for some reason or other. He's got very punctilious, all of a sudden—Rex. One would have thought, to hear him, that I'd asked him to force himself on a stranger. He objected because Estelle herself hadn't invited him—as if that mattered."

170

" Did you arrange about picking him up as we pass ? "

" Of course. It's all settled."

Sir Clinton's gesture of approval was purposely patronising.

" Very nice," he said in the tone of one commending a stupid but well-meaning subordinate. " And now that I've made all the arrangements, Elsie, I think I can take a rest for a while, till it's time for us to start."

He turned away before his enraged niece could find words to express her thoughts about this last remark, and walked out of the front door. He had no desire to encounter Francia at that juncture, so he took the path down to the lake, meaning to keep away from the others until it was time to drive them over to Estelle's house. His morning's experiences had given him enough to think over ; but he put them resolutely out of his mind and concentrated his thoughts on an earlier problem.

On the night when he arrived at Fern Lodge, his plans for the future had been cut and dried ; but more recent happenings had thrown a fresh light on things, and Sir Clinton was not the man to pursue a course doggedly for the mere reason that he had chosen it and had too much pride to allow himself to deviate from a prearranged plan. The things which had come to his notice within the last few days had their bearing on Elsie's welfare ; and, when that came into question, it would have needed a very strong inducement to keep Sir Clinton even neutral in the matter.

One thing seemed certain. To let Elsie and her companions go off to the Argentine unaccompanied by anyone except Francia was to run a very grave risk indeed. True, Sir Clinton had no definite proof of anything against the Argentiner ; but this was a case in which it might be criminal to wait for proof before taking action. One way out of the difficulty might be to send out Mrs. Thornaby with the party ; but, although he had perfect trust in his sister's capacity, Sir Clinton felt that this precaution was hardly enough. It would be so easy to contrive that Mrs. Thornaby should miss a train or be detached in some other way from the rest of the party ; and, in a difficulty, a woman cannot act in the same way as a man might do. No, if Francia needed watching, then only a man would be of any service. He would have to go himself, even though it disarranged his own cut-and-dried plans. Without flattering himself, he felt that he would be a match for Francia even in a foreign country.

Once he had made his decision, he felt in a more comfortable frame of mind. He still deliberately put aside the possible connection between Francia and the death of Roca, since he expected to pick up fuller details of that affair before very long, and it seemed hardly worth wasting time on the subject until he had all the facts in his hands. Instead of considering the question, he set himself to re-plan his own business to fit his fresh decision about the South American trip ; and in this task the time soon passed until it was necessary for him to go back and take the car out of the garage.

As he reached the front of Fern Lodge, he found Elsie bringing Mrs. Thornaby's car up to the front door, where some of the party were already waiting.

" Hurry up, uncle," his niece advised him. " I'll take the ones who are here, and you can pick up the rest."

Sir Clinton brought out his own car before the first party had time to embark, and the two motors set off in company. On the road to Raynham Parva they overtook the Fern Lodge maids walking towards the village ; and Sir Clinton felt a certain relief at finding that his sister had acted on his suggestion about letting the girls take the afternoon off.

When they reached their destination, they found that Estelle had come down to the gate to welcome them. She exchanged a glance of intelligence with Sir Clinton as he drew up his car, and a suppressed smile hinted that she regarded the success of her manœuvres as amusing.

" What's all this I hear ? " she demanded, with a very fair imitation of annoyance. " Elsie says you've faked up some engagement or other to get off spending the afternoon here. It's a sample of police manners, I suppose ? "

" Something of the sort," Sir Clinton agreed. " Nuisance, isn't it ? The loss is yours, which makes me sorrier still, of course."

" Well . . ."

She pretended to be breathless at this suggestion. Sir Clinton gave her no time to complete her phrase.

" You'll have quite enough of me before long," he said consolingly. " I'm thinking of changing my mind and taking the trip to South America with you."

He shot a glance at Francia as he spoke ; but the Argentiner's control over his features seemed perfect, for he betrayed nothing to show that this decision put him out in any way.

" You will ? Really ? " Estelle exclaimed in obvious delight. " Hear that, Elsie ? Your esteemed and doddering uncle means to inflict his company on us. He'll sit about the decks with some more of the prehistorics and comment angrily on the manners of the new generation, and enjoy himself simply no end. We must arrange to shock him, or he won't enjoy himself a scrap."

She turned back to Sir Clinton.

" Well, I'll book you for the first dance we have on board, Uncle Clinton," she announced, in a tone which showed her real pleasure at learning that he was coming with them.

Sir Clinton did not wait for any further discussion. With a warning gesture, he re-started his engine, turned his car, and drove off towards the main street of the village, leaving Elsie and Estelle exchanging congratulations on his change of plans.

Once out of sight, he slowed down the car and moved along the street till he came to the ironmonger's shop, where he stopped and got out.

" I've lost one of my keys," he explained to the shop-keeper. " Most annoying, since I want to get the thing open, and it's locked, I find. I suppose you could let me have something that would do—a bunch of assorted keys, or a pick-lock or two, if you happen to have them. It's most important that I should get the thing open at once."

The ironmonger had recognised him, apparently. Sir Clinton's arrival had furnished a certain amount of gossip in the village which did not often find a well-known man among its visitors.

" I'll send a man up to fix it for you as soon as I can, Sir Clinton."

" Oh, don't bother about that. I think I'm in good enough practice to manage the thing myself."

His smile convinced the shopman that the picking of locks was part of the normal work of a Chief Constable.

" I'm sure you are, sir," he agreed, with a knowing look, as he bustled about to procure what Sir Clinton wanted. " Here's some keys for you to look over and see the size you want. I'll get you some false keys in a moment, too."

On his return, he found his customer looking dubiously at the assortment on the counter.

" A bit stupid of me," Sir Clinton confessed. " I for-got to measure the size of the keyhole ; and I can't be quite sure of the kind of key I need. Do you mind if I take the lot? I'll let you have them back in an hour or so."

The ironmonger readily agreed ; and Sir Clinton set off for Fern Lodge again, armed with a very fair selec-tion of keys. He let himself in with his latch-key and went up to his own room, where he extracted from a suitcase a pair of rubber gloves. Putting these on, and taking the keys, he made his way to the room which Elsie and Francia shared.

174

Normally, nothing would have persuaded Sir Clinton to break the ordinary rules of hospitality and to pry into other guests' affairs ; but this was no ordinary occasion, and too much was at stake to allow him to respect conventions. His niece's life might be in the balance, and he had no intention of abstaining from the task before him merely because it involved breaking some of the unwritten rules of society. Things had got to such a pitch that he intended to learn, by hook or crook, all that could be discovered about Francia's affairs.

He set about the business methodically, knowing that he would have the house to himself for some hours to come ; but his work proved very much simpler than he had anticipated. None of the drawers or cupboards in the bedroom was locked ; and it was obvious that he was hardly likely to find anything important in the open.

A large attaché-case attracted his attention ; and, on trying its catch, he found it locked. Two or three of the ironmonger's keys failed to open it ; but in a very short time Sir Clinton found one which fitted, and the case clicked open. Placing it on the floor near the window, Sir Clinton bent over it and memorised the appearance of the top layer of papers which was exposed ; and when he felt quite certain that he could replace them in exactly the original arrangement, he began carefully to remove them and distribute them on the carpet in a definite order which would make repacking simple. He removed paper after paper without reading them and then, as he lifted those in the last layer, he came across what he had expected to find : an automatic pistol. Along with it, on the bottom of the attaché-case, lay a small bottle with a druggist's label.

Sir Clinton picked up the bottle, examined the label, and placed the bottle aside. The druggist had not misled him ; for this phial in Francia's case contained the same preparation of ipecacuanha as had been supplied

175

to himself when he asked for a repeat order. Evidently his surmise as to the origin of Elsie's sick turn had been accurate. That was so much cleared up, at any rate.

He turned next to the automatic pistol. The smooth surface of the weapon was of the kind which takes finger-prints sharply, and Sir Clinton congratulated himself on the fact that he was wearing rubber gloves. They were a relic of his police career ; and they had certainly come in handy on this occasion.

He gingerly loosed the catch of the magazine, slipped out the container from the butt of the pistol, and counted the cartridges. There were two short of a full load.

" One in the barrel now, I suppose," Sir Clinton reflected.

He slid back the jacket of the pistol far enough to let him look into the breech, and, on turning the weapon towards the window, he caught a glimpse of the brass of the cartridge-case.

" So he must have fired one shot, evidently," Sir Clinton noted.

He lifted the pistol to his nostrils and sniffed at the muzzle. A faint, but unmistakable odour of pistol-fumes was easily recognisable. Sir Clinton's face showed more than a trace of contempt.

" Hadn't even the thoroughness to clean his pistol after firing," he reflected acidly. " A man might at least have the thought to keep his tools in good condition. The acid will eat into his rifling, apart altogether from the value of the reek of the powder as a clue. I seem to have over-estimated the fellow."

He replaced the pistol along with the bottle in the attaché-case, and then began a methodical study of the papers which he had laid out upon the floor. As he finished each one, he replaced it in its proper position in the case. Some of the documents he glanced over without much apparent interest ; but as he read on his countenance darkened. Finally he reached the sheet of

paper which had lain on the top of the pile—an un-
finished letter which Francia had apparently slipped
into the attaché-case, meaning to complete it at some
convenient time. It was in Spanish ; but Sir Clinton's
knowledge of the language was sufficient to allow him
to translate it roughly as follows :

" DEAR MENDOZA,—Fifi la Commande reports that
the Martigue has quarrelled with her and stopped
negotiations ; so our commissionnaire is still one short
in his consignment. He writes himself to say he is in
touch with another Franchucha who might do. One
hopes so. He will advise you direct.
" The remount trade is very bad at present. I have,
however, secured four green articles of 21, 22, 23, and
25 kilos., which I am bringing out with me by the
S.S. *Malta* on her next voyage. You can meet the
Mihanovich and look them over before they go up
country. Well worth your trouble, I assure you—
something quite uncommon, and picked up marvel-
lously cheap. The *cedullas* will be all right, so there
will be no chance of trouble this time with the Vigil-
antes. Tell La Gallina to be ready for them.
" I am holding back this letter till the next mail in
case Henri sends word about the three Polaks he was
negotiating for. If he gets them, they are to go via
Danzig as usual. One of them is an underweight."

Sir Clinton had sufficient knowledge of criminal argot
to make most of this cryptic epistle clear to him. The
first paragraph apparently dealt with an unsuccessful
attempt by a *commissionnaire* to secure a Marseillaise girl,
and his later operations to obtain a second Frenchwoman
as a substitute.
The second paragraph of the letter meant more to
Sir Clinton. The " four green articles of 21, 22, 23, and
25 kilos." he easily translated as " four decent girls of

177

the ages 21, 22, 23, and 25." *Cedullas*, he knew, was the technical name for cards of entry into the Argentine, which would save any trouble with the police. La Gallina was obviously the nickname for one of the harpies of the Centre, into whose charge the girls would be given when they arrived in South America. Sir Clinton grimly reflected that Elsie was 22 and Estelle 23. The Anstruther girls would be about 21 and 25, as near as he could judge. There was not much doubt now in his mind as to what Francia was. The reference to the Polak girls in the last paragraph clinched the matter ; for Sir Clinton knew something about the way in which the traders of the Centre took advantage of the peculiarities of the Danzig corridor to further their ends.

He re-locked Francia's attaché-case and replaced it carefully in its original position, dropping the key which fitted it into his waistcoat pocket. Then, stripping off his rubber gloves, he collected the remainder of the keys and left the room. The whole affair had occupied him less than an hour ; and it had given him material for an immense amount of hard thinking.

CHAPTER XIII

THE GOVERNMENT MISSION

Inspection of his wrist-watch showed Sir Clinton that he had still plenty of time in hand before it would be necessary to go back to Estelle's and pick up her visitors. He went downstairs, hesitated for a moment in the hall, and then entered the smoke-room, which had become his favourite lounging-place at Fern Lodge. The most comfortable chair stood between the fireplace and the window overlooking the verandah ; but the sun was shining brilliantly upon this very spot, so Sir Clinton stepped across the room to draw the curtains and shield the place from the direct rays. When he reached the window, he paused for a moment, gazing out over the still surface of the little lake ; then his eyes fell on the shelf which formed the sill of the window, and mechanically he began to straighten out the books which stood upon it. Books were among his weaknesses, and he hated to see them untidy.

When he had reduced the confusion to some semblance of order, he drew the curtains sufficiently to protect the chair from the sun ; then, taking a cigarette from his case, he sat down to review the whole series of events which had led him up to his present position. Although some pieces were still lacking from the puzzle, all the facts in his possession fitted neatly together if certain assumptions were allowed.

Roca, by some means or other, had tracked to Raynham Parva two of the people concerned in the fate of Marcelle Barrère ; and he had succeeded in squaring

179

his account with one of them—Quevedo. That seemed plain sailing, except for the fact that Roca must have had reliable information about Quevedo's movements on the night of the killing, although he himself had not appeared in the village until after the murder had been committed. That implied a confederate who played the spy on the *commissionnaire* and passed on to the doctor the information which he needed. The identity of this confederate Sir Clinton put aside for the present, since he had no data from which to draw an inference.

The fact that Roca had been able to produce an alibi for the night in question did not trouble Sir Clinton much. Ledbury had been satisfied with the evidence of the people at the inn at Micheldean Abbas, who had testified that Roca had been in bed at the time of the murder. That simply meant that he had gone to his room and locked the door. But a door is not the only means of exit from most rooms ; there is generally at least one window also : and the fact that his room was upstairs was not likely to prove much hindrance to a man like the doctor, if he wished to leave the house unobserved. The sergeant had made a slip when he accepted that alibi as conclusive.

Then there was the question of the car which undoubtedly Roca had used when he put an end to Quevedo. Roca professedly had no motor—certainly he had brought none to the inn at Micheldean Abbas or to the Black Bull. But, if he had a confederate, the problem of the car had its obvious solution. The doctor's accomplice could have brought the car into Micheldean Abbas by appointment, handing it over to Roca, and receiving it back again after the killing of Quevedo. Or he might even have been present at the murder itself.

After the death of Quevedo, the doctor had evidently turned to the second task which he had set himself ; and the two telephone messages which he had sent to Fern Lodge were sufficient to indicate clearly enough the identity of his second quarry : Francia. Roca had evidently intended to utilise the inn at Micheldean Abbas once more to provide him with an alibi ; and he had left Raynham Parva on the afternoon before the night of his own death in order to avoid any suspicion falling upon him owing to his presence on the actual spot. He had, in all probability, rung up from some country call-office ; and he had expected in this way to leave no trace of his communication with his victim. A letter would have been dangerous, since it might have been preserved, and eventually might have fallen into the hands of the police.

What bait Roca had offered to attract Francia to the Bale Stones was an immaterial matter now. The activities of agent 7-DH might easily have suggested something which would serve the purpose. Probably the doctor, posing as one of the Centre agents, had proposed to supply Francia with an " article " or a tender " beef-steak " at a remunerative rate. But the matter was of no importance, since clearly enough Francia had not been deceived. Quevedo's death had put him on the alert. He had suspected something in it beyond the ostensible motor accident ; and he had been on his guard when he went to the stone circle.

The next point to be fitted in was Francia's visit to the druggist. There seemed to be very little difficulty in accounting for that. Roca had made his appointment in the small hours of the morning—probably alleging some quite reasonable excuse for such an unheard-of time. Francia, having his own suspicions, would find that the hour suited the course of action he had planned, and would agree to it readily. Then he would be faced with the obvious fact that he shared a room with Elsie. If he got up in the middle of the night and left the house, she might awake and miss him—and the whole affair would come out. But if Elsie turned ill, what could be more natural than that Francia should spend the night in the

181

dressing-room and so be free from her observation ?
She herself would probably suggest the arrangement,
if she felt sick. Sir Clinton was not an expert in phar-
macology, but he knew that ipecacuanha is com-
paratively slow in its action. Francia had forced a card
by his offer to make a tamarind cocktail—with no
tamarinds—which he alone could concoct. He had
dropped some of his drug into Elsie's glass, knowing
that it would not act for half an hour or so—long
enough to conceal the direct connection between the
cocktail and her sickness. In a new kind of drink, she
would be prepared for an unfamiliar taste, and hence the
tang of the ipecacuanha would not attract her attention.

As to what happened in the night, Sir Clinton could
do no more than sketch out an imaginary course of
events. Francia had waited till the household was asleep.
Then he had come downstairs, secured the garage key
from the drawer in the hall where it was left at night, let
himself out of the house, and taken Sir Clinton's car
from the garage. He had chosen it instead of Mrs.
Thornaby's saloon because a touring car would be less
likely to be remembered by anyone who happened to
notice it on the roads at that time of night. He had overlooked the danger of the trip-dial of the speedometer,
and had simply driven straight to the Bale Stones.

Apparently he reached the stone circle ahead of Roca,
left his car round the turn of the road, and went up to the
prehistoric temple, where they had arranged to meet.
He must have been suspicious. A man of that sort would
be suspicious of everyone ; and Quevedo's death had
given him reason enough, if he guessed what lay behind
it. He would be ready to seize any chance that was
offered.

Roca arrived in due course ; and it seemed safest to
assume that he had left his confederate behind him.
Francia's suspicions would have been aroused instanter
if two men had appeared. The doctor had taken his

precautions, obviously. The false number plates proved clearly enough that he was bent on hiding the identity of his car in view of the coming tragedy. He also arrived before his time ; for clearly enough he did not expect to find Francia on the spot when he himself reached the stone circle. Had he thought that likely, he would have had his automatic pistol ready for instant action instead of leaving it with the safety-catch up and no cartridge in the breech.

One hypothesis fitted the case neatly, whether it was correct or not. Suppose that Francia, on his arrival, had concealed himself behind the big monoliths beside the altar-stone, and had waited there, pistol in hand, ready for anything that might turn up. Roca had arrived, gone up to the circle, and, failing to notice Francia, had sat down on the altar-stone to wait. After that, it was of very little importance whether Francia shot him in the back at once or held him in talk until at last he confronted Roca's empty pistol with his own deadly weapon. Roca had been taken by surprise in any case ; and the first alternative seemed the more likely. Probably Roca had presumed too hurriedly that his own real identity was unknown to the Argentiner and had taken a risk for which he had paid with his life.

The rest was easy enough. Francia had carried the body down to Roca's car, poured petrol over it from the spare tins, cleaned up the blood on the altar-stone, set fire to the car, and then gone off to Fern Lodge again, overlooking the evidence of the milometer dial once more when he put up the car.

" It's no use trying to guess what gave Roca away," Sir Clinton reflected. " Nobody's ever likely to puzzle that out. And it doesn't matter very much, in any case."

Satisfied that he had arrived at approximately accurate conclusions about the course of past events, Sir Clinton then turned his mind to the future ; and here he found a much more intricate series of problems awaiting him, some of which demanded almost immediate solutions.

Two major possibilities presented themselves at once to his mind : either Francia would escape detection or he would be arrested for the murder of Roca.

In the first case, the obvious thing would be for Francia to leave the country as soon as possible. All his arrangements were already made, his berth had been booked long in advance, and, if he got clear away, it was doubtful if anyone would think of him as flying from justice, unless they already had some ground for suspicion. And what grounds had the police for suspecting Francia ? As Sir Clinton reflected, he himself had discovered all the really telling evidence against the Argentiner : his relations with the White Slave traffic, Roca's telephone calls, the use of the drug to clear Elsie out of his way that night, the employment of Sir Clinton's car with its tell-tale milometer, and the uncleaned automatic. Ledbury knew nothing of all this ; and without evidence the case must seem almost hopeless.

As Ledbury's name crossed his mind, Sir Clinton was struck by a fresh possibility. Ledbury undoubtedly knew that a Fern Lodge car had been on the spot when the murder was committed ; and the sergeant was the last person in the world to drop a clue of that sort. In a muddle-headed way, he had begun to suspect Sir Clinton himself, it seemed ; and the late Chief Constable recognised that this might lead to difficulties. If he were seriously accused, he knew that he could produce no alibi ; and he was undoubtedly the only person at Fern Lodge who had made Roca's acquaintance, so far as the public knew. It might lead to an awkward state of affairs if Ledbury carried his suspicions into action and managed to secure a warrant for Sir Clinton's arrest.

If that happened, then Sir Clinton could clear himself only by accusing Francia and producing his evidence ; and in that case his earlier suppression of the facts would constitute him an accessory *ex post facto*. Should he suppress the evidence until Francia had time to leave the country, the Argentiner might take the girls with him, whilst Sir Clinton was in gaol on suspicion and thus unable to intervene. It would certainly produce an awkward situation if Ledbury pushed things to that stage.

" Elsie's the keystone of the whole business, so far as I'm concerned," Sir Clinton summed up his personal position ; and he began to reconsider the matter from a fresh angle.

If Francia fell into the hands of the law and Sir Clinton supplied the evidence in his possession, then Francia would undoubtedly be convicted. No jury could do anything but bring in a verdict of guilty with the facts before them. Everything fitted together far too neatly to leave any room for doubt. But this meant that Elsie would be stamped as the wife of a murderer and a trader in women—for the whole story of Francia would come out if the police once began to investigate his career. That was an ugly possibility for Sir Clinton : to publish the very evidence which would put a stain upon his niece. On the other hand, if he suppressed the evidence, he would be deliberately conniving at the escape of a murderer from his proper punishment.

An awkward dilemma for a late Chief Constable ! On the one side, a sensitive girl made miserable for life owing to the action of one of her nearest relations ; on the other, a late high official voluntarily thwarting the course of justice.

Sir Clinton ground his cigarette-stub in the ash-tray at his side, got up restlessly, and walked over to the window to look out. He drew back the curtains again and gazed out over the lake ; but it was evident that his eyes saw very little of the scene before him. He threw back the two valves of the casement and leaned out, as though he found the room too close. Then, mechanically restoring the window to its original state, he fingered the row of books in front of him, glancing aimlessly from title to title, but obviously paying no real attention to the names which he read.

At last a thought struck him. There was still another possibility, one which he had overlooked. Suppose that before the police got upon Francia's track, something happened to Francia himself? That would be a solution of the problem. Roca's confederate was still lurking somewhere in the background. What if he took a hand in the game and eliminated Francia? The police would have no reason for pushing the Roca case into public view then, since they could not secure a conviction. He himself could offer his evidence if necessary—but only if it *was* necessary in order to get the whole matter hushed up. Elsie would come out of it with her credit safe, since the most that anyone could do would be to pity her for the loss of her husband. The whole White Slave business would be buried once for all. And when Elsie had got over the shock of Francia's death, Rex would have a chance of coming into his own if he played his cards properly.

" I wish I could find out something about that confederate of Roca's," Sir Clinton mused. " If he had any direct interest in the affair, he may be the man to carry the business through by avenging Roca. If he does, I certainly shan't lend a hand in bringing him up for it."

This fresh view of the case seemed to have relieved his mind considerably. At least it gave him an excuse for delaying the choice between the two horns of the original dilemma ; for if the confederate meant business he would obviously act before Francia slipped away out of the country. Sir Clinton decided that in the meantime he would keep his own counsel, so far as the evidence against Francia was concerned.

He turned back to his original problem again. There

was now no doubt in his mind as to Francia's character ; and clearly there must be a break between Elsie and her husband sooner or later. If the whole thing came to light in this country, or even if he was able to prove—as he suspected—that Elsie's marriage had been merely one of Francia's business deals involving bigamy, Elsie would suffer. But there was an alternative scheme which had marked advantages. Suppose the whole party went out to South America as arranged and that he sprang his mine as soon as they had landed. It would be easy enough to come home again with the story that Francia had been taken ill suddenly and had died almost on their arrival. Estelle could be counted on to back up the tale when all the facts were laid before her ; and, from his knowledge of the two Anstruther girls, he thought he could reckon on their gratitude when they found the fate from which he had saved them. It would be a complex affair and would involve a good deal of hard lying ; but he knew that he himself would not stick at a mere lie or two when it was a case of ensuring Elsie's happiness.

" That seems to cover the ground," he said to himself at last. " If I draw blank with the confederate, and Francia's still alive by the time we've got to leave for South America, then I'll go with them and arrange to explode my mine under Mr. Francia as soon as the proper occasion presents itself. We'll be clear of everyone who knows us then, and we can fix things up to suit ourselves. I'll undertake that Francia won't come back to this country to give the show away. I have the whip-hand of him there, with the evidence I could hand over to the police as soon as he turned up."

His reflections seemed to have ended in cheering him up ; for now he briskly set about effacing any traces of his stay in the house during the afternoon. He picked up the ash-tray which he had used, threw the contents into the garden, and replaced it in its original position. Then he went across to the window and examined it carefully, as though to make sure that it was precisely the same as when he had entered the room. Satisfied on this point, he collected the bunch of keys and pick-locks and went out to get his car.

In the village, he stopped at the ironmonger's, and, handing over the keys, paid the man's charges. As he crossed the pavement on the way to his car, Constable Peel happened to pass along ; and Sir Clinton hesitated for a moment so as to give him the chance of speaking if he wished to do so. The constable seemed only too glad of the opportunity.

" Good afternoon, sir," he said tentatively.

" Good afternoon, Peel. Got everything cleared up now at the Bale Stones ? "

" Oh, yes, sir. We finished up there before very long. The body's in safe keeping, waiting for the P.M., sir. And the sergeant's been working double tides. Wonderfully zealous, he is. He spares no pains."

Something in the tone of the constable's voice suggested that he thought little of the results of his superior's zeal. Sir Clinton gave him the opportunity of amplifying his criticism. It was no time to consider the niceties of etiquette.

" Has he found out anything ? " he asked, half-indifferently. " He dragged me into the affair much against my inclination, so I suppose I may as well hear what's come out of it all."

" Well, you were quite right about its being a murder, sir," Peel hastened to inform him, with a malicious expression in his eyes. " Ledbury, he's had to admit that he made another bloomer and that you put him straight a second time. Suicide, says he ! Why, when we came to examine that corpse really careful like, there was the mark of the shot square in the back. That was a nasty one for Sergeant Ledbury to swallow, after having been so ready with his theories in the morning."

" Well, well," Sir Clinton interjected, " we all make

188

mistakes now and again, and think no worse of ourselves for doing it.''

Peel was evidently sublimely unconscious of any personal application which this statement might have.

" Don't worry yourself to sympathise with Ledbury, sir," he advised. " That sort of thing runs off him like water off a duck's back. He's been worrying half the countryside already with this here case. I've been sitting in the office listening to him a-wearing out the telephone with calls. Sometimes I laughed fit to split over it when he'd turn away with a " Damn ! " and hunt up a new number. It was real funny, that was."

" Did he make anything out of it in the end ? " Sir Clinton inquired in a tone which suggested that he was almost tired of the conversation.

Constable Peel was manifestly enjoying his share of it, and, lest Sir Clinton should turn away, he hastened to admit that Ledbury had discovered something after all.

" He's found the burned car was garaged once at Friar's Bush—that's about thirty miles away from here ; and once at Silvergrove—that's a matter of six-and-twenty miles off in another direction. The garage people think they recognise the car from the description, but the numbers they remember don't tally with each other. So he must have been changing the number-plates between times, sir. But my impression is that all that evidence is just 'all my eye and Betty Martin,' as one might say ; for the descriptions of the man who brought in the car at these places don't tally with Roca at all. The garage people can't give any clear description themselves—they never noticed the man particularly ; but they're sure it wasn't anyone like Roca."

Sir Clinton nodded as though in mere politeness ; but actually he was keenly interested. Here was Roca's confederate appearing at last in the solid flesh. Hitherto he had been a purely hypothetical figure ; and Sir

189

Clinton was not sorry to find the accuracy of his con-
jectures established by this evidence.

" Roca was on the tall side, if he was anything,"
Constable Peel continued. " Now these garage people
say the car—if it *was* the same car, which the sergeant
hasn't proved yet—was brought in by a man who was
middle-sized at the most. In fact, sir, that's about all
the description they can give of him ; so there you have
it ! A lot of help that'll be to anyone ! A middle-sized
man ! Why, nearly every stranger that comes to this
village is what you'd call middle-sized."

He seemed to be struck by the acuteness of this observation, and apparently racked his memory for examples.

" That Mr. Brandon, now, that's staying at the Black
Bull," he went on, " *he's* middle-sized. Then there's a
Mr. Scotswood that's taken a house for the summer—
he's middle-sized too. And the commercial traveller
that stopped here last week or so, *he* was middle-sized.
A funny bloke, that was, sir. He kept the bar of the
Black Bull in fits, he did. Amusing wasn't the name for
it, I heard. But he wasn't so good at his business, they
say. Didn't sell a pennyworth of stuff in the place to
my knowledge."

He broke off and glanced up the street.

" And this little pest that's coming along now, sir,
you'd call him middle-sized too. You'll see, he'll stop
and ask me some of his silly questions. He always does."

Sir Clinton followed the direction of the constable's
glance and caught sight of an unmistakably middle-
sized man moving towards them on the opposite pavement. He was dressed in loud-patterned tweeds, which
seemed incongruous with his short, tripping steps and
general air of bird-like alertness. Catching sight of the
constable's uniform, he turned at once in their direction
and crossed the road. Constable Peel made an inarticu-
late sound of disgust.

" Didn't I tell you he would ? " he demanded in an

undertone. " I'm fair polluted out of my life with him and his questions, and here he comes with more of them."

His forebodings were speedily justified. The stranger came up to them ; and, with a jerky gesture which seemed to ask Sir Clinton's permission to interrupt, he at once addressed the constable.

" Good afternoon. A very pleasant day, very pleasant. By the way, constable, if it wouldn't be troubling you too much, I'd like to ask you something."

His voice had a chirping intonation which enhanced the effect of his other bird-like characteristics ; and his eager glances from face to face inevitably suggested the curiosity of a sparrow.

Constable Peel, with an air of gloom, gave his permission with a nod.

" Then perhaps you could tell me this," the stranger went on. " Yesterday evening I was walking along the right of way beside the wood on Staff Hill. Naturally I inspected the wood as I went by ; and I was struck by the amount of wild life in it. A very interesting spot, indeed. Weasels—I saw two—and several squirrels. The squirrels were brown ones, *Sciurus vulgaris*. Evidently the grey Canadian squirrel has not yet penetrated into this district. And I was fortunate enough to observe a badger in the dusk. At least, I am almost sure that it was *Meles taxus*, though it was fairly far off and the light by that time was poor. And there is an extensive rabbit-warren only a little way inside the fence. I watched the rabbits coming out of the wood to feed. Very interesting animals, rabbits. I hope to study their habits if possible."

" Ah ! You're interested in rabbits' habits," interrupted the constable, evidently in the hope of bringing his interlocutor to the point.

" Rabbits' habits," the stranger repeated, as though his attention had been caught by the phrase. " Quite a tongue-tangler, that, isn't it ? Yes, I'm interested in *Lepus cuniculus*."

191

Quite manifestly he was delighted to exhibit his acquaintance with the technical names he had used.

" I was about to enter the wood," he continued, glancing for sympathy from face to face, " when I discovered in front of me a large notice-board : ' TRESPASSERS WILL BE PROSECUTED.' I am all on the side of the law, constable, so I refrained from crossing the fence. But I was disappointed, very naturally disappointed. Now could you tell me how I could obtain permission to go into that wood ? To whom should I apply. I ask you, since you're sure to know."

Constable Peel was evidently relieved to reach something definite in his inquirer's discourse.

" If I was you, sir," he answered slowly, " I'd write to Mr. Keppel—he owns the ground—and tell him all about your interest in leppuses and taxies and vulgaries. He'll know what's what, then ; and I expect he'll give you permission. You write to Mr. Keppel, High Thorn, Raynham Parva ; that's all you need do, Mr. Yarrow."

Yarrow put his hand into a pocket of his loud tweeds, drew out a notebook, and made a jotting of the address. But, to the constable's evident disappointment, he did not replace the notebook.

" There's just another thing I'd like to ask," he explained, his glance taking Sir Clinton into his confidence as well. " The other day, I walked up the road over yonder "—he pointed vaguely—" and I saw a little lake with a house at the end of it. With my telescope, I made some observations. I noticed on the water some specimens of the *Gallinula chloropus*. These I should like to examine at closer quarters, if possible. But perhaps the owner of the house might object to my going there."

Constable Peel hastened to divert the stream of information from himself.

" That would be the lake beside Fern Lodge, sir," he suggested. " This is Sir Clinton Driffield, here. He's at Fern Lodge. He'd perhaps be able to say."

" Charmed to meet you, Sir Clinton. Most opportune,"
Yarrow said effusively. " Would there be any objection
to my going down to the lakeside to study the habits of
the water-fowl ? I am, as you can guess, an amateur
naturalist. Very much of an amateur, I'm afraid—merely
a beginner. But keenly interested, now that I have begun.
If you could give me leave . . ."

" So long as you don't come near the house itself, I
can see no harm in it," Sir Clinton interjected, cutting
short Yarrow's explanations. " If anyone offers to hinder
you, give them my name. It'll be all right."

He glanced at his watch.

" It's later than I thought. By the way, Peel, there's
one other thing I want to know . . ."

His gesture politely excluded Yarrow from the conversation, and the amateur naturalist reluctantly
separated himself from the group.

" I've nothing to say," Sir Clinton admitted, as he
watched Yarrow retreating along the pavement. " But
I thought perhaps you'd like a rest, Peel."

The constable glared malevolently after the figure of
the naturalist.

" That's him, sir. Talk, talk, talk, and dashed little
in it all when you come to put it through a sieve. He's
fair got on my nerves. Thanks for shaking him off."

" Anything further that Sergeant Ledbury's un-
earthed ? "

" Ledbury ? " Constable Peel brought his mind back
to the original theme of conversation. " Oh, Ledbury's
had another bad drop. You'll remember how he went
off and interviewed Roca over the Quevedo business,
sir ? And how he found Roca had been in bed when
Quevedo got his dose. Well, when they overhauled Roca's
luggage, what d'you think they found amongst it ? "

" A rope or a rope-ladder, I expect," Sir Clinton
suggested.

Constable Peel stared at his companion with something as near admiration as was possible to his nature.

" The very thing, sir ! " he admitted. " Wonderful guess, that. Yes, he had a rope-ladder in his suitcase. That was how he got out of the window and none of the inn-people suspected he'd been out. Simple, wasn't it ? "

" Pretty nearly obvious," Sir Clinton assured him. " And that's all up to date ? "

" That's all, sir," Peel concurred, after consulting his memory. " But that was a nice drop for the sergeant, after all his fuss. There's fussers and fussers, in this world," he continued peevishly. " That man Yarrow . . ."

" Sorry I must go, Peel," Sir Clinton interrupted hastily as he retreated to his car. He had obtained all the useful information which the constable seemed to have ; and the charm of Peel's company hardly attracted him in itself.

At Estelle's he found the major section of the party ready to return to Fern Lodge ; but Johnnie was still engrossed in his fishing and had to be dragged away from the stream almost by main force. He had actually secured five fish in the afternoon ; and was exceedingly bitter at being interrupted, since he had just had a rise when he was summoned away.

" I'd have caught it with the next cast, I'm sure," he protested, with the eternal optimism of the true angler.

Despite his almost tearful pleadings for " just one more cast," he was bundled into the car, clutching his rod in one hand and his rather dishevelled catch in the other.

When they reached Fern Lodge, a telegraph boy was just leaving the door, and Sir Clinton found that the message was for him. Tearing open the envelope, he scanned the form and saw that the message opened with : " *Altazimuth, declination, meteorite, focus* . . ." He put it in his pocket, glanced at his watch, and found he had just time to decipher it before dressing for dinner, since the message was very short. Rather bored by the prospect, he went slowly up to his room and set about his task.

When decoded, the communication proved to be an order—or at least a demand so urgent that it was practically an order. His services were again required on the Continent, and he was to be at a certain spot without fail on a given date. With a certain foreboding, Sir Clinton refreshed his memory from his pocket-book, and found that his misgivings were accurate. He would have to be in Central Europe on the very day when the S.S. *Malta* left Havre ; and his business would detain him until it was too late to overtake her in the course of her voyage down the Spanish coast. The Government wire had cut clean across his plans.

" H'm ! " he reflected. " That shortens the time available for Roca's confederate to take a hand in the game, if he wants to. I wish I could run across him and give him a polite hint."

He smiled grimly at this idea as he began to slip the links into the cuffs of a dress shirt. While he was thus engaged, his quick ear caught the sound of Johnnie's easily recognisable step coming up the stair ; and he went to the door of his room to summon his nephew.

" Here, Johnnie ! Cut along and get me some stout thread. Your mother will give you some. Say it's the thick stuff for sewing on buttons that I want. She'll know what I mean."

CHAPTER XIV

THE LETTER WITH THE PARIS POSTMARK

Sir Clinton, coming down early for breakfast, arrived in the hall just as Staffin took the letters from the postman. He held out his hand for the bundle of correspondence, and began in a leisurely fashion to pick out his own share, when his eye was caught by an envelope addressed to Francia. A glance at the stamps revealed the Paris postmark, and Sir Clinton moodily speculated on the nature of the contents. Probably some more of Francia's " business correspondence," he concluded, with a faint twitch of his brows.

He put the letter down and was proceeding to sort out the remaining envelopes when Johnnie came downstairs at a run, clearing the last four steps at a bound.

" Here's a letter for you, Johnnie," Sir Clinton observed, flicking over to his nephew an envelope addressed in a sprawling and immature hand.

" It's from Spink Faraday," Johnnie announced, after studying the calligraphy of his schoolmate. " He promised to write to me about some rabbits."

He tore open the letter, read it in a hurry, and seemed relieved by what he learned from the contents.

" I was afraid something had gone wrong about these rabbits," he explained, as he caught his uncle studying his face. " It's all right, though."

His eye wandered to the spot where Sir Clinton had laid down Francia's letter.

"Foreign stamps ! They must have changed the colour of the French forty centimes. This one's different from the ones I've got already. I wonder if he'd give me these if I asked for them ? Do you think he would, uncle ? "

Johnnie's stamp-collection contained nothing of interest to an expert philatelist. Despairing of ever acquiring rarities like the two-penny post office Mauritius or an early Moldavian issue, he had taken a line of his own and become seized with the ambition to have the biggest collection in his school. Quantity, not quality, was what he concentrated upon ; and all was fish that came to his net. He hesitated longingly over the Paris letter before he could tear himself away and join his uncle in the breakfast room.

During the meal, Sir Clinton seemed busy with his thoughts ; and he answered only abstractedly when his nephew addressed him. Just as they were about to rise from the table, the door opened and Francia came in, with the letter in his hand.

"I say, Vincent "—Johnnie attacked him in a tone blending courtesy with determination—" would you let me have these foreign stamps, please ? I'd like them. I haven't got a specimen of that French forty centime yet for my collection."

Francia agreed without hesitation, opened the letter at once, and handed the envelope to Johnnie. The letter itself he slipped into one of the side-pockets of his jacket before sitting down at the table. Sir Clinton, not feeling eager to talk to his niece's husband at that particular juncture, rose from his chair, paused for a moment to light a cigarette, and moved out of the room. It seemed needless to put an unnecessary strain upon himself to conceal his real feelings towards Francia, as he would have to do if he fell into conversation. Much better to avoid the fellow as far as possible.

On the previous evening, he had dealt with the reply to

197

the code telegram which he had received. There was no getting out of the mission : it was too important a piece of business to be set aside ; and he was well aware that he had been selected for special reasons, so that no one else would do as well. So, with the feeling that he was burning his boats, he had drafted a cypher reply agreeing to do as he was asked.

It was a still morning, with a heat-haze which promised a scorching afternoon. Johnnie had gone off on some affair of his own, so his uncle was free from his attentions. Sir Clinton decided to get his telegram sent off at once. He had some matters in his mind which he wished to consider carefully, and a stroll into the village would give him an opportunity of dealing with them uninterrupted.

When he returned to Fern Lodge, the day was already growing hot under the brilliant sunshine. Linda Anstruther was sitting out on the lawn under a tree, and he crossed the grass to a chair beside her. She had been busy with some papers, but at the sight of him she put them down on her knee and looked up with a rather worried expression on her face.

" I'm afraid these sketches we've been writing aren't really much good, Sir Clinton," she said, in a disappointed tone. " When we were writing them, they seemed all right ; but now, somehow, they sound as dull as ditch-water. Isn't it annoying ? "

Sir Clinton endeavoured to be reassuring.

" That's quite a common trouble with some authors," he encouraged her. " When they write a thing, they think it's all right so long as the pen's in their hands. Then, when the hot fit passes off, they under-estimate at once. It's only after they've forgotten it a little and can come back to it with a fresh eye that they can give it fair judgment. I expect you're in the cold-fit stage just now. Are these the sketches ? "

" Yes, I've just been re-reading them, and they do

seem simply rubbish—not a bit of good. I'm almost ashamed to show them to Mr. Francia now ; and we've promised to let him have them to-day."

With a glance which asked permission, Sir Clinton leaned over and took up the papers.

" You've certainly been industrious," he observed, as he picked up the heavy bundle and made a pretence of weighing it in his hand. " Look here, Miss Anstruther, I'd like to read these, if you'll let me. I'm not an expert ; but I go to a show now and again, and I've a fair notion of what catches a foreign public. Do you mind if I see them ? I'll hand them on to Mr. Francia this afternoon, without fail."

His desire to help seemed so genuine that Linda Anstruther made no futile protestations.

" Well, if you would take the trouble," she said in a tone of mingled gratitude and shyness. " I'm honestly depressed about the stuff, now I come to read it over ; and I'd really like a candid opinion about it. Only, you will be candid, won't you ? It's no good telling us the things are first-rate when you really think they're hopeless."

" When you ask for my opinion, you'll get it quite frankly," Sir Clinton assured her in a voice which satisfied her completely.

He patted the loose sheets into a neat pile and kept them in his hand.

" By the way," he asked, " are there any special arrangements for this afternoon ? I haven't come across any responsible members of the family yet to-day."

" Mrs. Francia said she's going to ask some people over to play tennis. There'll be enough to fill the two courts— if you play." She counted the party on her fingers. " There's Miss Scotswood, Mr. Scotswood, and Mr. Brandon from the village ; then there's yourself and Mr. Francia, that makes five ; Mrs. Francia, six ; and my

199

sister and myself, eight. Mrs. Thornaby doesn't want to play. You see, we're depending on you, Sir Clinton. You'll play, won't you ? "

Sir Clinton seemed almost in doubt for a moment. He glanced at the horizon, from which the heat-haze had cleared almost completely.

" It'll be frightfully hot," he pointed out, with no great enthusiasm in his tone. " My impression is that we'll all have had enough of it pretty soon. Of course I'll play as long as I'm wanted—delighted to get a game."

Quite obviously the prospect of tennis on a blazing afternoon had few charms for him. He considered for a moment or two.

" Suppose we work it in this way," he suggested. " We can play for the best part of an hour. By that time, most of us will want a rest—certainly Mr. Scotswood will, if I know him. You and your sister have never been out on the lake yet. I'll take you in a boat for a short time, if you like—until tea appears. Meanwhile, if Mr. Francia has nothing better to do, he can look at your sketches ; and that leaves four to go on playing if they want to. Would you care for that ? "

" If you don't think Mrs. Francia would mind . . ." Linda consented doubtfully. " It doesn't seem quite right to be making arrangements behind her back, does it ? "

" I'll make it all right with her," Sir Clinton assured her. " In fact, if the day develops as it seems to be going to do, I shouldn't wonder but the rest of the party will take the second boat out themselves. The lake will be the only decently cool place this afternoon."

Before Linda could raise any further objections, Johnnie flew out of the house with a long paper parcel in his hand.

" It's come, uncle ! " he called, as he rushed up to them, waving his prize.

" Your new air-gun ? " Sir Clinton inquired. "Here, pass it over and I'll cut the string for you."

He drew out his penknife as he spoke ; and Johnnie set to work to unwrap the little weapon.

" Oh ! A new box of darts, and a big box of slugs as well ! " he exclaimed, as the paper tore apart under his eager fingers. " Thanks ever so much, uncle ! I forgot to say anything about slugs and darts when you said you'd get me a new gun. It's awfully good of you to have thought about them."

He disengaged the air-gun from its last wrappings and examined it with the eye of a connoisseur.

" Did you ever shoot with an air-gun, Miss Anstruther ? " he demanded, loading the toy as he spoke.

" No, but I should like to."

" You would ? Well, come on now with me and I'll show you how," Johnnie invited her cordially. " I've got a target stuck up at the back of the garage, and we can shoot with darts. Are you coming too, Uncle Clinton ? "

His uncle shook his head.

" No, Johnnie. I've some reading to do just now."

" Then come on, Miss Anstruther," Johnnie directed. " We can get through the shrubbery this way ; it's the shortest."

When Miss Anstruther and her companion had vanished among the bushes, Sir Clinton reseated himself and took up the manuscript which she had left with him. As he read, his face showed a smile which was not entirely a proof of amusement.

" Smart enough," he commented as he turned the final page of the first sketch. " Just the sort of thing one would expect a rather nice girl to turn out if she had a sense of humour—quite funny. But, good Lord ! Fancy her imagining that *this* is what Francia expects them to put into the show in an Argentine cabaret-hell ! "

201

He continued his reading, an occasional smile crossing his features at some turn of peculiar humour in the sketches. But when he laid down the last sheet, he sat for a time thinking of the contrast between the hopes of the two girls and the reality which Francia had planned for them. He was more anxious than ever that Roca's accomplice should prove a *deus ex machina* in the whole complicated tangle of events.

The afternoon proved to be all that Sir Clinton had prophesied : a cloudless sky, a blazing sun, and not a breath of wind to bring coolness.

" We proceed according to plan, I think," Sir Clinton observed to Linda Anstruther as they stood at the door watching the visitors' car drive up. " No one will want much tennis on a day like this. I'll take you on the lake at four o'clock."

Linda glanced up at the unflecked sky.

" It is frightfully hot," she admitted. " Poor Mr. Scotswood looks as if he felt it already, even though he's in flannels."

Rex Brandon was in the car with the Scotswoods ; and the party moved at once to the tennis-courts. They played several sets ; but even the most energetic soon admitted that the heat was unpleasant. By tacit consent, play was abandoned and they retreated to the shade of some trees. Mr. Scotswood, with a crimson face, thankfully dropped into a chair beside Mrs. Thornaby. Rex, Estelle, and Elsie formed a group by themselves a few yards away ; whilst Francia moved over and joined the Anstruther girls.

" It's really far too hot for you people to be running about in the sun," Mrs. Thornaby commented, glancing round at the unmistakably heated party. " Suppose you stop playing until tea comes out ? Later on, when the sun's down a bit, you can begin again and play till dinner-time. You'll all stay to dinner—flannels don't matter, Mr. Scotswood—and after that we can make up a couple of bridge-tables until there's some dance-music on the wireless."

Mr. Scotswood, who had looked at first as though he might refuse the invitation, stifled his protest when he heard the last sentence. The chance of a game of bridge was a godsend to him in Raynham Parva, where he found the evenings very long on his hands. Rex Brandon also seemed to be inclined to object at first ; but apparently it struck him that his withdrawal would unbalance the party, and he gave way gracefully without any verbal demur.

" Then that's settled," Mrs. Thornaby announced. " Aren't you going to sit down, Clinton ? "

Sir Clinton shook his head. He took out his cigarette-case, selected a Turkish cigarette, and, after asking permission, lit it. He had been watching with outward impassivity the conversation between Francia and the two girls ; but apparently he thought it time to break up the party, for he moved over to the little group.

" Where's my cigarette-case ? " Elsie demanded. " Oh, I left it in my room. Nuisance, that."

Rex offered his own case, but she shook her head.

" I can't smoke any brand but my own favourite," she said, after a glance at his cigarettes. " And if I don't smoke, these mosquitoes are sure to begin to bite. They come up in hundreds from the lake."

She hurried off up the path towards the house.

" That's a good notion about a smoke-screen," said Estelle, warding off an enterprising mosquito with a gesture. " Give me a cigarette, please, Rex. I'm not so refined as some people, and I expect I'll survive your tobacco, no matter what it may be."

She took a cigarette from his case and allowed him to light it for her.

" That seems to discourage them," she said, blowing a cloud of smoke in the direction of several mosquitoes which were hovering near her.

Sir Clinton disliked to see Francia beside any decent girl, and he deftly inserted himself into the conversation with the Anstruther sisters, though without appearing to force himself on the party. After a few minutes desultory talk, he seemed to recollect his promise to Linda Anstruther, and glanced at his watch as though to gauge the time which they had in hand.

" It's just four o'clock," he said.

Then, turning to Noreen Anstruther, he added :

" Care to have a row on the lake, Miss Anstruther ? Your sister's going out with me in one of the boats, and you might come too. It'll be cool on the water ; and parts of the lake are rather pretty."

Noreen hesitated for a moment, consulting her sister with a glance ; but Linda quite evidently had no objections to a party of three. She liked Sir Clinton, but she had no special eagerness to have him to herself. Noreen accepted the invitation with obvious pleasure.

" It will be nice to have cool water round one," she owned. " It's a perfectly blazing day. I haven't felt so hot for ever so long."

To Sir Clinton's annoyance, Francia showed signs of attaching himself to the party. Without exactly making his intrusion obvious, he managed to include himself in the group as Sir Clinton moved towards the house with the two girls. The late Chief Constable, however, had no intention of allowing this incubus to be thrust upon him. As they came to the porch, he turned to Francia.

" Oh, you've nothing on your hands just now," he pointed out. " Miss Anstruther's finished these sketches ; and she says you promised to read them to-day. You won't have any time later on, if we're playing bridge after dinner. Suppose you look over them now. I'll get you the manuscript."

If Francia had thought of objecting, there was an

undertone in Sir Clinton's voice which warned him that he was most obviously not welcome as a member of the water-party. Apparently he recognised this, for, with an almost imperceptible shrug of his shoulders, he turned away from the girls and followed Sir Clinton into the hall.

" Please go on down to the boat-house," Sir Clinton suggested to his guests. " I'll follow you in a moment or two."

Linda Anstruther walked slowly towards the entrance to the boat-house path, and her sister followed her.

" Wait in the smoke-room," Sir Clinton directed Francia. " I'll bring you the stuff in a minute. I have it upstairs."

In a very short time he reappeared with the pile of manuscript in his hands.

" It'll pass the time for you until tea," he said in a tone which made it quite clear that he expected Francia to begin reading at once. " I'd take that chair there, if I were you. It has the light behind you from the verandah window ; and there's a table handy, if you want to put down the sheets you're finished with."

Francia held out his hand, took the manuscript, and sat down. He seemed frankly bored with the task which had been set him ; but quite obviously he did not care to risk friction with Sir Clinton.

" Clever girls, those," Sir Clinton went on in a casual tone, as though to efface any impression which his firmness might have left. " One or two of these sketches are not at all bad—quite funny. H'm ! That sun's shining directly on your paper."

He stepped to the window behind Francia and drew the curtains across it to shield the Argentiner from the blaze of the afternoon sun.

" That right ? " he asked, when he had adjusted the curtains. " Want a pencil to make notes with ? They'll probably expect a detailed criticism, you know. Read the one about the two girls at lunch, first of all. It's really not bad."

Francia made a vague gesture as though he were already engrossed in his reading and wished to be free from further interruption. Manifestly, he bore a grudge against Sir Clinton for defeating his scheme to join the party. Sir Clinton suddenly bethought him of the fact that there were two boats, and that the Argentiner had probably intended to detach one of the girls and take her out alone in the second boat. He turned at the door, and there was a faint touch of malice in his smile as he examined Francia engaged in his uncongenial task.

Sir Clinton hurried after the girls, but they had evidently been waiting at the boat-house for a minute or two, for they had brought out cushions and placed them in the stern seats of one of the skiffs. Sir Clinton steadied the boat while the girls stepped on board ; then, getting in himself, he pushed off, and picked up his oars. After a few strokes he paused and drew out his cigarette-case, which he offered to his passengers.

" You're not smoking yourself, Sir Clinton," Linda pointed out as she selected a Virginian from the mixed contents of the case.

" No, I must have put my cigarette down somewhere when I was in the house. It doesn't matter," he assured her. " One can't smoke comfortably when one's rowing."

Noreen Anstruther trailed one hand in the water.

" Well, it *is* cooler here," she said thankfully. " What a day ! "

" We'll go over yonder, if you like, under the shade of the trees," Sir Clinton suggested, as he took up his oars again.

Linda glanced lazily over the smooth waters.

" I don't see Johnnie anywhere about. Isn't he fishing ? "

" No, his new air-gun's keeping him busy, I expect," Sir Clinton explained. " Nothing but a fresh toy would keep him away from the lake. I expect he's gone off intent on slaughter, somewhere ; for I haven't seen him since lunch. I don't think he'll do much harm."

CHAPTER XV

THE BURSTING OF THE BUBBLE

When Elsie left the remainder of the party beside the tennis-courts, she went straight to the drawing-room of Fern Lodge, where she believed she had left her cigarette-case. A cursory search failed to reveal it anywhere in the room, however ; and she passed to the smoke-room, thinking that possibly she might have laid it down on one of the tables when she had gone in there to telephone some orders before lunch. Again she drew blank ; and for a moment or two she stood racking her memory for some clue. At last she remembered having put it down on her dressing-table earlier in the day, and she could not recall having used it since then.

She went lightly up the stairs and, crossing the hall, entered her room. The cigarette-case was there, lying on the dressing-table ; and she moved over to pick it up, glancing out of the window at the empty lawns before the house as she did so. Almost without thinking, she opened the case, and extracted a cigarette which she put between her lips. Then it occurred to her that she had no matches, and she went to the mantelpiece in search of some ; but when she lifted the box there, she found it empty.

Men always carry matches, she reflected ; and she turned to the wardrobe where her husband's clothes were kept. When she opened the door, the nearest garment was the jacket which Francia had worn that morning and which he had replaced on its hanger when he

changed into tennis-flannels in preparation for the afternoon's play. Elsie slipped her hand into one of the pockets
at random, felt a match-box under her fingers, and tried
to extract it ; but apparently it had become entangled
with a paper ; and in order to get at the vestas she had
to pull out the paper first. She transferred it to her
left hand and continued her search for the match-
box.

It was the contents of the envelope with the Paris postmark which she had come upon thus accidentally.
Francia had thrust it into his jacket-pocket at the break-
fast-table, since it was hardly the sort of document which
he felt safe in reading with someone at his elbow. After
breakfast, when he was alone, he had taken it out, run
his eye over it, and replaced in it his pocket. There were
some questions in it which required answers, otherwise
he would have destroyed it immediately. As it was, he
retained it until he could put it under lock and key in
his attaché-case ; and when the time came to change
into flannels he had overlooked it and hung up his coat
in the wardrobe with that damning piece of evidence at
the mercy of anyone. But for the chance that Elsie needed
a match, it would have been perfectly secure.

Elsie was devoid of any inquisitiveness and it was
her nature to trust people ; so she had never manifested
the slightest curiosity about the business correspondence
of her husband. As she stood beside the wardrobe,
fumbling in the jacket-pocket, it was by the merest
accident that her eyes fell on the paper she held in her
left hand, and she read, half-unconsciously, one of the
sentences of the letter.

That sentence was enough. Francia's correspondent
was not skilled in wrapping up her meaning in vague
phrases ; and the French was plain enough to Elsie.
Half-incredulous, she took her hand away from the
jacket, opened up the letter, and began to read it through
from the beginning. The first page of it put the nature

of Francia's trade beyond any doubt. Before she reached the signature, she had seen enough to gauge the vileness of the woman who had written it and of the man who had received it. Francia must have revealed his whole plot to his female coadjutor ; and this epistle conveyed her congratulations on his ingenuity in such unmistakable terms that the whole business was laid bare.

Elsie's knees threatened to give way under her ; and she moved uncertainly across the room to a chair beside the dressing-table. The blood pulsed like a hammer in her temple, and she felt physically sick under the shock of her emotion. The thing had struck her like a thunderbolt, leaving her whole being numbed ; and faintly, at the back of her mind, something clamoured that this was impossible, that there must be some mistake.

She spread out the letter again, but her wrists trembled so violently that she had to rest her hand on her knee before she could read the ill-formed handwriting. On re-reading it, she found the note even more atrocious than it had seemed the first time. Phrase after phrase cut her like a whiplash. The illusory hope of a mistake vanished as she scanned the lines.

She wanted to cry, but something seemed to prevent her ; and she sat, dry-eyed, staring blankly in front of her out of the side-window which overlooked the lake, conscious only of the pulse in her temple and the lump which had risen in her throat. Tears would have been a relief.

She had been so proud of Francia ; and so much in love with him. Ten minutes before, she had reckoned herself one of the happiest girls alive ; and to have the flagrant proof of his depravity thrust upon her in this brutal fashion seemed more than her nerves could bear. If she could only break down and let all this pent-up emotion find its escape ! And at last she got the relief she wanted and lay curled up in the armchair, her face in her hands, and her whole frame shaken by the violence of her weeping.

The fit did not last long. She sat up, wiped her eyes with her handkerchief, and, finding it insufficient for this emergency, she got up and hunted for another in a drawer. The action seemed to steady her nerves ; and she sat down again with a cooler mind. The letter had fallen on the floor, but she picked it up again, and once more read it from start to finish.

The third reading made things no better. The bubble of her illusion had burst, and nothing could ever reshape it. Her husband—that ! She shivered with disgust as she thought of him. What cut most deeply now was a phrase in the letter which showed that Francia had been laughing at her behind her back. While she had been giving him all she had, he had been grinning in amusement at her innocence and simplicity ; and he had made a joke of it to this creature from whom the letter came. All she had meant to Francia was something which he could sell at a good price. His love-making had been a sham from the start—just a few moves in the game. That wounded her pride as well as her heart ; and somehow this second stab seemed to bring her into a cooler frame of mind.

Elsie had inherited some of the characteristics which served Sir Clinton well in his work ; and, now that the first storm of her emotion had blown over, she began to collect herself and think ahead. She folded up the letter and put it away in a drawer. As she was about to turn the key in the lock, a fresh idea occurred to her. She hated Francia now ; all her love for him seemed suddenly to have been transmuted into its opposite in the short space since she had entered the room ; and, with something of her uncle's clarity, she bethought herself that Francia might have other damning letters in his possession. These would be worth having in any case. She had not got the length of considering clearly what her next

211

step would be ; but some instinct urged her to secure all possible weapons against the brute who had treated her like that.

As she glanced round the room, her eyes caught Francia's attaché-case, standing in one corner. That would be where he would keep confidential matter, obviously ; because she knew that he never locked up any of the places in which he kept the rest of his belongings.

She picked up the attaché-case, and brought it to the dressing-table. The catch refused to open, and she looked round for some lever which would serve to wrench up the hasp. A shoehorn-buttonhook seemed fit for the work ; and for a moment or two she struggled with the fastening. It gave way suddenly at last, and she opened the attaché-case. The sight of the papers satisfied her that she had got what she wanted.

One by one she picked them up and glanced over them ; but only here and there did she find anything she could understand. A good many of the documents were in Spanish, which she could not read ; but there were several in French and English ; and as she read them her loathing and hatred for Francia increased.

She was almost cold by now. The first shock was over ; and anger was mingling with the bitterness of her disappointed love. What beasts men were ! Why, no beast could ever sink so low as this man whom she had adored. And all the time he had been laughing in his sleeve, sharing the joke with his confederate, getting ready to sell her into something worse than slavery. She bit her lip as she thought of it. And not only she, but Estelle and the other girls were to be dragged into the net. She was to be the bait that caught them. She recalled phrases he had used, stored up unconsciously in her memory because she loved him, which now seemed to carry a fresh significance. And to think that she had lived side by side with *that* ! She would never feel clean again ; the very touch of such a reptile was contaminating.

Elsie had very vague ideas about the divorce laws. In her set in London, divorce had been looked upon as unimportant ; and she had never had the curiosity to inquire into the subject. She had no definite knowledge of the value of the papers in the attaché-case ; but since they had come into her possession she felt she might as well make them secure. One or two documents still remained in the case. She lifted them out, and caught sight of what lay below them. Then, making up her mind, she took up the contents of the case, crossed over to the open drawer, and put the papers under lock and key. After that, she closed the attaché-case and replaced it in its original position. As she did so, a curious expression crossed her face. It seemed a needless precaution ; for, if she could prevent it, Francia would never enter that room again.

The sound of voices under the window roused her from her absorption. She heard her uncle speaking ; and the sound gave her back some of the courage she had lost. Here was someone who would stand by her and see her through her troubles. She could throw the whole thing on his shoulders, make him shield her from any harm. At least there was one man in the world she could trust implicitly.

The voices fell silent ; and in a moment she recognised Sir Clinton's light step on the stairs. He passed her door and went to his own room, further along the hall. She had a sudden impulse to call him in as he passed back again ; but it died out almost as soon as it entered her mind. She felt it would be better to wait before appealing to him. He would always be there to help when he was needed.

She crossed to the window overlooking the lake and gazed out vaguely while her mind worked furiously, reviewing the whole situation. Dimly realising that anger

213

hurt less than disappointed hopes, she concentrated her thoughts on the wound to her pride, and succeeded in lashing herself into bitterness against her husband. That was better than brooding over the wreck he had made of her life.

Sir Clinton's figure came into her range of vision as he left the house and went down to join the Anstruther girls at the landing-stage ; then he disappeared among the bushes which fringed the path. A few moments later Elsie saw the boat, with the three of them in it, push out on to the lake.

She turned back to the dressing-table and picked up the thing she had taken from the bottom of Francia's suitcase. For a moment she examined it curiously. Then, leaving the room, she went softly down the stair. At the front door she paused and looked about her, fearing that someone might come upon her at this time when she especially wished to avoid people. Seeing no one about, she walked along the front of the house to-wards the steps leading up to the verandah outside the smoke-room window.

CHAPTER XVI

A SURPRISE FOR SIR CLINTON

Behind her outward flippancy, Estelle possessed a fund of shrewdness and discernment, and her mind had been exercised in the last day or two upon the situation presented to her by the affairs of the group which centred round Fern Lodge. The glamour which Francia exercised upon Elsie had no influence on Estelle ; and, although she had done her best to like the Argentiner for his wife's sake, she could not succeed in rousing herself to any enthusiasm over him. Though she had been careful to conceal her real opinion from Elsie, in her own mind she had summed up Francia with the vague phrase : " Not quite it, and more than a bit of the other thing." And the fact that she perceived a kindred feeling in Sir Clinton had helped to reinforce her own views on the subject.

Rex was the man who ought to have married Elsie. Estelle, with even better sources of information than Sir Clinton possessed, was quite convinced that things would have taken that turn inevitably if it had not been for the sudden incursion of Francia into the field. Rex certainly was not the sort of man she would choose for her own husband ; but that very fact enabled her to appreciate him all the more accurately ; and she was convinced of one thing : Rex would never let a girl down. Somewhere at the root of his simple character lay a stratum of fundamental decency—even in her own mind she shrank from using the word " chivalry "—which would make him an asset to any girl who relied on him.

Francia did not leave that impression on her, for all his attentiveness and surface courtesy.

Where Estelle parted company with Sir Clinton was in the matter of inviting Rex to Fern Lodge. Without being able to formulate her reasons, she inclined unconsciously to Mrs. Thornaby's view ; and she felt that Sir Clinton was running unnecessary risks of friction by bringing Rex into so much direct contact with Francia. Her vague distrust of the Argentiner made her apprehend trouble between him and Elsie, sooner or later ; and if trouble arose when Rex was on the spot . . . She did not feel inclined to probe the possibilities. Rex had one of those deceptive tempers which flash up only at times of deep disturbance, and it was often difficult to say where things would stop if once he were roused.

She had caught Rex's expression as he glanced after Elsie when she left the group to go up to the house for her cigarette-case ; and she had mentally filed that along with the very different look which was on his face as he watched Francia attaching himself to the Anstruther girls and Sir Clinton. Though she laughed at herself for over-imaginativeness, she could not help fancying that there was danger in the air when two such opposite feelings were lodged in a single mind.

" Care to take me for a row on the lake, Rex ? " she inquired lazily. " I don't mind going, if you're very keen."

Rex shook his head.

" Nothing doing, when you put it in that tone of voice," he answered, meeting her with her own weapons.

Estelle waved her cigarette disconsolately.

" How manners degenerate—all except mine. Now a couple of generations ago you'd have said : ' Indeed, you honour me too much, my dear Miss Scotswood. Permit me to procure a duenna for you, and then conduct you to the wherry.' Or something like that."

" I daresay," Rex answered abstractedly. " They all had no-trump hands in the politeness game then."

Estelle saw that he was disinclined to talk, so for a time she devoted her whole attention to discouraging the mosquitoes by means of her cigarette-smoke. At last, thinking that Rex would be none the worse of having his attention diverted from his thoughts, she broke the silence.

" Elsie seems to have been a long while looking for that cigarette-case."

Rex woke up suddenly at the sound of her voice.

" Yes, hasn't she ! "

Then he seemed to recollect something, and his face clouded.

" Confound it ! I'd forgotten I had a sort of half-engagement to-night."

Seeing that Estelle seemed curious, he added in explanation :

" There's a weirdish bird staying at the Black Bull—a fellow Yarrow. He's by way of being interested in the wild life of the countryside—so he tells everyone. An Amateur Naturalist, in capitals. Accent on the adjective, I should think ; for the beggar would be hard put to it to tell a dragonfly from a kingfisher, so far as I've gathered. I half promised I'd give him the benefit of my expert knowledge—take him for a stroll in the evening and explain the difference between a frog and a toad, and all that sort of thing. I'll need to put him off, or he'll be hanging round the place waiting for me all evening. He's no call to complain, really, for we fixed up nothing definite ; but I'd better ring up the Black Bull and leave a message for him."

He rose to his feet with a gesture, asking her permission to go and send his message.

" Give me another cigarette, please ? " Estelle begged, as he was about to leave her. " These mosquitoes are a bit too enterprising."

217

He offered his case and she helped herself to a cigarette, which he lit for her. Then he took one himself and struck a second match.

" Turkish ? " Estelle inquired. " A bit heavy for me ; but anything's better than a mosquito-bite."

" An Abdullah won't do you much harm," he re-assured her as he turned away.

Estelle watched him take the path up to the house.

" This party's going the way of the Ten Little Nigger Boys," she reflected. " It seems to dwindle as one looks at it. I'll be Old Maid in a minute or two if this goes on."

She crossed the grass and took a chair beside her father and Mrs. Thornaby ; but she felt no inclination to join in their conversation. The heat of the afternoon was apparently having its effect on Mr. Scotswood, for by degrees his contributions to the talk were approaching the monosyllabic stage. Estelle leaned back and amused herself by warding off the cloud of midges and mosquitoes which had gathered about the party.

Suddenly, across the hot, still lawns, came the report of a firearm, muffled but unmistakable.

" What's that ? " Mr. Scotswood ejaculated, starting up from his chair as the sound reached his ears.

" A shot, it sounded like," Estelle's eyes showed something which looked like fear, though it was not of herself she was thinking. " Come on, Daddy. I think it came from the house."

She started to her feet and took a step or two before her father could restrain her.

" You stay where you are ! " Mr. Scotswood directed in a tone that admitted no disobedience. " I'll go and find out what it was."

Estelle hesitated. Then, glancing at Mrs. Thornaby's face, she saw in its expression a counterpart of her own emotion. She allowed her father to go off alone, and turned to her hostess.

" It may have been only Johnnie with his air-gun,"

Mrs. Thornaby suggested, but her tone betrayed that she did not take her own supposition seriously.

Estelle made no pretences.

" That wasn't an air-gun," she said. " But who'd be firing a gun up here ? There's nothing to shoot at."

And she cast an anxious glance after the retreating figure of her father as he cut across the lawn in the direction of the house.

As Mr. Scotswood drew near the front door of Fern Lodge he heard a fresh and even less reassuring sound : the scream of a girl in panic ; and on the doorstep he encountered Staffin flying from the house, her face a mask of terror. Deftly he intercepted her.

" What's all this about ? " he demanded, in the same tone that he might have used in inquiring why his afternoon tea had been overlooked.

His apparent calmness brought Staffin up sharply and avoided the attack of hysteria which he had dreaded.

" Oh, sir, I heard shooting in the smoke-room ; and when I went to the door, there was Mr. Francia lying on the floor and Mr. Brandon standing over him. And there was a great pool of blood on the hearthrug. Oh, such a shock I got ! I'll never forget it as long as I live. I won't dare to go to sleep at night for fear of dreaming about it . . ."

Mr. Scotswood had little patience with useless emotion. He took the terrified girl by the arm, swung her round, and directed her towards the path leading down to the boat-house.

" Go down to the lake and wave to Sir Clinton. He's out in a boat there. Tell him to come up here immediately. Now get off, and don't waste any time."

Staffin responded to this mechanically. Evidently she had feared that he might want her to go back into the house again ; and the prospect of getting away was a relief. She set off immediately ; and Mr. Scotswood, after seeing that she was obeying his orders, stepped

219

into the hall. At the end of it he caught sight of two terrified faces ; and his first act was to send the maids back to their own quarters. Then he turned the handle of the smoke-room door and walked in with a steady step.

Staffin had given him the essentials of the scene in two sentences. Francia's body was lying contorted on the hearthrug before the fireplace ; and from its attitude there was little difficulty in seeing that, if he had died quickly, the end had not been painless. His flannels were splashed with blood and a great pool was slowly extending itself on the floor. Bending over the body was Rex Brandon, and at the sound of the opening door he swung round and turned upon the intruder a face which puzzled Mr. Scotswood even at that extraordinary moment. Horror and amazement seemed to have had their moulding influence on Rex's expression ; and in addition there was something which hinted at a hardening resolution struggling to the front in the turmoil of conflicting emotions. Somehow, Mr. Scotswood had not expected a murderer to look quite like that, if he were caught red-handed. Then, suddenly, Rex gained control over his countenance ; and he straightened himself up with a sullen look on his face which obliterated the earlier expression.

" What's all this about ? " Mr. Scotswood repeated.

He could not help giving himself a good mark for the way in which he was succeeding in repressing his own emotions in this unexpected situation.

Rex gulped for a moment before he could find his voice.

"He's been shot," he said at last, with a gesture towards the body at his feet.

Mr. Scotswood's glance followed the gesture and he shivered slightly. After an instant's inspection of Francia's body, he turned his eyes again to Rex's face.

" Damn it, man ! " he broke out. " Did you do it ? "

Rex's face hardened at the question, but he made no

reply. Mr. Scotswood was suddenly impressed by the strangeness of the whole affair. His world seemed to have been given a twist since he had heard the shot a couple of minutes before. Here he was, with a dead man at his feet, asking a boy whom he had known for years the plain question : " Did you do it ? " And the boy did not take the trouble to reply ! What was one to make of it ? There seemed to be no key to this puzzle, for Mr. Scotswood had no inkling of the state of affairs brought about by Elsie's marriage. To him, the whole situation was inexplicable to the verge of incredibility. He had come up in the car that afternoon with a sane youth who had discussed batting averages in the most matter-of-fact fashion ; and now . . . He simply could see no glimmering of meaning in the whole affair.

Some sheets of manuscript scattered over the floor added to the complexity of the puzzle. He stooped to pick one up ; then, recalling that nothing should be disturbed, he straightened his back, and found Rex, with a white, set face, giving him stare for stare in silence.

" Damnation, man ! Say something ! " Mr. Scotswood exclaimed in a tone of mingled anger and appeal.

Rex's only noticeable response was an almost imperceptible movement of his head—a mere involuntary action which conveyed nothing to Mr. Scotswood. Then another glance of Rex's directed the older man's attention to the floor, and he found that the ever-widening pool of blood from Francia's body had almost encroached upon his tennis-shoes. A sudden qualm attacked him at the sight ; and he crossed the room to the window overlooking the verandah, in search of fresh air. One of the curtains was drawn back ; he leaned out through the open casement ; and as he did so his eyes fell on the figure of Sir Clinton hurrying up the path from the boat-house. Staffin must have found him as he was bringing the boat in to the landing-stage.

221

" Thank God ! He'll tackle this business," was Mr.
Scotswood's softly-breathed expression of relief at the
sight.

In a moment or two, quick steps sounded on the
parquet of the hall, the door opened, and Sir Clinton
appeared on the threshold. For a moment he stood there,
and even his long training was unable to conceal his
surprise and consternation at the spectacle before him.
Then his eyes narrowed and his face seemed to grow
grimmer as he looked about the room.

" H'm ! " he said, in a perfectly expressionless voice.
" This is a surprise."

The callousness of this remark put the coping-stone
on Mr. Scotswood's edifice of new sensations. He had
never seen Sir Clinton engaged on a case, and this
matter-of-fact way of treating a murder seemed convincing proof that the whole world had gone mad. He
stood silently at the window, watching for the next
incredible happening.

Sir Clinton advanced into the room, closing the door
behind him. For a moment he stooped over Francia's
body, as though merely to satisfy himself that life was
really extinct. Then he confronted Rex.

" You didn't do it ? " he asked in an almost conver-
sational tone, which gave Mr. Scotswood yet another
jar.

Rex's eyes wandered round the room for a moment ;
but he brought them back to face Sir Clinton's glance
when he replied :

" I've nothing to say."

Sir Clinton was obviously puzzled by this response ;
and he did not take the trouble to conceal his surprise.

" Look here, Rex," he said kindly, " I suppose you're
keeping your story for the police when they arrive. But if
you'll tell me about the business, it'll help to get the
details fixed in your mind while they're fresh. And perhaps we could sift out the main points together, so as to

have a cut-and-dried tale ready. That would save time."

Rex shook his head definitely.

" I've nothing to say," he repeated.

Sir Clinton examined him with more attention than he had hitherto seemed to give him ; and under the scrutiny Rex's face grew even more dogged in its expression. Quite obviously, he had determined to withhold any explanation whatever ; and Sir Clinton could make nothing of this decision. Mr. Scotswood, studying the two faces before him, imagined that Sir Clinton really had discounted the possibility of Rex's guilt and was doing his best to help ; but at the same time Rex's sullen refusal to give information seemed inexplicable on any hypothesis except that of culpability.

With a gesture which betrayed his dissatisfaction, Sir Clinton turned away and began methodically to examine the room. He went first to the open window and glanced out, as though to gauge what could be seen by a person standing outside and looking into the smoke-room ; but he was careful to disturb nothing. The row of books on the window-shelf was half concealed by the section of the curtain which was still drawn ; and Sir Clinton inspected them sideways, apparently without finding anything worth noting.

Turning round, he came next to the cane chair in which Francia had been sitting when he was killed. There was a splash of blood on the back of it ; and, in the centre of the stain, the cane had been smashed and torn by the passage of the bullet. Mr. Scotswood saw Sir Clinton's glance pass back from the bullet-hole to the window ; and he inferred that the shot must have travelled in a line joining the casement to the chair.

As he stood watching the late Chief Constable's proceedings, an adventitious thought crossed Mr. Scotswood's mind. Here he was, thrust by accident into the

223

position of a Watson to Sir Clinton's Holmes ; but Watson never seemed to have felt as he himself felt at this moment. Watson could encounter all the accessories of a violent death without turning a hair. In fact, he hardly noticed them, so far as one could gather from his accounts. Mr. Scotswood, on the other hand, was acutely conscious of the spreading pool of blood on the floor, the contorted body on the hearthrug, and the cold detachment with which Sir Clinton was going about his work.

" I suppose it's sound enough," he reflected inconsequently. " Watson was a sawbones, so blood wouldn't disturb his nerves as it disturbs mine."

Sir Clinton's glance went back to Rex's face for a moment ; and again Mr. Scotswood read in his expression a perplexity which seemed the counterpart of his own feelings. So far as Mr. Scotswood's knowledge went, there was not the slightest reason for Rex to disagree with Francia, much less to shoot him. They had been perfectly polite to one another when they were playing tennis together not twenty minutes before. And yet, if Rex had not killed the Argentiner, why did he remain silent under what was practically an accusation ? Mr. Scotswood felt that he was completely out of his depth. Unless . . . but he dismissed the idea that Rex could be a homicidal maniac whose madness had come suddenly to the surface. That was out of the question.

His attention went back to Sir Clinton, who was obviously hunting on the floor for something which he could not find. Mr. Scotswood had not given a thought to the weapon, up to that moment, but now he seized the opportunity of doing something, and he joined in the search.

" You can't find the pistol ? " he demanded, as he began to ferret about on the floor near Sir Clinton.

As he uttered the remark, he heard a faint sound behind him ; and, turning round, he found Rex staring at him with hate and dismay written plainly on his white, set face.

" There's no pistol here," Sir Clinton said, rising to his feet and mechanically dusting the knees of his trousers.

Mr. Scotswood was puzzled for a moment by this. Then a wave of relief passed over his mind.

" Of course not," he said, meeting Rex's stare. " The shot must have been fired through the window."

He had expected to see Rex's face brighten at the announcement of this positive proof of his innocence ; but, instead of that, the expression on Rex's features seemed to grow more sullen. He relaxed his lips momentarily as though to say something ; then, apparently, he thought better of it and remained silent. Mr. Scotswood, turning to Sir Clinton to see how he was taking the remark about the pistol, found him examining Rex's face in an abstracted fashion as though he were thinking of something which puzzled him completely. A few seconds passed before Sir Clinton spoke.

" I'll have to ring up the police, Rex. Can't you be frank with us ? It's really the safest thing in the end. You can talk to me alone, if you like. I must have the facts if I'm to be of any use to you. Once Ledbury gets this business into his hands, you'll have to speak, whether you like it or not."

Rex shrugged his shoulders almost impatiently.

" I've nothing to say," he repeated in the same dogged tone.

Sir Clinton made a gesture of despondency.

" Then there's nothing for it," he said.

After a final glance round the room, he moved over to the telephone on the table beside the door. As he did so, his eye was caught by the receiver, which lay at a little distance from the telephone-stand, as though it had been put down hurriedly on the table-top. Mr. Scotswood, watching his face, saw it light up with a gleam of hope. Sir Clinton swung round to where Rex still stood impassively in the middle of the room.

" You were telephoning just now ? " he demanded. " Or was it Francia ? "

Rex paused for a few moments before replying, as though he wished to consider where this question might lead. Then, moistening his lips before he spoke, he made the first voluntary statement which Mr. Scotswood had heard him utter since the tragedy.

" I used the 'phone. I was ringing up the Black Bull."

He closed his lips firmly again, as though afraid that he might let slip some further admission. Mr. Scotswood, eyeing Sir Clinton, could not determine whether this answer had been expected or not. It elicited no comment. Sir Clinton turned away from Rex and sat down before the telephone desk. As he was about to pick up the displaced receiver, Mr. Scotswood made a gesture of warning.

" If you pick that thing up, you'll perhaps destroy some finger-prints on it, Sir Clinton," he pointed out quickly.

" My finger-prints are on it already. So are those of most of the family," Sir Clinton explained mildly. " Another set will hardly matter. But, if you think it advisable, we'll take precautions."

He pulled out his handkerchief, gripped the receiver gingerly through it, and called up the exchange. In a few seconds he had got through to the police station and acquainted Sergeant Ledbury with the state of affairs so far as Francia was concerned. Mr. Scotswood noticed that Rex's name was left completely out of the conversation. Sir Clinton rose up as he laid the receiver back on its catch.

" Ledbury will be here in ten minutes," he said. Then, turning to Rex, he added, " You'd better give up this line, Rex. It does no good, really."

Rex's mouth tightened a little ; then he broke his silence with another voluntary statement.

" You think you know a lot, but there's a lot you don't know."

Mr. Scotswood was surprised at the substance of this remark, but still more by the tone in which it was uttered. Whatever his motive might be, Rex evidently resented bitterly any attempt of Sir Clinton to come to his aid. Anyone could see from Sir Clinton's manner that he wanted to help ; and yet Rex had thrown away the chance of that assistance almost insultingly. It seemed all of a piece with the general inversion of the normal order of things which had followed on the pistol-shot. Then a sudden thought crossed Mr. Scotswood's mind. What if Rex were shielding the real criminal at his own expense ? Assume that, and the situation appeared to grow clearer.

CHAPTER XVII

SERGEANT LEDBURY'S
INVESTIGATION

Although obviously puzzled, Sir Clinton showed no sign that he resented Rex's violent rejection of his proffered assistance. He seemed to ignore it completely, and for a few moments he appeared to be considering some point quite alien to the latest incident. At last he turned to Mr. Scotswood.

" I'm rather worried about our womenfolk," he said. " They'll be a bit nervy, probably ; for Staffin will have spread the news of this. Someone ought to look after them, just in case they take it into their heads to venture up here. I leave that to you, if you don't mind. I can't very well go myself. The police may be here at any moment now."

Mr. Scotswood was only too glad of an excuse to betake himself elsewhere, as probably Sir Clinton had guessed. Between Rex's incomprehensible reserve and the almost brutal, matter-of-fact methods of Sir Clinton, he felt completely out of his element ; and the ghastliness of the environment in which the play was staged had affected him more than he liked. He muttered a phrase which might have been anything for all his audience made of it ; then, pointedly avoiding the hearthrug with his eyes, he let himself out of the room.

When his retreating steps had died away down the hall, Sir Clinton's manner changed abruptly.

" He's out of the road now," he said in a tone of

228

hardly suppressed eagerness. " Now you can make a clean breast of it, Rex. It's quite safe ; you know I won't give you away. Quick ! Ledbury may be on top of us at any moment."

His new method of approach yielded exactly the same success as his earlier ones. Rex simply shook his head, not even taking the trouble to put his refusal into words. Sir Clinton seemed dashed by this rebuff. He retreated a step or two and sat down on the arm of one of the big chairs. Mechanically he put his hand into his pocket, pulled out his cigarette-case, placed a cigarette between his lips, and held out the case to Rex, who refused the offer with another head-shake.

" Smoking might steady your nerves," Sir Clinton pointed out, as he struck a match for his own cigarette. " You're all jarred up. Bound to be."

Then his eyes caught Rex's glance wandering towards the body, which lay almost at their feet.

" Oh, it's that, is it ? Don't waste any grief over *that*. Not worth it, really."

If the brutality of these sentiments was intended to show Rex where his sympathies lay, Sir Clinton's latest line of approach ended, like the others, in a *cul-de-sac*. Rex refused to let himself be drawn ; and Sir Clinton, recognising that it was hopeless to question him further, smoked in silence until a noise of boots on the parquet of the hall announced the arrival of Ledbury and his subordinates. Sir Clinton got up.

" You're a young fool," he said, in a tone completely devoid of heat. " But from what I've seen here, I don't think you'll come to much harm, if that's any encouragement."

If Rex had any intention of replying to this, he got no opportunity. The door opened, and Sergeant Ledbury appeared on the threshold. His little gimlet eyes passed from the white, sullen face of Rex to that of Sir Clinton, who had composed his features instantaneously as the

handle turned. Only after that inspection did the sergeant look at the body on the floor. He went forward,
knelt down, and subjected the corpse to a careful examination without saying anything. Then, after making a
jotting or two in his notebook, he rose to his feet and
spoke impersonally.

" Better take things in their order, p'raps. That maid
in the hall seemed to know something about the start of
affairs. Might begin with her, if there's any place one can
talk in. Not here, of course."

He cast a glance at Francia's body as he spoke,
evidently to amplify the meaning of his last phrase.
Then, moving to the door, he made a gesture as though
ushering his two companions out into the hall. Rex
obeyed mechanically ; and Sir Clinton followed him.
Ledbury waited until they were out of the room, then
he called to Peel, who was posted near the front door,
and put him in charge of the smoke-room.

Sir Clinton led the way to the drawing-room, followed
by Rex and the sergeant. Apparently Mr. Scotswood had
fulfilled his mission, for there was no one to be seen
about the house. In a moment or two, Staffin appeared
in answer to the sergeant's summons. Ledbury looked
her up and down critically as she came in—a process
which did not seem to reassure her much. She threw a
glance at Sir Clinton, as though begging for his support
against the rigour of officialdom.

" Now, then," said Ledbury in a tone which sounded
like an attempt to ingratiate himself with the girl, " we're
not going for to bother you more than we can help, you
understand ? But we want to know what you've seen
about this murder in there."

He pointed crudely with his thumb over his shoulder
to indicate the smoke-room.

The girl was obviously anxious to tell what she knew,
but apparently she had difficulty in determining where
her story should begin.

" Better start about lunch-time," Ledbury advised,
seeing her difficulty. " Just begin about lunch-time and
tell us all you can remember."

This seemed to give Staffin the help she needed.

" There was just the usual people at lunch," she
began. " Sir Clinton, there, Mrs. Thornaby, Master
Johnnie, and Mr. and Mrs. Francia, and the two Miss
Anstruthers."

" Did you notice anything remarkable about them ? "
the sergeant demanded as he noted the names in his
book.

Staffin shook her head.

" There was nothing different from other days. Later
on in the afternoon, Mr. Scotswood and Miss Scotswood
came in a car. They brought Mr. Brandon here with
them. Then they all went down to the tennis-courts."

The sergeant nodded encouragingly. Sir Clinton, with
a faint touch of amusement, noted that Ledbury did not
think it worth while to lick his pencil in dealing with this
witness.

" The next thing I saw," Staffin went on, " was when I
went into the pantry opposite the smoke-room door.
I was cleaning silver and the pantry door was a bit
open, because it was stuffy in there with all this heat. I
heard voices, and then Mr. Francia came past my door
and went into the smoke-room. That would be somewhere about four o'clock, I should think ; but I don't
know for certain."

" It was four o'clock," Sir Clinton confirmed.

" Then, in a minute or two, I heard Sir Clinton come
down the stairs, and he went into the smoke-room
too."

Ledbury seemed to prick up his ears at this, and threw
an involuntary glance at Sir Clinton. Their eyes met
for a moment ; then, at the sight of the smile on Sir
Clinton's lips, Ledbury looked disconcerted and turned
back to the maid.

" They were in the smoke-room together for a minute or two, and I heard them talking," Staffin went on.

" Ordinary voices, or angry ? " the sergeant demanded, keeping his face averted from Sir Clinton.

" Oh, just ordinary," Staffin answered.

" Quite ordinary," Sir Clinton confirmed, his smile growing slightly more accentuated as he met the eyes of Ledbury. " I'll tell you all about it in a moment, if you wish."

" Well, what happened after that ? " the sergeant demanded, as though to cover his annoyance at having mistaken the situation.

" Sir Clinton came out of the room again, leaving Mr. Francia behind."

" Anyone else in the room except him ? " Ledbury asked, as though he feared she might have overlooked something.

" Nobody that I knew of," Staffin answered frankly.

" Nobody at all," Sir Clinton testified. " He was quite alone when I left him in the room."

" Well, what next ? " the sergeant urged.

Apparently he was anxious to get away from the point, since he had betrayed himself in a slip.

" Not very long after Sir Clinton had gone out of the front door," Staffin pursued, " I saw Mr. Brandon here go into the smoke-room and shut the door behind him."

Ledbury swung round and studied Rex's face with increasing interest for a second or two ; but this time he was careful not to say anything which might betray what he thought.

" The next thing I heard," Staffin went on in obedience to a gesture of the sergeant, " was the telephone bell ringing and then Mr. Brandon speaking. I didn't hear what he said, of course, through the door."

She paused, as though the next part of her story was harder to tell.

" After that, I heard a shot behind the door and a horrid noise—an awful noise . . . "

" Come, come now ! None o' that," said the sergeant. " Just say what you heard and be done with it. You heard a noise ? A cry, or what ? "

" Somebody hurt and calling out," Staffin described it. " And a noise like something falling on the floor."

" A big thing ? A man's body ? "

Staffin pulled herself together with an effort which evidently cost her a good deal. For a moment or two she seemed to be racking her memory for the exact details.

" Yes, a noise like a man falling in a lump. But there was another noise too, like . . . I can't think exactly what it *was* like. Oh, well, like a brass candlestick falling, or something of that sort. That's as near as I can re-member it. I'd know it again if I heard it. That's all I can say."

Ledbury looked rather glum at this description.

" You'd better try to remember more about it, if you can," he cautioned her. " Now, then, what did you do after that ? "

" I didn't know what I was doing," Staffin admitted. " I came out of the pantry, and I must have walked over to the door of the smoke-room without thinking. And the next thing I heard was Mr. Brandon's voice, quite loud it was and I could hear it quite plain. It said : ' Go away ! At once ! ' Like as if he was hustling some-one out of the room."

" Quite so ! " Ledbury said reflectively.

He turned sharply round on Rex, as though hoping to surprise something ; but the set face which confronted him seemed to give him as much food for thought as any self-betrayal could have done. For some seconds he examined Rex's features as though he wished to mem-orise them ; then he turned away again and seemed to reflect before he spoke again.

" There's a French window in that room. Was that open or shut when you went out, Sir Clinton ? "

" Shut, I should imagine. Otherwise I'd probably have gone out by it instead of by the front door," Sir Clinton answered. " I was on the way down to the boathouse, and the French window would have been the shortest way if it had been open."

" Just so ! " Ledbury agreed.

He turned back to Staffin.

" And what next ? "

" I didn't know what I was doing. I must have got my hand on the handle and turned it without thinking. The door opened, anyhow, and I looked in—just for a moment."

She was shaken by a quiver like the symptom of St. Vitus's dance.

" Well, what did you see ? " Ledbury demanded, giving no time for further developments. " Come along now. You may as well get it over, and then I shan't have to bother you any more just now."

This promise seemed to give Staffin back her control.

" I peeped in. Mr. Francia was lying on the hearthrug, all in a pool of blood. Mr. Brandon was over at the window, behind the chair Mr. Francia had been sitting in. He was looking round at me when I opened the door. Then he seemed to think of something, and he said : ' Get out ! ' Just like that. So I shut the door and ran. I expect I called : ' Murder ! ' or something like that. I know I was shrieking when I met Mr. Scotswood at the front door. He sent me off down to the lake for Sir Clinton, and I waved him ashore."

Sir Clinton reflected that if all witnesses could give their evidence as well as this girl had done, police work would be very much simplified. She had omitted nothing essential ; and she seemed to have fastened upon the really salient points in a very confusing series of events.

Ledbury put only one further question :

" When you looked in at the door, did you see whether the French window was open or not ? "

Staffin shook her head.

" I didn't notice it. I was in such a state I hardly noticed anything," she admitted frankly.

" Just so ! " Ledbury said. " Well, that'll be about all we want with you, just now."

Staffin needed no further hint. She turned at once and went out of the room. When she had gone, Ledbury swung round to examine Rex's face again ; but it was Sir Clinton whom he addressed.

" I'm not quite clear about this, sir," he explained. " What were you and the deceased doing in the smoke-room ? "

Sir Clinton gave him a brief account of the Anstruther girls' sketches, and how he had left Francia engaged in reading the manuscript.

" Quite so ! Now I begin to see what it was all about," Ledbury said when he had finished. " And now, Mr. Brandon, perhaps you'll give us your story. But I've got to caution you that you need not say anything to incriminate yourself. What you do say will be taken down by me and used as evidence against you."

At this blunt declaration Rex winced. There was no mistaking its purport.

" Then I'll say nothing," he answered in a hard voice.

" I'll make a note of that," Ledbury answered, writing in his pocket-book. " Murder's felony, and I can arrest without a charge made. You'll have to come along with us."

Rex seemed to have anticipated this. After Staffin's evidence there was obviously nothing else to be expected. He threw a glance of inquiry at Sir Clinton, and apparently read in the answer a confirmation of Ledbury's statement.

" Very well," he said. " I'm ready."

Ledbury summoned one of his constables and handed

Rex over to him with some instructions. When he had completed his arrangements, he caught Sir Clinton eyeing him ironically. The expression on the late Chief Constable's face seemed to take him rather aback.

" Sorry to have to do it, sir. But it's my duty, isn't it ? The case's as plain's a pike-staff."

" Quite plain," Sir Clinton conceded, with no attempt to conceal the possible double meaning in his phrase.

" Ah ! Just so ! You think so ? " said Ledbury, with a tinge of discomfort in his tone. " Well, I'll have a look at the smoke-room now."

" You'd better see Mr. Scotswood," Sir Clinton suggested. " Then you'll have all the evidence of witnesses in your hands."

The sergeant agreed, and Mr. Scotswood was summoned. He gave his account of what he had noticed when he burst into the smoke-room ; and, as his narrative drew near its close, Ledbury evidently felt surer of his ground. He threw a look at Sir Clinton as much as to say that the case was now clearer than ever.

" There's one thing I ought to add," Mr. Scotswood wound up. " Neither Sir Clinton nor I could find the pistol anywhere in the room. In fact, I'm sure it wasn't there."

" So am I," Sir Clinton threw in.

" We went over the place together, side by side," Mr. Scotswood elaborated, " and, if one of us had missed it, the other would have been sure to find it. I was most careful in searching."

" Just so ! " Ledbury said non-committally. " We'll need to have a look for it."

At the door of the smoke-room, Mr. Scotswood turned away. Quite obviously he had no desire to re-examine the scene of the tragedy. When Sir Clinton and the sergeant were left to themselves, Ledbury's first act was to subject Francia's body to a minute inspection.

" Shot in the back it seems," he said, looking up at

last, " and the bullet's made fair hay of him in front.
Must have been a heavy one to do all that damage."

" Or an expanding one ? " Sir Clinton queried.

" Or an expanding one, as you say, sir," Ledbury
admitted after a pause for consideration. " Anyhow,
the shot was fired in this room, that's clear. I can smell
the stink of the powder strong enough."

" Quite so," Sir Clinton answered, but the tone of his
voice left it in doubt whether he agreed with the sergeant
or was merely amusing himself by turning Ledbury's
favourite non-committal expression against its author.

Ledbury showed no sign that he had noticed the faint
caricature of his own manner. He rose to his feet and
went across to the window which looked out on the
verandah.

" You were in here with the deceased, weren't you,
before Brandon came in ? " he demanded. " Is this
window just as it was when you were in the room ? "

" I was in the room before *Mr.* Brandon entered it,
certainly. When I left it, both curtains were drawn across
the window, which was open. Your eyes will assure you,
sergeant, that one of these curtains has been slid aside
since then, leaving a clear view out into the garden. It
was in that state when I came back into the room after
being summoned up from the lake. Quite clear, I trust ? "

Ledbury seemed to take the hint about Rex's name.

" Then it must have been drawn back by either the
deceased or Mr. Brandon ? "

" How should I know, sergeant ? It's drawn aside ;
I see that with my own eyes. I didn't see who drew it."

" Has anything else been disturbed that you know
of ? "

Sir Clinton noticed a distinct change in the sergeant's
manner, which was reflected in the tone of his voice. In
their previous intercourse, Ledbury had been in the
position of a more or less docile pupil ; but now it was
only occasionally that he interjected " sir " into his

sentences ; and his general air was one of dissatisfaction.

" The receiver of the telephone was off its bracket when I came into the room after the shot," Sir Clinton explained, with no outward sign that he noticed anything peculiar in Ledbury's attitude. " I replaced it after telephoning to you. It was lying on this exact spot on the table."

He put his finger on a place about two feet from the telephone stand.

" That fits in with the maid's evidence, all right," Ledbury admitted. " He'd been telephoning. Then he put the receiver down, came over here to the window, and shot the deceased through the back of the chair. Um ! That would be it."

He flashed a glance from his sharp little eyes at Sir Clinton's face as he spoke, evidently hoping to surprise some expression which might give him a key to the views of the ex-Chief Constable on this particular point ; but his hopes were disappointed. Sir Clinton seemed to accept the statement as the most natural thing in the world, though he refused to be drawn into any verbal comment on it. Ledbury's glance travelled on till it reached the figure of the constable on guard, who was standing in one corner of the room, evidently much interested in the whole affair.

" You can wait outside now," Ledbury ordered, much to the manifest disgust of his subordinate. " We don't need you."

The constable retreated and closed the door behind him ; and, as soon as his steps showed that he had moved away along the hall, the sergeant brought his eyes back to Sir Clinton's face.

" Isn't it a rum sort of coincidence the way you seem to have got mixed up with all this business ? " he asked in a voice which showed that he was making a tentative move. " There was Quevedo, now. Who was the last person to meet him on the road before he was done in ?

Sir Clinton Driffield. Then there was Roca, him that was killed up at the Bale Stones. Didn't you strike up an acquaintance with him at the Black Bull ? So they're saying, anyhow. And I've got a sort of notion it was one of your cars that was up at the Bale Stones that night, too. That's a lot of coincidences. And now, here's another man murdered, and who was on the spot again ? You ! If one was a fanciful sort of person, now, wouldn't these strike you as being things that wouldn't be the worse of some explanation ? "

Throughout the whole of his speech ran an undercurrent of doubt which evidently prevented him from saying more plainly what he was evidently thinking. Rather to his confusion, Sir Clinton laughed heartily instead of taking offence.

" You've struck a fresh parlour game, sergeant," he said rather cruelly when he stopped laughing. " *Find the coincidence !* Causes shrieks of laughter from young and old, eh ? Well, let's play it, if you insist. My move ? Isn't it remarkable that all three victims should have been foreigners ? There's a coincidence worth noting. And another coincidence is that I never set eyes on any of them before the night I came to Raynham Parva. Now it's your turn to guess, I think."

Ledbury flushed angrily, but seemed in difficulty about his next move.

" Can't go on ? " Sir Clinton inquired with mock sympathy. " Then it's my move again."

His voice lost its tinge of amusement and grew colder.

" Final amazing coincidence. I wasn't on the spot when any of these murders was committed. That seems an interesting fact, doesn't it ? "

Ledbury still remained obstinately silent ; but the increasing redness of his ears showed that he was feeling far from comfortable. If he thought the worst was over, he was mistaken.

" It's evidently time I did some plain speaking," Sir

Clinton said, with a complete disregard for the sergeant's feelings. " You've got a bit above yourself lately—perhaps with getting your name into the papers. You seem to think you can run about throwing out insinuations all over the place, and no one may dare to pull you up. It's not done, sergeant. You've made two howlers already this afternoon, and that's quite enough. If Mr. Brandon chooses to make it hot for you, I shouldn't care to be in your shoes. These stripes of yours aren't tattooed on your skin, remember. A pair of scissors will soon bring them off."

Ledbury's little eyes betrayed his anger, but they showed also that the suggestion about his stripes had gone home. What if he *had* been a bit hasty in arresting young Brandon ? But when he reflected on the evidence, he felt reassured.

" You think he didn't do it ? " he demanded, with only the faintest tinge of a sneer in his tone. " The man that tries to prove that to a jury'll have his work cut out for him, he will."

" I haven't got all the evidence yet," Sir Clinton admitted frankly, " but I expect to secure it very shortly. You've made a muddle of it, sergeant."

The certainty in his manner convinced the sergeant against his will. Quite unconsciously he glanced at the stripes on the arm of his tunic. If he *had* " made a muddle of it," as Sir Clinton said, and if Rex Brandon (with Sir Clinton to advise him) chose to cut up rough . . . a lot of unpleasant things might happen.

Sir Clinton evidently felt that he had given Ledbury a much-needed lesson ; but he had no desire to push the man into a corner. The sergeant had forgotten, evidently, that he himself had very little claim to any credit in the unravelling of the Quevedo and Roca affairs. He had discounted the help which had been given him and had allowed his conceit to get the better of him. That, after all, was nothing out of the common.

" Here," he said. " Run your hands over my flannels. Find the pistol there ? No ? Well, then, add to that the fact that, when the thing happened, I was out on the lake in a boat with the two Miss Anstruthers. Does that seem enough to keep you from flinging insinuations about at random in future, so far as I'm concerned ? If it doesn't, then I'll point out that from the time I got out of the boat I've been under the eyes of people, and so had no chance of disposing of a pistol if I'd had one."

" You didn't find the pistol when you looked for it ? " Ledbury inquired in a much more polite tone than he had been using ·before.

" No. Neither Mr. Scotswood nor I could see it anywhere. You'd better look for yourself."

The sergeant seemed only too glad of the excuse to do something. The positiveness in Sir Clinton's manner carried conviction to his mind, and he began to have more than a glimmering of how his bounce must have appeared to the man who had gone out of his way to help him earlier in the week. He moved over to the window overlooking the verandah and began to search the floor in that neighbourhood. Sir Clinton, manifestly letting bygones be bygones, walked across the room and swung himself up on to the table which held Johnnie's Meccano, from which position he could overlook the sergeant's proceedings.

" What's that you've got hold of ? " he demanded, after a moment or two.

" Seems like one of the nuts off those toys up there," the sergeant suggested, passing up the tiny object.

From the tone of his voice it was clear that he also was inclined to let bygones be bygones, possibly in the hope that if he conciliated Sir Clinton he might have a friend to help him should Rex Brandon's arrest turn into an awkward matter.

" Meccano nut," was Sir Clinton's verdict.

He turned and compared it with facsimiles on the piece of machinery which Johnnie had abandoned before completion. Then, putting it down on the table, he was just in time to see Ledbury make another find.

" One of the bars out of that toy," the sergeant declared as he passed it up.

He returned to his minute search of the floor.

" Your housemaid doesn't half seem to do her job," he complained. " There's a regular litter of bolts, and nuts, and odds and ends scattered about here."

" My young nephew has a compact with her that she's only to sweep up this particular bit of the floor once a week—under his personal supervision. It seems he was losing components right and left in the daily sweeping until he made his bargain," Sir Clinton explained.

" H'm ! " was Ledbury's comment. " It doesn't make the job of hunting through it any easier. Here's a bit of spring. I suppose that's one of the Meccano bits too ? "

Sir Clinton took it from his hand and examined it.

" No," he reported. " That's a broken bit of an old air-gun spring. Here's the other bit lying on the table."

" A fish-hook and two ordinary pins," Ledbury continued, handing up his prizes for examination. Then his voice shot up a couple of tones. " Ah ! here's something ! A cartridge-case ! "

" Let's have a look at it," Sir Clinton requested after the sergeant had inspected his catch in the light from the window. " H'm ! A .38 by the look of it."

He threw a glance at the body on the hearth-rug.

" An ordinary .38 wouldn't have made a mess of him like that. They must have filed the tip off the bullet and turned it into a dum-dum, to judge by the results. That seems suggestive, sergeant."

Ledbury welcomed the return of Sir Clinton's earlier tone.

" What do you make of it, sir ? "

Sir Clinton shrugged his shoulders faintly.

" One might make a guess. If it had been an ordinary bullet, Francia might have lived long enough to say something. The makeshift dum-dum didn't give him much opportunity to split on anyone, if he'd a mind to."

This was evidently a fresh light on the situation to Ledbury. He made no reply, however ; but went down again on his knees and resumed his search.

" Here's the stub of a cigarette, sir."

" What's the make ? " Sir Clinton asked, with a certain eagerness in his voice.

" Abdullah's the word on it, sir. Turkish blend."

Sir Clinton's eagerness died out.

" Too common in this house to be much help," he said, with a tinge of disappointment in his tone. " There's another one of the same brand lying on the hearth, and another in that ash-tray. You'll not get much help there."

Ledbury resumed his grovelling on the floor, extending his search wider and wider ; but, except for two more pieces from a Meccano outfit, he discovered nothing further. The pistol was nowhere in the room.

" Well, you were right enough, sir," the sergeant admitted, rubbing his dusty hands together as he got to his feet at last. " There's no pistol here. And there was none on his person, either ; for I gave one of my men the tip to search him in the hall, and he'd have brought me the gun if he'd found it. It's a rum start, that is ! "

His eyes wandered round the room until they came to the open window, and at the sight of it the expression on his face altered suddenly.

" Ah ! " he ejaculated. " That would be it ! "

Without a word to Sir Clinton, he went across to the French window, drew back the heavy curtain which screened it, and let himself out on to the verandah. Sir Clinton, with a faint tinge of amusement in his

243

expression, watched the sergeant's figure disappear over the balustrade.

" So he's seen it at last," he reflected. " Well, he took the deuce of a time over it ! "

Without troubling to follow Ledbury, he left the room and made his way to the garage. Taking out his car, he drove straight into Raynham Parva.

CHAPTER XVIII

THE MAN WITH THE TELESCOPE

It was not long before Sir Clinton returned to Fern Lodge ; and, as he pulled up his car at the front door, he found Sergeant Ledbury waiting for him with a look on his face which betrayed mingled feelings of triumph and a malicious joy at having scored a decisive point. In his hand he held a dinner-plate, on which rested an automatic pistol ; and quite evidently he was far too cock-a-hoop to consider how incongruous a spectacle he presented.

" I'd just like to hear what you think about *that*, sir," he said, in the tone of an unsporting player putting down a trump with open satisfaction.

" Anything to oblige you, sergeant," Sir Clinton answered as he got out of the driving-seat. " I think it's a pistol. And I think it was thrown out of the smoke-room window into the bushes."

" Just so ! " said Ledbury, slightly taken aback by this. " And perhaps you've been thinking something more about it ? "

" Perhaps I have," Sir Clinton admitted, refusing to be drawn.

Ledbury looked at him doubtfully for a moment ; but apparently he was unable to postpone his triumph.

" It's got somebody's finger-marks on it," he announced in a tone which threatened a revelation.

" So I gathered, when I saw the dinner-plate," Sir

245

Clinton confessed blandly. " Not mine, by any chance, are they ? "

Ledbury was evidently annoyed by this ; and he hastened to stab at what he thought would be a weak spot in Sir Clinton.

" No, they're not yours. As soon as I saw them, I telephoned down and got one of my men to take young Brandon's finger-prints . . . "

" Better go cautiously, sergeant." Sir Clinton interrupted, spoiling Ledbury's effect completely. " You seem to be treating your prisoner rather too much like a convict. He's not that yet, remember. There's still a trial to come—if it ever comes."

" Well, anyways, I had his prints sent up here with a man on a bicycle, so as to lose no time ; and when I compared them with the prints on this pistol here . . . "

" They were identical, of course. When a man picks up a pistol and throws it out of an open window, it's only to be expected that he'd leave his finger-prints on it."

" And when a man *fires* a pistol, he leaves his finger-marks on it too, doesn't he ? " Ledbury suggested with more than a touch of tartness in his tone. " Brandon fired that shot. That's my belief, and you won't shake it."

Sir Clinton's eyebrows lifted slightly.

" A bit unsafe, isn't it, when you count chickens in the shell ? There's one you needn't reckon on, sergeant : a conviction of Rex Brandon for this murder. You've made the biggest blunder of your life over this business. And now come along with me, and I'll prove it to you."

Ledbury's confidence was badly shaken by the certitude of Sir Clinton's tone. Once again, uneasy feelings began to surge up in his mind ; and it was with an apprehensive face that he obeyed instructions. As he passed into the smoke-room, Sir Clinton swung round on him abruptly.

"Now, let's have no more bungling. First of all, when you left me here not long ago and scuttled off in search of that pistol, you pulled back the curtain which was hanging over the French window, didn't you ? "

"Yes," Ledbury admitted sullenly. "What's the harm in that ? "

"And you unlatched the window and went out through it ? "

"Didn't you see me do it ? " Ledbury asked querulously. "What's the good of asking me about it ? "

"Because I want you to remember it and not go getting your souvenirs tangled up. Understand ? "

Ledbury quite obviously could not see what this was meant to lead up to in the next stage ; but he contented himself with nodding his acquiescence. Sir Clinton led him over to the window overlooking the verandah.

"You didn't pull back this curtain ? " he asked, pointing to the one which had been drawn back.

"No. Better to leave things as they were. I was thinking of getting the place photographed as it was when the murder happened."

"Well, pull it forward now."

Evidently resenting the order, Ledbury apparently thought it best to fall in with Sir Clinton's wishes. He put out his hand and drew the curtain out to meet its companion at the middle of the window.

"See anything now ? " Sir Clinton demanded.

Ledbury's astonished eyes fell upon a small hole torn in the material of the curtain—the obvious mark of a bullet's passage through the stuff.

"Well, I'm damned ! " he ejaculated in a tone of dismay, as he appreciated the bearing of this discovery on his case against Rex. "You think that means the shot was fired from outside the room, sir ? "

Sir Clinton had evidently grown tired of sarcasm.

"You've asked what I think about things before,

247

sergeant. Use your own wits for a change. Anything peculiar about the position of the hole, for instance ? "

Ledbury examined the tear in the cloth attentively for a few seconds, then he turned round. By this time, all trace of bumptiousness had vanished from his manner.

" Meaning that it's low down, sir, rather below the level of the casement."

" Yes. Can you see how that could happen ? "

Ledbury pondered for some moments.

" You mean that a man was outside with the pistol, and when he pushed it against the curtain the cloth ran up on the muzzle, and the farther he pushed it into the room, the lower down on the curtain the hole would be ? "

" Or else the curtain was waving in a draught. Either would fit. So much for the curtain. Now for the telephone. What's the length of the cord attaching the mouthpiece to the desk-stand ? "

Ledbury extracted a measuring-tape from his pocket and took the length of the cable.

" Three and a half feet, sir."

" How far is it from the stand to the dead man's chair—the back of the chair—roughly ? "

Ledbury measured the distance with his eye.

" Close on thirty feet," he estimated.

" So no man could stand behind this chair and talk into the mouthpiece at the same time ? "

" No."

Sir Clinton's questions evidently suggested a fresh idea to the sergeant, and he looked more uncomfortable than ever.

" You mean, sir . . . ? "

" I mean this. If you'll go down to the Black Bull, as I did just now, and ask for the girl who answered Mr. Brandon's telephone call, you'll learn this. In the middle of a sentence, and while Mr. Brandon was still

248

speaking, she heard a bang. Then there was a jar as if the transmitter had been slammed down. She didn't know what it all meant, of course ; but she's put two and two together now that she's heard the stir in the village about the murder. What she heard was the firing of the shot. And at that very moment Mr. Brandon was speaking through the 'phone. Grasp the inference ? If I were you, I'd pick up that 'phone and offer Mr. Brandon your humblest apologies immediately. It doesn't do to waste time. Every minute he'll be getting angrier, if I know him."

Ledbury saw the ground cut completely from beneath his feet by these new facts. Sir Clinton hadn't been far out, after all, when he had termed it the biggest bungle of the sergeant's life ; and the prospect of having to straighten out the results of his rashness was anything but pleasant.

" You're quite sure of your evidence, sir ? " he asked in a very dejected tone.

" Quite," said Sir Clinton definitely.

Ledbury took the hint. He picked up the telephone, rang up the police station, and gave orders for Rex's release. He added some instructions about the removal of Francia's body from Fern Lodge, in readiness for the necessary inquest. When he put the telephone down, he found Sir Clinton inspecting the pistol which the sergeant had laid down on the table when he came into the smoke-room.

" Do you make anything of that, sir ? " he asked, rather humbly. " Does it suggest something to you ? "

Sir Clinton gave an almost imperceptible shrug, as though the matter were almost outside his purview.

" On the face of it, one or two things look clear enough," he said. " The shot wasn't fired by Mr. Brandon ; and yet Mr. Brandon's are the only finger-prints on it, so far as one can see. Therefore the man who handled it before Mr. Brandon took special care not to leave his prints on it. Premeditated crime, evidently. And done by someone who takes trouble to think things out.

" The bullet came through the curtain ; the cartridge-case was on the floor ; and the window was open. One might infer that whoever fired the pistol was just outside the window, leaning in over the sill, perhaps. The pistol itself must have been inside the window at the moment of firing, or else the cartridge-case would have been on the verandah, since the ejector works backwards and sideways in its throw. That seems to dispose of the possibility of the shot having been fired from any distance outside the window, quite apart from the fact that a man at a distance couldn't see through the curtain to aim, whereas a man actually at the window would be able to peep through any gap between the drawn curtains. By the way, know anything about these automatics, sergeant ? "

Ledbury shook his head.

" Never had much to do with them," he confessed.

" They're neat bits of machinery," Sir Clinton explained. " See that little pawl that can be moved up to engage in the notch in the sliding jacket ? If that's home, you can't fire. Safety-catch No. 1. Now, see that moveable bit on the pistol-grip ? Safety-catch No. 2. It's depressed when you grip the butt of the pistol for firing ; and the gun won't go off unless it's pressed down. So even if you drop the pistol on the floor, the jar won't set it off."

" Can't be fired unless someone's holding it ? " the sergeant said, to show that he had grasped the point. " So that's why it didn't explode when it fell out of the murderer's hand immediately after he'd fired the shot ? For of course it was the pistol falling that made the noise the maid described, wasn't it ? The noise like a candle-stick falling ? "

Sir Clinton nodded in agreement.

" Suppose you take out the magazine and count the cartridges," he suggested. " That is, if you can do it without finger-marking the pistol."

" Six cartridges, sir," Ledbury reported after a second or two. " That makes seven in all, with the empty case we found on the floor."

" If eight's a full load, it looks as if more shots than one were fired," Sir Clinton pointed out. But we needn't bother about that just now."

He moved towards the open French window, passed out on to the verandah, and stepped up to the window from which the fatal shot had come. From that position, he looked to right and left for a moment or two ; then, without explaining his actions, he re-entered the room. In the short interval a change had come over Ledbury's expression.

" There's just one point I've overlooked, sir," he said, with a light recrudescence of suspicion in his tone. " You'll mind what the maid said ? What d'you make of her hearing Mr. Brandon say : ' Go away ! At once ! ' That'll want explaining."

A flash of comprehension lighted up his face.

" You've explained away Mr. Brandon very neatly," he said slowly. " Mighty neatly indeed, you've explained him away. But p'raps I was a bit hasty in taking your advice and letting him out of the jug. What about his being an accomplice, *ex post facto*—shielding the real criminal, like ? How would you look at that, sir ? "

" I shouldn't look at it at all," Sir Clinton said, taking hardly any trouble to conceal his contempt for the idea. " Use your brains, sergeant."

The flame of suspicion was blazing up in Ledbury's eyes now even stronger than before. With a complete disregard of Sir Clinton's implied warning, he picked up the telephone, rang up the police station, and made some inquiries. From what he heard, Sir Clinton,

251

gathered that Rex had been set at liberty and had immediately set off for Fern Lodge.

The sergeant put the telephone back on its bracket with a gesture of relief.

" No harm done yet," he said half-aloud. " I'll lift him when he turns up here."

At that moment there came a knock on the door of the smoke-room ; and, in answer to Ledbury's summons, one of the constables put his head into the room.

" There's a Mr. Yarrow wants to speak to you, sergeant. He says he's got some important information to give you. It won't keep, he says."

" All right, I'll see him—in the drawing-room, say." He turned to Sir Clinton with a politeness which seemed rather forced. " I suppose you've no objection to our using your room, sir. Perhaps you'd like to hear this new evidence ? "

If the last sentence was ironical, Sir Clinton was apparently obtuse, for he took it at its face value.

" Certainly, sergeant," he agreed, following Ledbury from the smoke-room.

Waiting in the hall was the amateur naturalist, dressed in his incongruous loud tweeds. Ledbury ushered him into the drawing-room ; and, almost before the door was closed behind them, Yarrow had launched eagerly into a long, detail-encumbered narrative.

Stripped of its irrelevancies, his story ran thus. That afternoon, taking advantage of Sir Clinton's permission, he had come up to the lake to study the habits of the water-fowl—" *Gallinula chloropus* " ; and for that purpose he had brought his new telescope. He installed himself under cover of some trees and kept a look-out on the lake. About four o'clock, he noticed two girls on the landing-stage. Shortly afterwards, Sir Clinton joined them, and the party went out in one of the boats. Yarrow confessed quite frankly that he had spied on them through his telescope—" merely with the friendliest

252

interest." Then, tiring of this, he turned his glass towards Fern Lodge.

From his position, he could see the verandah and also the porch of the house ; and when he brought the front door into his field of view he caught sight of a girl standing on the steps—" a very pretty girl, brown-haired, and dressed in a flimsy frock—a tennis-costume or something of the sort." She had riveted his attention immediately, and he tried to keep her in sight. " But I am unused to my telescope, or any telescope, and I find difficulty in holding the instrument steady and in keeping my second eye closed." From the spasmodic glimpses he obtained, he got the impression that she was disturbed about something. " She seemed, if I may put it so, agitated—nervous."

This natural phenomenon had fixed the attention of the amateur naturalist. He watched the girl walk along the front of the house towards the lake, and sit on a garden seat which stood a yard or two away from the foot of the stair leading to the verandah. Then, for a few seconds, his telescope wavered ; and when he picked up the seat again it was empty. He wasted a moment or two before he found the girl's figure, and by this time she was at the window of the smoke-room. He described the window with an accuracy sufficient to make it manifest that he had identified it correctly.

Then something happened which he had not understood at the time. The girl had her left hand on the window-sill when he saw her again. Where her right hand was, he could not see. Suddenly, the curtain of the window was drawn aside and he caught a glimpse of a man standing within the room. The girl appeared to have had a shock of some sort, for she tottered for a moment and caught with both hands at the leaves of the open window in order to support herself. Then, in obedience to an abrupt gesture of dismissal from the man in the room, she ran along the verandah towards the front of the house and disappeared out of Yarrow's field of vision. Meanwhile, the man in the room made another gesture—" as if he were throwing something out of the window." After that, he turned away from the casement into the room and Yarrow lost sight of him.

The amateur naturalist kept his telescope fixed on the window to the best of his ability, in the hope of seeing more ; but in this he was disappointed ; and at last he turned his attention once more to the front of the house. He witnessed the meeting of Staffin and Mr. Scotswood, and followed the maid's arrival on the landing-stage and her signalling to Sir Clinton in the boat. After this, the house yielded nothing of interest to him, and he had finally given up his spying, feeling very much puzzled by what he had already seen.

Not venturing to trespass near Fern Lodge, he had made the best speed he could back to Raynham Parva, frankly in the hope of picking up some gossip. When he reached the village, the whole place was astir with the news of the third murder ; and he saw that his evidence was vital. He resolved to volunteer it at once—" as a mere matter of public duty."

To his credit, Ledbury refrained from any display of exultation during Yarrow's narration. He had no need to question the amateur naturalist ; all the details he wanted were poured out upon him to the last tittle. Occasionally he stole a glance at Sir Clinton to see how this latest turn of the wheel was affecting him, but the face of the late Chief Constable had fallen into its habitual impassiveness. Only when Yarrow had exuded his last item of evidence did Sir Clinton open his lips.

" This is the telescope you were using ? " he asked, as though the matter was one of casual interest only. " May I look at it ? "

Yarrow handed it over, and Sir Clinton drew out the slides. He walked over to the window, turned the telescope towards the lawns, and brought it to the focus.

Ledbury, obviously unable to see the bearing of this experiment, waited rather impatiently for the end of it.

Sir Clinton shut up the telescope and turned to Yarrow.

" Magnifies a good deal, doesn't it ? I suppose you couldn't get much into your field of view ? " he asked. " The window itself, and a bit of the wall on either side, perhaps ? "

" Yes," Yarrow confirmed, evidently flattered by the praise of his instrument's power. " That's just what I saw ; the window with the girl's figure and perhaps a yard of wall on each side of it, just as you say."

Sir Clinton turned to Ledbury.

" If you're thinking of calling Mr. Yarrow as a witness, sergeant, you'd better impound that telescope. It'll be an important exhibit at the trial."

Yarrow began at once to protest against the confiscation of his telescope ; but the sergeant made short work of his objections. Ledbury had got all he wanted from Yarrow, and now he practically turned him out of the room under the pretext that he had better put his statement in writing immediately. A constable took charge of the naturalist and led him off in search of writing materials so that he could put his narrative on paper in another room.

Closing the door, Ledbury came back and confronted Sir Clinton. He made no effort to conceal his satisfaction with the latest development of the case.

" Greatest bungle of my life ? " he said softly, as though merely thinking aloud. " 'A very pretty girl, in a tennis-frock, and brown-haired.' There was four girls here this afternoon. Two of 'em was on the lake when the shot was fired. Another of 'em was Miss Scotswood —and she's fair-haired. So that leaves Mrs. Francia. She's ' a pretty girl, brown-haired, in a tennis-frock.' I begin to see a bit o' light in this case."

He paused in his soliloquy and stared hard at Sir Clinton with an expression of triumph on his face.

" She was the one your young friend Brandon was shielding with his : ' Go away ! At once ! ' That explains why he kept his mouth shut so tight and wouldn't tell us anything. *She* was the one that fired the shot ! "

CHAPTER XIX

THE FRENCH METHOD

" *She* was the one that fired the shot ! "

When the words had escaped him, Ledbury remembered, too late, that the girl he was accusing was the
niece of the man he was addressing. He waited uneasily,
expecting a verbal storm to break over his head. To his
surprise first, and then to his discomfort, Sir Clinton
gave no sign that he had been touched on a sore spot.
If anything, his face set more firmly into a mask which
the sergeant scanned vainly in an endeavour to see what
mental reaction his ejaculation had produced. When
he spoke, his voice betrayed no more than his features.

" Another arrest, sergeant ? In your own interest, I
suggest you should hear Mrs. Francia's story before you
go that length."

Ledbury, having burned his boats, greeted this
proposal with a shrug which was almost cavalier.

" You don't imagine she'd tell anything ? " he
demanded in a tone that was almost contemptuous.
" Why should she incriminate herself ? And you're at
her elbow, aren't you, to shut her up if she gets near a
dangerous bit ? *You* know I'm not supposed to put the
screw on anyone, once I've made up my mind to charge
them."

" You haven't quite caught the idea, sergeant," Sir
Clinton explained, in a tone which Ledbury vainly tried
to interpret. " I shall be present, of course. And I shall
do my best to persuade her to tell you everything she
can, without reservation of any sort."

257

The sergeant took his eyes from Sir Clinton's face and stared thoughtfully at his own boots for some seconds. This was the last move that he had expected ; and he could not help feeling that it must conceal a trap of some sort. Nobody in Sir Clinton's place would voluntarily throw the girl open to this attack, unless he had something clearly in view which would turn the affair to his advantage. Try as he would, Ledbury could not conceive why this suggestion had been put forward at all.

" I'll send to fetch her," he agreed reluctantly, in the end. " But understand, sir, I've my duty to do. I'll have to arrest her, whether she makes a statement or not. I'll send someone to look for her now."

He left the room to make his arrangements. Sir Clinton followed him out into the hall and, rather to the sergeant's surprise, entered the smoke-room, where a constable was again on guard. He stayed there only a couple of minutes ; and Ledbury encountered him once more as he returned to the drawing-room. Just at that moment, Rex Brandon appeared in the porch and came forward to intercept them. He ignored Ledbury completely.

" What's happened since they took me away ? " he demanded, going up to Sir Clinton, with a white and anxious face. " What game are they up to now ? "

" Sit down there for a little, Rex," Sir Clinton ordered, evading any answer to the questions. " You can't wait in the dining-room—it's occupied by a Mr. Yarrow, who mustn't be disturbed. Find a chair here in the hall. I'll need you in a few minutes."

He paused, and then added :

" You're a good sort, Rex."

Ledbury overheard the low-toned sentence. Evidently it gave him something to think about, for his brows knitted as though he was making a violent effort to grasp something which eluded him. The whole affair, as he saw it, had taken on an increasingly suspicious aspect. He had an uneasy feeling that all these people were in league together to hoodwink him ; and yet he knew that there had been no opportunity for a private consultation between uncle and niece since the firing of the fatal shot. For all his guessing, he could not imagine what Sir Clinton had up his sleeve.

They waited patiently for a long time before anything happened. Sir Clinton seemed to have no desire to say a word ; and Ledbury was only too glad to have an opportunity of reconsidering the whole case in the hope that he might be able to forestall Sir Clinton's coming move. At last steps sounded in the hall, the door opened, and Elsie was ushered in. As she entered, the voice of Rex sounded in the hall.

" Don't say a word, Elsie ! For God's sake, don't tell them anything ! "

Sir Clinton stepped swiftly to the door.

" Leave things to me, Rex," he said decisively. " We'll need you in a minute or two. Till then, keep quiet."

He closed the door and turned to Elsie ; and as his eyes fell on her, he was astonished, for all his forebodings, at the change in her whole aspect. At four o'clock she had been a care-free creature in the height of happiness ; now, as she turned her haunted eyes upon him, he could almost feel in his own flesh the work that anguish, shock, horror, and terror had wrought on her in the interval. His little Elsie, the child who used to run to meet him in the old days—brought to this ! She was at the end of her resources ; and as he turned to her, she held out her hands in a pitiful, involuntary gesture which begged for help.

" It's all right, Elsie," he reassured her, as he guided her gently to a chair. " You've nothing to be afraid of— nothing. I want you to tell the sergeant here the whole story."

He felt her wince in his clasp.

" I can't," she said, " Oh, I can't ! "

259

Sir Clinton had the key to that lock.

" Rex is cleared," he assured her.

Elsie half-started from her chair at the words.

" He can't be," she cried. " I saw him with the pistol in his hand. . . . Oh ! What have I said ! "

" Nothing that'll do any harm," Sir Clinton reassured her. " All you've got to do is to tell us everything you know "—he corrected himself suddenly but naturally— " everything that's happened since you left the house about four o'clock, so far as you know it. It's all right ; you know I wouldn't lead you wrong. You must trust me then it'll be all right. You're quite safe."

Ledbury suddenly interrupted.

" I've got to caution you . . . "

Sir Clinton swung round, his face white with anger.

" Damn you, man ! " he said in a fierce undertone. " You've nearly ruined everything. Be quiet ! "

He turned back to Elsie, and gradually he was able to soothe her. She made a gallant effort to pull herself together, and under the influence of his voice she seemed to gather courage. At last he succeeded in bringing her to the state of mind that he wanted.

" You came out of the front door . . . " he suggested, to give her a starting-point in her story.

" I came out of the front door," she repeated, keeping her eyes on her uncle's as she spoke. " Then I went along towards the verandah. I wasn't feeling quite well . . . "

" Never mind about that," Sir Clinton interjected.

Something in her eyes suggested that here they might be on thin ice, though he could not understand what she actually meant.

" Tell us what you saw, and what you did—nothing more."

Elsie nodded faintly to show she understood. Quite obviously she was nearly at the end of her nervous strength.

" I sat down on the garden seat just below the steps

leading up to the verandah. I wasn't feeling . . . I wanted to be alone, I don't know how long I sat there. I don't, really."

" Never mind about that," Sir Clinton advised her. " What was the next thing you did ? "

" The next thing that happened was I heard the sound of a shot. It seemed to come from the smoke-room. There was a horrible cry, too. I thought someone had had an accident."

In the pause that followed, Sir Clinton heard Ledbury turn over a page of his notebook in which he was evidently writing furiously in an attempt to keep pace with the narrative. Sir Clinton dared not take his eyes away from Elsie's for fear of directing her attention to the uniformed figure.

" And then ? " he asked gently.

" When I heard the shot, I ran up the verandah steps and along the verandah to the nearest window of the smoke-room. The curtains were drawn."

" Yes ? " Sir Clinton encouraged her, for he knew the next sentences would be the worst.

" Then suddenly one curtain was torn back—and there was Rex face to face with me at the window. I saw a black pistol in his hand. He tried to keep me from seeing what was on the floor ; but I could see it was Vincent's body. Then Rex said : ' Go away ! At once ! ' or something like that."

She stopped abruptly and seemed to collapse in the chair. It was some time before Sir Clinton, even with all his efforts, could bring her back again to a state in which she could give a coherent narrative.

" I didn't know what I was doing," she continued at last. " I knew Rex had shot Vincent. I couldn't tell why. Everything seemed to be happening in a nightmare . . . "

" Don't bother about that," Sir Clinton urged soothingly. " Keep to what you did."

" I ran away along the verandah, down the steps, and

261

down one of the paths—the one that leads to the summer-house. I just got to the summer-house. Then I expect I fainted. I can't remember anything after that for a long time. When I came to again, I was in the summer-house. I tried to walk, but I was too sick and faint to do it. The police found me there."

She halted for a moment.

" Are you *sure* . . . are you *really* sure no harm'll come to Rex ? "

Sir Clinton seized the opportunity to divert her mind from the main tragedy.

" Rex thought you'd fired the shot yourself. And when we questioned him, he stood in and allowed the blame to be thrown on his shoulders instead. No one could have done more for a . . . friend."

As Sir Clinton had hoped, this swung Elsie's thoughts into a fresh channel. Manifestly it threw the whole affair into a new light, and her mind concentrated on a re-interpretation of the facts.

" Rex did that for me ? " she asked half-wonderingly.

" Rex did that," Sir Clinton echoed. " Now that's all we want with you just now, Elsie. Go upstairs and lie down. You're absolutely worn out. I'll come up to you very soon and tell you all about it if you wish."

He gave her his hand and helped her to her feet. Then, as he was about to lead her to the door, a thought struck him.

" Get me that picture from the wall there," he ordered Ledbury, pointing to a sketch framed in passe-partout. " Clean the glass carefully and keep your fingers off it."

Ledbury obeyed ; and Sir Clinton took the glass from him.

" Now, Elsie, I want you to grip this—first with your right hand, and then with your left—as if you were catching the end of a door and swinging it open."

He held the little frame vertically in the air, ready for her to catch. Elsie hesitated for a moment, as though in sudden mistrust. Then, after a glance at her uncle's face, she did as he wished. Her exhaustion touched her attitude with a trace of the unquestioning obedience of a little child, and Sir Clinton found something uncomfortable in the reminiscence.

" Now, that's all, Elsie. I'll see you upstairs," he said, putting the passe-partout carefully on a table. " You're not fit to go up yourself."

Ledbury seemed for a moment inclined to object to this, but after a look at Sir Clinton's face he decided to let things take their course. Even yet, he had not been able to see a plain solution of all this tangle ; and he could not repress the feeling that some gigantic game of bluff was being played upon him. Here was a man murdered, and two people on the very spot—within a couple of yards of the body—and Sir Clinton was trying to persuade him that neither had a hand in the crime. Absurd on the face of it ! And yet . . .

He was still pondering over the problem when Sir Clinton returned, bringing Rex Brandon with him.

" Now, Rex, the plain truth and the whole truth, please. I've cleared you completely ; and we need your evidence to clear Elsie. Tell us exactly what happened from the time you went into the smoke-room up to the moment when Staffin looked through the doorway."

Rex listened with a heavy cloud of suspicion on his face.

" I think I'll say nothing," he said bluntly. " You've no power to force me to make a statement ? "

" None at all," Sir Clinton agreed. " But Elsie has told her story—after she learned that you were cleared— and we need your confirmation of it in the details. If we don't get that, it'll be more difficult to prove that she had no hand in the thing. The only way you can do her harm is by refusing to tell us the whole truth—leaving out nothing whatever."

Rex scanned Sir Clinton's face for a moment.

" Well, I can trust _you_, I suppose," he said at last. " Only, I hope you're not making a ghastly mistake over it. I'll tell you what you want, now you've put it that way. Where do I begin ? "

" You went into the smoke-room . . . " Sir Clinton prompted.

" Yes, I went into the smoke-room and shut the door. Francia was reading some papers in the chair by the window. I didn't interrupt him. I sat down at the telephone and called up the Black Bull. There was a message I wanted to leave for a man Yarrow, so I spoke to the girl at the desk in the hotel ! "

Sir Clinton nodded.

" That's all been checked already," he told Rex. " Now, go on with what happened next."

" I was in the middle of talking to her," Rex continued, " when suddenly there was a bang—a pistol-shot—and a cry. I swung round in my chair just in time to see Francia's body fall to the floor. He writhed a bit . . . "

" What did you do ? " Sir Clinton demanded, bringing him back to the main line.

" I must have dropped the telephone when I started up out of my chair. The shot had come through the window. By the way, I forgot that. Just as Francia fell out of his chair, I heard the pistol drop on the floor. I got up and went over. Francia was done for—anyone could see that at a glance. My eye caught the pistol lying behind his chair, and I stooped and picked it up. I wasn't very quick in thinking just then, a bit dazed by the suddenness of it all, I expect. It was a second or two before it dawned on me that the murderer must have been behind the curtain—the curtains over the window, I mean. So I jerked one of them aside and looked out, hoping to see the beggar running away."

He halted abruptly.

" Is that enough ? "

Sir Clinton shook his head.

" The next is the important bit."

Rex paused for some moments, evidently in grave doubt.

" Elsie told you what happened next ? " he demanded.

" We know all about it," said Sir Clinton impatiently. " The only thing that counts is that your story and hers should check each other. Don't fake a single detail. You understand ? "

" Oh, very well," Rex answered. " I'm in the dark about it all ; but I'll take your word for it. When I pulled back the curtain, Elsie was standing behind it, out on the verandah."

" We know that," Sir Clinton repeated.

" Well, what was I to think ? " Rex continued. " On the face of it, she'd shot him. The noise of the pistol would bring a crowd in no time. I hadn't much time to grasp the affair and I blurted out : ' Clear out ! ' or something of that sort to her, to get her off the spot before anyone came. She seemed frozen or numbed or something. Couldn't act herself, it seemed. But she took what I said, and she went off along the verandah towards the front of the house."

" That fits perfectly," Sir Clinton assured him. " It's all right. Now what next ? "

Sir Clinton's manner seemed to satisfy Rex that he was doing no harm.

" Well, there I was left standing with the pistol in my hand. I had enough wits left to see what things would look like if anyone came into the room. So I hove the pistol clean out of the window amongst the bushes, meaning to collect it later on and bury it, or something."

Rex saw Ledbury start slightly at this last phrase ; but a glance at Sir Clinton's face revealed that the ex-Chief Constable attached no importance to the point, and Rex continued :

" I'd hardly got it out of my hands than the maid poked her head in at the door. There was the body on the floor—no sight for a girl—so I said : ' Get out ! ' and off she went, screaming ' Murder ! ' for all she was worth. That fairly started me thinking. There I was, the only person in sight, alone with the body. If I told the truth, I'd be giving Elsie away. I wasn't going to do that. If I faked up a yarn, it would go to pieces under the very first half-dozen questions they put to me. I hadn't time to make up a decent set of lies—I was too flurried to think clearly at all. The only thing to do was to keep my mouth shut and refuse to say anything. That would give me time enough to think out a yarn that would hold water, when I had to talk. Whatever happened, I wasn't going to give Elsie away. I drew the line at that. You did your best to draw me—in different ways. But quite obviously you didn't know anything about Elsie having been there, so I fended you off."

He seemed afraid that he had been too frank, but a glance at Sir Clinton's expression of relief evidently reassured him, though he could not understand what the ex-Chief Constable was driving at.

Sir Clinton turned to Ledbury, whose facial control had failed completely under the revelations of the last few minutes. The sergeant was manifestly amazed by Sir Clinton's action in forcing out this apparently damning series of facts.

" If Mr. Yarrow's still busy with his writing, I think we'll have him in again, sergeant, just to test his memory on a point or two."

Ledbury, his face a mask of bewilderment, went and fetched the naturalist.

" Now, Mr. Yarrow," Sir Clinton began suavely, " we should like to be sure of one or two minor points in the evidence you gave us. You didn't notice the report of a pistol—or a cry ? "

Yarrow shook his head.

"No," he admitted, as though he feared he was making a mistake, "I can't say that I heard anything—at least, at the time I didn't think of a pistol-shot, so it doesn't look as if I heard the report, does it?"

"Another point," Sir Clinton pursued hurriedly, in order to cut short the naturalist's habitual verbosity. "We'd like to know how much detail your telescope showed. Could you see the rings on the girl's hand, for instance?"

"No, I couldn't have done that," Yarrow protested. "The image was far too small to see things of that sort."

"H'm!" Sir Clinton commented doubtfully. "I want to get this clear. Could you see her hands? Could you have seen if she'd had gloves on, or anything like that? Or if her hand was open or shut?"

"Oh, I could have seen that sort of thing clearly enough," Yarrow hastened to assure him. "If she'd been wearing gloves, I'd have noticed it. And I could see when she gripped the casement to keep herself from falling. That was quite obvious."

Sir Clinton nodded.

"Would you mind adding these points to your written statement, Mr. Yarrow?" he asked, as he made a gesture to show that he had no more questions to put.

The naturalist agreed effusively, and Ledbury ushered him out of the room. Rex's face showed that all this had been quite beyond him; he had not heard Elsie's statement and could not put two and two together. All he had gathered was that some of Sir Clinton's questions had been of no importance and had been put in merely to avoid throwing the main point into too sharp relief in Yarrow's mind. But which of them was the crucial one, he had not the means to guess.

Ledbury's face, when he returned to the room, showed that he also had been at work on the problem; and Rex thought he saw signs that the sergeant was now

267

thoroughly uneasy. He looked as though he were on pins and needles ; and his first words as he closed the door made the thing clear.

" You seem to have got something there, sir," he admitted to Sir Clinton. " Now would you mind telling me what it is ? I can make a guess at it already."

" Then bring along that passe-partout thing with you, and we'll have a look at the smoke-room window," Sir Clinton proposed, leading the way.

When they reached the smoke-room, Sir Clinton took them out through the French window on to the verandah ; and for a short time he examined the glass of the open window at which Elsie had stood, comparing some marks on it with the finger-prints on the passe-partout. Satisfied at last, he made way for Ledbury.

" Here are the prints of Mrs. Francia's fingers, made when she caught at the leaves of the window to steady herself. See them ? Now compare them with the prints she made on the glass of the passe-partout with her hands in the same positions. Identical, so far as one can see, aren't they ? If she left prints on the panes, she'd have left prints on the pistol if she'd ever had it in her hand, wouldn't she ? But there were no prints of her fingers on the pistol—Mr. Brandon's were the only ones on it, as you established yourself. And Mrs. Francia didn't strip off a pair of gloves after firing the shot ; because Yarrow's evidence proves she had no gloves and because she would hardly be likely to strip off gloves specially in order to make a finger-print on the window, would she ? It follows, sergeant, that she didn't fire the pistol. And I've proved that Mr. Brandon didn't fire it. So where are you ? "

Ledbury's hand stole up to scratch his ear ; but it was clear enough that this time the action was involuntary and not merely a piece of camouflage. He was apparently completely puzzled.

" What do you make of it yourself, sir ? " he

demanded. " It fair beats me. There's no denying that. I chuck my hand in."

Sir Clinton did not trouble to triumph over the sergeant, although the occasion might have justified it.

" Ever hear of the French method—reconstituting the crime, they call it ? Suppose we try something of the sort, and we'll have a real test of whether this notion of mine's practicable or not. Mr. Brandon will represent himself ; you can play the part of Mrs. Francia ; and, since the murderer's rôle demands a bit of accurate timing, I'll take it myself to save explanation. You, sergeant, will go and sit on the garden seat near the foot of the steps leading to the verandah. I'll go down among the bushes. Mr. Brandon will go and sit at the telephone table. I'll draw the curtain over this window, so that everything will be exactly as it was."

As Rex was moving off to take up his position, Sir Clinton stopped him.

" Everything has to be just as it was when the shot was fired. Shut the French window after you, and draw that curtain across it. Now when I, representing the murderer, come up to the window, I'll shove my cigarette-case against the curtain and say : " Crack ! " That represents the firing of the shot. You'll then act precisely as you did when the real shot was fired, making the proper allowance of time for each move. You, sergeant, will pause for a moment or two, as though you were really startled. Then you'll run up here, following Mrs. Francia's description as closely as you can till you're off the verandah again. Now, away to your posts."

He swung himself over the balustrade of the verandah and disappeared among the bushes. Rather to their astonishment, minute after minute went by without his partners hearing the signal. Sir Clinton meant to exhaust their patience, and so take them off their guard when the crucial moment arrived.

269

Suddenly, just as he was beginning to fidget, the sergeant heard the catch-word and sprang to his feet. He ran to the steps, mounted them, turned on to the verandah—and found it empty. Remembering his rôle, he hurried to the fatal window, and, just as he reached it, the curtain slipped back and he found himself face to face with Rex. The cigarette-case in Rex's hand showed the sergeant that Sir Clinton had played his part successfully. At Rex's gesture, Ledbury turned away as Elsie had done and retraced his steps along the verandah ; whilst Rex turned back into the room again, after pitching the cigarette-case out among the bushes.

At the foot of the verandah steps, Ledbury halted, since he had not been told to carry the play further than that. As he waited, he was surprised to see Sir Clinton emerge from the screen of bushes close beside him.

" See now how it could have been done, sergeant ? " he asked.

" I'm not just sure yet," Ledbury replied. " You were really on the verandah, for I heard your voice plain enough from that direction. And yet I didn't see you when I got up there. And I'd have seen you plain if you'd bolted for the bushes."

Rex joined them at this moment.

" Simple enough," Sir Clinton explained. " I could reach the verandah without your seeing me, sergeant, because the corner of the verandah hid me from you as I crossed the space between the bushes and the balustrade. I got up to the window unobserved. I peeped through the curtains, then I shoved the cigarette-case inside the sill, low down ; and I was careful to keep my shadow off the thin curtain, or Mr. Brandon would have seen it. I then pretended to fire, and dropped the pistol on the floor.

" In the real affair, Mr. Brandon got a bad shake-up, naturally. He wasn't likely to be over-observant. Now what I did, as soon as I'd given the signal, was simple enough. I just took a step or two along the verandah *and slipped into the deep recess of the French window*. When you came tearing up the steps, I was already under cover so far as you were concerned. And at my back was the heavy curtain of the French window, which transmitted no shadow that Mr. Brandon would have noticed.

" Then came the scene at the window, and you rushed off to the steps while Mr. Brandon turned back into the room. All I had to do was to move off the verandah at the opposite end from you, taking care to keep outside the range of the window where Mr. Brandon was, until I got under cover of the bushes."

The sergeant considered this for some time without speaking.

" You've beaten me, hands down, sir," he admitted frankly at last. " That's how it could have been done—and I never thought of that deep recess. What a fool I was ! But we're still as far away as ever from getting hold of the man. Who could he be ? "

" Dr. Roca had an accomplice," Sir Clinton pointed out. " In the Quevedo business he had someone who collected information for him. That was clear enough. Now the whole of these foreigners seem to have been at sixes and sevens, so far as one can judge. What about this confederate ? "

A flash of enlightenment crossed Ledbury's face.

" You mean . . . was it this man Yarrow that's in there ? He might fit the case, sir. And, of course, coming up here and offering himself as a witness would be just a bit of bluff."

Sir Clinton shook his head.

" No good, sergeant. If Yarrow had been standing in the recess of the French window, he couldn't possibly have seen all the details which he described and which we checked. Besides, Mr. Yarrow isn't so expert in taking cover as he seems to imagine. I saw him down at the lakeside myself, just as he stated. The brass end of

271

his telescope was catching the sun and shining like a small heliograph. No, he's all right."

" Then it must have been the commercial traveller, sir, the one that was here just before the Quevedo murder."

Sir Clinton refused to commit himself definitely.

" Certainly," he admitted, " if I wanted to pick up local news I'd hang about hotel bars just as your commercial friend seems to have done. But that's not a criminal offence when it's done within legal hours, sergeant. And suspicions aren't much good alone, you know."

He felt for his cigarette-case mechanically and found it missing. The action seemed to remind him of a point.

" Of course the murderer, whoever he was, had gloves on so as to leave no marks on the pistol. And, as there were no marks on it, he might think it safer to leave the weapon behind rather than risk being found with it in his possession if he were spotted."

Ledbury nodded to show that he grasped this point. Then he turned to Rex.

" I'm not quite sure what your position is, sir. You may hear more of this, I'm afraid. You're an accomplice *ex post facto*, you see."

Sir Clinton made no attempt to conceal a smile.

" An accomplice of *whom*, sergeant ? Mr. Brandon connived at Mrs. Francia's escape. But Mrs. Francia is a witness in the case and not a criminal. I don't quite see where the felony comes in, really."

" You have me there," Ledbury admitted, scratching his ear furiously. " That's a way I hadn't looked at it, but it's right enough now you point it out."

" One more thing," Sir Clinton added. " I hate to leave loose ends. The murderer knew that Francia was in the smoke-room. How could he have found that out ? you might ask. Simple enough. Suppose he was lurking amongst those bushes when I came up to the house at four o'clock. We stood at the front door and I offered

272

to give Francia these sketches to read. We both went into the house. He'd have no difficulty in overhearing what I said. He'd know Francia would be left alone. And when I pulled the curtain of the smoke-room window, he'd see me there and guess Francia was there also. As soon as he saw me leave the house again by the front door, he'd know the coast was clear."

" That would be it, likely enough," Ledbury admitted. " It does fit neatly together, now you've explained it. I wish I'd seen what that deep recess meant."

Sir Clinton's hand made another futile search in his pocket.

" You might hunt up that case of mine for me, Rex. You know whereabouts it fell when you pitched it out of the window. And when you've found it, please wait for me. I must go up and see how Elsie's feeling."

He turned to Ledbury.

" You'll get everything put through now, sergeant ? There'll be an inquest, of course. I'll have to give evidence there, I take it. But, beyond that, I hope I'll never hear another word about this case. I've had all the experiences I'm in need of this time ; and I hope I'll never touch criminal work again."

CHAPTER XX

IN SAFE DEPOSIT

In his study, Sir Clinton Driffield was busy clearing up his affairs before leaving on his impending mission abroad. On the desk beside him lay a number of freshly written sheets of manuscript ; and, when he had completed his work, he rose and rang the bell.

" Get Orton," he said to the servant who answered his summons, " I want you both to witness my signature."

While this formality was being carried out, Sir Clinton took the precaution of screening the wording of the document from the eyes of his witnesses with a sheet of blotting-paper. Then, dismissing the servants, he picked up his pen again, and began to write a short note.

" DEAR SHIELBRIDGE,—Before leaving for the Continent, I shall send you a key and instructions which will give you access to my safe—No. 8039—in the Oxford Street premises of the Central and Suburban Safe Deposit Co. This safe contains a single document enclosed in an envelope inscribed ' The Vicente Francia Case.'

" Unless you get convincing proof of my decease, you need do nothing in the matter.

" If I die—a motor accident may happen to any of us—you are to do nothing unless someone is brought to trial for the murder of the late Vicente Francia. But should I be dead, and should anyone be put on trial, you will take immediate steps to procure the document and hand it over to the Public Prosecutor.

" Yours,

" CLINTON DRIFFIELD."

Sir Clinton addressed the envelope of this letter to his lawyer, one of the few men whom he trusted implicitly. Then he picked up the written sheets bearing his witnessed signature and re-read his statement once more, to ensure that no errors had crept in.

" Since by mischance an innocent man might be accused of the murder of the late Vicente Francia at Fern Lodge, Raynham Parva, I leave the following statement of the case, for use in the event of my unforeseen death.

" There fell into my hands certain documents proving beyond doubt that Vicente Francia was engaged in the White Slave traffic ; that he had gone through a ceremony of marriage with my niece merely to further his trade ; and that he was planning to secure three other girls as well, using my niece as his bait.

" Further, I had clear evidence that he murdered the late Dr. Esteban Roca at the Bale Stones, near Raynham Parva. Since Francia's death, I have communicated this evidence to the police ; and, owing to the death of the murderer, the case has been dropped without the public learning the inner history of the affair.

" With all this evidence in my hands, I had four courses open to me :

" 1. *To stand aside completely.* The four girls would then have accompanied Francia to the Argentine, where they would have been wholly at his mercy. The Centre's organisation is quite good enough to compass the complete disappearance of a girl out there. Naturally, I dismissed this course immediately.

" 2. *To intervene privately.* This would have saved a public scandal ; but, since my niece was married to Francia, it would have left her tied for life to him and unable to contract a fresh marriage even if she separated herself from him. This course, also, I rejected.

" 3. *To offer the evidence in my hands to the police ; and get*

275

Francia hanged as he deserved. This would have freed my niece, certainly ; but simultaneously it would have stamped her as the widow of a peculiarly loathsome parasite and murderer. After careful consideration, I rejected this course also.

" 4. *To eliminate Francia.* This course had three main advantages. It would liberate my niece completely from her marriage entanglement. It would also leave her the widow of a murdered man and not of a convicted murderer ; and of the two states, the former seems a shade less derogatory. In all probability, if there was no trial, Francia's career would not come to public knowledge. Finally, Francia's elimination would atone for the fact that I had become his accomplice *ex post facto* by failing to denounce him as soon as the evidence in the Roca murder case fell into my hands. By suppressing that evidence, I had saved him from execution by the law ; but if I removed him myself, I should be restoring the balance which I had thus disturbed.

" There were two obvious objections to this fourth course : one moral, the other practical. The moral one did not trouble me greatly. No one would carry humanitarianism to the extent of protecting a plague-stricken rat ; and Francia's trade put him, in my mind at least, on a level with any other type of vermin. Quite apart from my personal feelings in the matter, he was the sort of person who is much better dead.

" Remained the practical objection. I had not the slightest intention of risking much in the matter. It would have been mere quixotry to take any appreciable risk in order to wipe out a thing like Francia. Consequently I spent some thought upon the problem of providing myself with a complete alibi ; and finally I worked out a detailed scheme.

" In the first place, I timed the smouldering of one of my cigarettes when it had been lit and laid down on the edge of a shelf. I then obtained some strong thread and soaked it in a solution made from chlorate of potash tabloids. When dry, it was converted into quite a good slow-match which could be ignited at a smouldering cigarette.

" I then removed from Francia's attaché-case the automatic pistol he had used in the murder of Roca. To avoid repetition, I may say that in handling the pistol I was always careful to wear rubber gloves so as to avoid finger-prints.

" My young nephew had broken his air-gun, and, on opening it up, I found the spiral spring broken in two. The smaller fragment fortunately proved suitable for my purpose. I compressed this bit of spring—a powerful one—and fastened it, still compressed, by means of a bit of the slow-match thread which I had prepared. This compressed spring I jammed between the trigger and trigger-guard of the automatic pistol so that when the thread gave way the spring drove back the trigger and fired the pistol. One end of the slow-match thread was utilised to tie down the safety-catch embodied in the pistol-grip, since otherwise the pistol would not have been fireable.

" The other end of the slow-match thread I laid across a smouldering cigarette.

" This arrangement provided me with the means of exploding the pistol at a given moment, even though I myself were at a distance. I may say that I tested and re-tested the action of the infernal machine until I could gauge exactly how long a period would elapse between setting it and the explosion. At first I was troubled by a tendency of the slow-match to go out when it reached a knot ; but, by dosing the knot with a stronger solution of chlorate of potash, I got over the difficulty and made the contrivance thoroughly reliable.

" The rest of the matter needs no lengthy description. I arranged that Francia should occupy the chair in the smoke-room which had its back to the window. When he had sat down, I pretended to notice that the sun was on the paper he was reading ; and I went to the window to draw the curtain. Under cover of looking out of the window for a moment or two, I jammed the pistol in position among the books on the window-shelf ; put down my burning cigarette on the ledge ; laid the slow-match across the cigarette at a point which would be reached by the smouldering in a few minutes ; and drew the curtain over the window-recess. I then left the room and went down to the lake, thus securing a perfect alibi.

" The operation of the contrivance will now be quite clear. When the cigarette had smouldered away to the critical point, the slow-match which lay across it became ignited. It in turn smouldered away until the spark reached the part of the thread which was holding the spring compressed. The release of the powerful spring pressed home the trigger, firing the pistol and shooting Francia in the back. To make quite sure of the result, I filed the tip of the bullet.

" I had satisfied myself in my experiments upon a further point. The spring, after driving home the trigger, expanded sideways and jerked itself clear of the trigger-guard, carrying with it the remaining bit of thread which had been used to tie down the safety-catch on the pistol-grip. It is unnecessary to go into details ; but I had fixed up the thread in such a way that the slow-match burned along to a control-knot and made the operation certain. The result of this was that the spring and the thread, which might have suggested something if they had been discovered, were dropped on the floor when the pistol went off ; and the rest of the slow-match burned away so rapidly that in a moment or two all trace of it was gone and the main bit of evidence was destroyed. Luckily, my young nephew is rather careless with his Meccano fittings, and, as a number of these were strewn over the floor beside his table, the bit of spring seemed merely one of these odds and ends—the more so since the rest of the spring was lying amongst his Meccano toys on the table.

" When the pistol exploded, the sliding jacket of it flew backwards, and struck the back of the book-shelf ; and of course this resulted in the pistol being jerked from its position and thrown forward, so that it fell on the floor. This concealed the fact that it had been on the book-shelf at all.

" There were only two possible flaws in the scheme. One was that Francia might smell the cigarette smouldering behind him and might get up to see where it was. This seemed hardly on the cards, since he was smoking a similar cigarette himself when I left him, and the fumes of the one would cover the smell of the other.

" The second flaw lay in the possibility of someone coming into the room and throwing back the window-curtains. But that, when I arranged the affair, was so unlikely in the short time allowed for the action of the infernal machine that the risk seemed negligible. I had located everyone in the party at the house that afternoon, and Francia seemed unlikely to be disturbed. The advent of my niece and Rex Brandon was outside the calculable bounds. In any case, there was no direct evidence to connect me with the pistol. No one knew of any motive which would have made me contrive Francia's death. Other people might have a grudge against him, however ; and, the window being open, it would have been quite possible for an outside agent to steal up on the verandah and plant the infernal machine in position from outside the house.

" Of course, on the road down to the boat-house, I took the precaution of getting rid of the rubber gloves I had used in handling the pistol at the last moment. When I returned again to the house, I took care to muddle Sergeant Ledbury sufficiently by assisting him in his investigation ; and when the vital bit of evidence appeared—the spiral spring—he paid no real attention to it, but regarded it merely as something which had been dropped off the table at some time or other by accident."

Sir Clinton finished the perusal of this document, and once more glanced back at one or two sentences.

" H'm ! " he said to himself. " It seems clear enough. Any small omissions can be filled in by people of normal intelligence, I think."

He placed the papers in an envelope and sealed them up securely. Then he smiled, a trifle grimly.

" The County police are calling in the C.I.D. We'll see what they make of it, now that Ledbury has got off on the wrong scent and lost some of the evidence in his hurry. In any case, it's not likely to worry me. I'm off to-night on that Government mission abroad ; and if I don't find it convenient to turn up again, that packet of bearer bonds will be sufficient for my simple needs."

He reflected for a moment.

" Elsie's safe, that's the main thing. And I guess Rex will get what he wants now."

www.ingramcontent.com/pod-product-compliance
Ingram Content Group UK Ltd.
Pitfield, Milton Keynes, MK11 3LW, UK
UKHW040434280225
455666UK00003B/60

9 781471 906015